Dead Feint

by Grant Atherton

with grateful thanks to

JAKOB PAULUSSEN

for all his valuable help and advice

Cover art by
SelfPubBookCovers.com/Michelleleedesigns

Grant Atherton's Website
GrantAtherton.co.uk

WARNING

This book contains sexually explicit scenes
and adult language and may be considered
offensive to some readers.

CHAPTER ONE

It wasn't a conversation I would forget in a hurry. "How did she die?" I said.

Rusty bit on his lip before answering. It was just long enough to put me on guard for what came next.

"Her head and face was smashed in. Some sort of blunt object they reckon. Not a lot left to see."

"Jeez, man." I flinched and tightened a hand around my glass of beer. "I don't know what to say. What a nightmare."

I was rarely at a loss for words but how was I supposed to respond to that?

End-of-term parties are about letting your hair down, throwing off inhibitions and having some well-deserved fun once the pressure of exams is over. But Rusty wasn't in a party mood.

He'd asked for my help with what he'd called 'a bit of a problem'. In his place, I would have ranked my sister's murder at a somewhat higher level of magnitude. But what would I know?

We were in the Red Lion pub just down the road from the College. The management had laid on a heavy-metal rock band - a motley crew of leather-clad post-pubescent posers who hadn't yet worked out the difference between talent and volume. My other students, clearly in favour of volume, were already whooping it up, party lovers all. Bursts of excited chatter and hoots of laughter broke through the roar of music, and pounding bass rhythms hammered at the walls of the small crowded bar.

1

Rusty and I had pressed ourselves into a corner at the far side of the room in a futile attempt to escape the din.

"I can't hear myself think in here," I said. "Let's go find somewhere to talk."

We squeezed our way through groups of boisterous revellers to the front of the pub, taking our pints of bitter with us, and stepped out into the relative quiet of the forecourt. As we crossed it, I clasped his shoulder in a show of sympathy.

There was a wooden bench table over by the pub's kitchen annexe, and we parked ourselves on either side of it, facing each other under the amber glow of a metal-cased lantern hanging from the wall.

Apart from the occasional moth attracted by the light, we had the area to ourselves. The evening air had cooled as day faded to night, and all the other patrons had stayed inside. Out here, the hubbub from the bar was a muted blur of sound.

My throat was dry - the sudden surprise of Rusty's revelation no doubt - and I gulped down a large mouthful of beer.

Just as surprising was the matter-of-fact way he'd passed on this information. No trace of emotion. But that was Rusty. And, eventually, time dulls the emotional impact of even the most traumatic of experiences, so I guessed it couldn't have been a recent event.

I took a closer look at him.

Rusty Naylor was one of my psychology students. A late starter. But bright. He was older than the others, but, even with the grey hair and beard, appeared younger than his forty years.

After a change of direction in his life - something he was still cagey about - he had returned to college to seek new challenges.

I didn't know much about his background. But with that body, I guessed he'd worked at something physical. He was all hard muscle and corded veins. It was the kind of body used to labour.

We'd developed a friendship over the months, seeking each other's company outside class, and I thought I was getting to know him.

Until now that is.

"Why did you never tell me this before?" I said.

"Come on, Mikey, it's not something you'd drop into casual conversation, is it?" There was a trace of mockery in his voice.

"No, of course not," I said, apologetically.

Many of us are burdened by events we prefer to stay buried in the past. It's not as if the details of my own troubled life would make for suitable dinner-party chit-chat. On the other hand, my ongoing acrimonious divorce and the reasons for it weren't quite on a par with having a family member murdered. Near enough, but not quite. So his revelation came as a jolt.

"How long ago did this happen?" I said.

"Reckon it's getting on for two years. They never caught him."

Rusty didn't make a show of his emotions. He wasn't the demonstrative type. But nor was he the stoic, bereft of feeling, and so it disturbed me to learn he had carried the weight of such a harrowing event with such forbearance.

Knowing the killer was still at large, not being able to find closure, must be a real kicker, a source of continuing pain.

"It can't be easy for you," I said, "knowing he's still out there. But I'm not sure what it is you're asking for, what I can do to help."

He leaned toward me across the table, a pleading look in his eyes. "I thought - you know - 'cos of your work, you might nudge 'em along. Get 'em moving again."

That threw me, and I stammered.

My students knew of my relationship with the police; I used details of cases I'd assisted with as examples in my lectures. But Rusty's expectations about the extent of my influence were way off the mark.

"That's not how these things work," I said.

I could imagine how that would go down in police circles, checking up to make sure they stayed on top of an investigation.

I was momentarily spared the embarrassment of turning him down by the sound of the door behind me bursting open and expelling four well-oiled young men into the cool evening air. Laughing and joshing among themselves, they staggered away across the forecourt to the road beyond. Their lively animated exchanges contrasted with the sombre mood at our table.

Once they were out of earshot, I leaned towards Rusty, hands clasped on the table before me, and said, "My only involvement with the police is in an advisory capacity. It's limited to the expert advice I can offer as a Forensic Psychologist. And it's always at their instigation."

He squirmed on his seat and looked down at his half-empty pint pot.

I said, "I'd like to help, but my intervention outside the limits of my role wouldn't be appropriate. Or welcome. And you must appreciate that the investigation into your sister's death will be ongoing, anyway."

He looked up again. "I wouldn't ask if it weren't for your connection."

I stared at him blankly, unsure what he meant.

"She was killed in Elders Edge."

The light of understanding dawned.

My mind raced back, and I vaguely recalled some details about a gruesome murder around that time. The victim must have been Rusty's sister.

Elders Edge, my old hometown, was a sleepy seaside resort out on the east coast where nothing much happened. But it had its share of turbulent events like anywhere. And the brutal murder of a young woman in the heart of the town's idyllic woodland had been one such event, details of which had eventually reached my ears.

Rusty said, "I figured you might know some people down there."

Now my term as a guest lecturer at Flamstead College was over, there was nothing to keep me in London. It was common knowledge on campus that I was returning to Elders Edge. Rusty must have seen it as an opportunity to take advantage of my links with the place.

I said, "A friend of mine runs a boarding house back there. I remember her telling me about the murder. But I had no idea how it turned out."

"Well, now you know. They could be sitting on their arses all day for what good they've done."

I mulled this over as I considered my options. Rusty drained his glass and pushed it to one side on the table.

Perhaps, given the circumstances, it wouldn't be such a bad idea to make a few discreet enquiries.

"I know some of the guys in the local force," I said, and added reluctantly, "and I guess I could have a word in the right ear, see what I can find out."

My connection to Elders Edge's Chief of Police, DCI Nathan Quarryman, was about as personal as it could get, our relationship being the reason for my return. But that was a different matter.

I continued, "But I'm sure they'll be keeping a close eye on the case. In my experience, cold cases are kept under constant review."

Rusty cleared his throat. "Sorry, Mikey, but I don't share your high opinion of the old bill."

That put me on the defensive. "I've worked with those guys before. They're a competent and committed team."

A flush rose in his cheeks. "Look, my sister…." He paused for a moment and tugged at the cuff of his shirt. "Let's just say she was no Mother Teresa if you get my drift. She had some form. Nothing serious. Shoplifting. And she'd been on the game." He shrugged and pulled a face. "In her case, I don't think the bizzies would give it their best."

"Who was in charge of the case? Do you know?"

"Some bod called Baxter. Sgt Baxter. Snotty type."

I searched my mind, tried to recollect the name. But nothing registered. "Sgt Lowe is the man on the ground at local level. I don't recall a Baxter though. Unless he's based at Divisional HQ in Charwell."

"I remember Lowe. He interviewed me."

Adopting a more placatory tone, I said, "I know him well. So maybe I could have a quiet word without ruffling any feathers. I'll check in with him when I get back, and I'll call you as soon as I have something."

To lose someone close is always a tragedy. But to lose someone in such circumstances and wait so long in the hope of justice must be almost unendurable. The least I could do was have Lowe check the file and bring Rusty up to date.

He thanked me profusely, and rising to his feet, said, "Come on, I'll stand you a pint to seal the deal."

On the way back to the bar, he said, "We'll stay in touch anyway, won't we? I'd hate to miss out on our get-togethers."

"You bet," I said. "I won't be far away. And I'll be back on business on a regular basis."

Now his mind had been set at rest, he adopted a lighter tone and said, "So who's the woman then?"

"What?"

"Come on, don't tell me there isn't a woman back home. That is why you're going back, isn't it?"

I considered telling him the real reason but bottled out. I opened the pub door and stood aside to let him through. "Something like that," I said with a grin.

Rusty wasn't the only who kept secrets.

CHAPTER TWO

"No regrets?" Nathan's breath was warm against my cheek.

Forcing myself into wakefulness, I tried to focus through sleep-bleary eyes.

Daylight filtered through the three slatted wooden blinds covering the large picture window at the side of the bed.

I blinked in the half-light and brushed his stubbled cheek with the back of my hand. "Regrets? After last night? What kind of dumb question is that?" I yawned, wrapped an arm around his chest, and huddled up to him. "No, I have no regrets."

Those last few days in London had passed in a flurry of activity. So many last-minute chores; final arrangements for furniture removal and storage, chasing the bank, setting up insurance, redirecting mail. All those mundane tasks. There had been no time to think beyond each day as it passed.

But, at last, it was over, and I was back where I belonged. Back home.

And what a homecoming it had been. A night of passion, wrapped in my lover's strong arms, flesh against flesh, a shared urgent need released in a frenzy of heat and fire and lust. As homecomings go, it had been impressive.

And all I wanted now was to bask in the warm afterglow of satiated desire.

"No, no regrets," I murmured again.

He prodded me in the ribs. "That's not what I meant."

"Ouch." I squirmed away from him. "What was that for?"

"Come on, Mikey. You know what I mean."

"You're an idiot. What's to regret?" I cuddled up to him again, ready to drift off into another slumber.

"It's a big change. A whole new way of life."

The tone of voice was serious. It unsettled me, and I tensed. "What is this?"

Now wide awake, I struggled out from under the bedclothes, sat up, and tried to read his expression.

The strong square-jawed face was impassive. As ever. But those molten green eyes, so recently fired with passion, were now full of questions.

He was still so unsure.

A surge of tenderness, tempered by guilt, welled up inside me. I leaned down and momentarily pressed my lips to his. "I'm home again. That's all that matters."

Trust, once lost, is not something easily regained. But time and circumstance were on my side. And what I'd once forfeited, I was set on winning back. I was determined to make a go of it.

He traced a finger over my face and across my lips, and his firm-set expression relaxed into a smile.

I nestled back down against him, nuzzled his neck, and breathed in his musky scent. There was a stirring in my loins. "Now where was I before I was so rudely interrupted." I slid a hand slowly down his chest, running my fingers through the thick mat of hair, down and down.

He brushed my hand away. "Sorry to disappoint you," he said, "but it's time to rise and shine. I need to get a move on."

"But I was rising," I said. "The shining can wait."

He answered with a laugh.

Groaning, I turned away and sat up again. "You know what you were saying about regrets…?"

"I'll make it up to you another time." Grinning, he rolled out of bed. "Right now, duty calls."

He raised the blinds.

Daylight flooded in. A bright morning sun hit the mirror on the adjacent wall and bounced back, glinting off the metal window frames, and adding a glossy sheen to the highly polished surfaces of the beechwood furniture.

I rubbed my eyes and squinted up at him. "You pick your times," I complained. "I was hoping to have you to myself for a while."

"Believe me. If I had a choice...." He headed for the shower, padding across the parquet floor, and grabbed a white towelling robe from the back of the door on his way.

I called out after him, "Serves me right for getting involved with a cop."

"Better luck next time," he called back.

I raised my voice above the sound of the shower. "Next time, I'm going for a work-at-home accountant. Someone nice and boring, who doesn't run off when I need him."

Not that there would be a next time. This time it was for keeps.

Ironically, he was being called away to London just as I'd left it behind. Conferences weren't really his thing; he was more the hands-on type and liked to work in the field with his men. But when duty called, he had to follow.

Personally, I preferred other ways to utilise his need for hands-on experience. But as I had just been denied that particular pleasure, I reluctantly crawled out of bed and picked up my scattered clothing from the floor where I had so hastily discarded it the night before.

Moments later, Nathan's rumbling bass tones drifted out from the bathroom, and I was treated to a very off-key rendition of Imagine Dragon's 'I'll Make It Up To You'.

I chortled.

Once quickly dressed in a pair of crumpled Levis and a white cotton sweatshirt, I slipped on my loafers and followed him into the bathroom. He was standing in the bath under the shower, with the curtain pulled back. I sank onto the edge of the lavatory seat and watched him lather himself, his practised hands running over that hard firm body, his rippling muscles wet and gleaming in the steam-laden air.

I followed the movement of his hands across the broad chest, through its tangled mass of hair, and over the flat plane of his stomach to the solid muscular thighs that flexed as he raised each one in turn.

I swallowed hard and said, "Need any help in there?"

Laughing, he turned to face me, facecloth in hand, and threw it at me. "What part of 'I need to get a move on' didn't you understand?"

The facecloth missed its mark as I ducked away and hit the wall behind me.

I feigned a loud sigh of dismay and said, "It was worth a try."

"And, anyway, don't you have some work to do?"

This time I groaned for real. My publisher was spitting fire after another missed deadline. "Great. Thanks for reminding me. That's all I need." I reached behind me, grabbed the wet facecloth and threw it back at him. It hit him square in the face.

He growled as it fell away and dropped into the bath. "So that's how it's going to be?" he said, a gleam in his eyes. "You're throwing down the gauntlet, eh?"

"Er, no. It was a facecloth."

"Near enough." He reached for the shower hose.

It didn't need a genius to see where this was going. I pushed myself up and leapt towards the door as a stream of water hit the lavatory seat where I had been sitting.

"Bastard," I shouted from the safety of the hall.

A moment later, he appeared in the doorway, pulling his robe around him, a wide grin on his face. "Seriously," he said, "you need to get on with your work."

"I'm already way behind," I said. "What's a few more days?"

"It'll give you something to do while I'm away. And I asked Lowe to dig out that case file you wanted to see. Something else to keep you busy."

I followed him back into the bedroom and sat on the end of the bed while he dried his hair on a hand towel. "What time will you be back?"

"Sometime this evening. Think you can survive till then?"

"You can make it up to me by buying dinner."

He turned towards me, laughing, and said, "It's a date."

For a moment, he stood where he was, the towel hanging loose in his hand. He looked down at me, his eyes wide and full of warmth, and the broad grin faded to a gentle smile. "It's so good to have you home again," he murmured.

I caught his look and held it.

And in his eyes, I saw the man behind the mask, behind the rough and ready exterior, the man I rarely saw, vulnerable and tender.

And a tightness spread across my chest.

"Where else would I be?" I said and held his gaze a moment longer.

And then, from somewhere in the street below, the harsh metallic blast of a car horn cut through the silence, interrupting the distant hum of traffic.

And the moment passed.

Nathan went back into action-man mode. He threw the towel onto the bed, grabbed some underwear from a nearby chest of drawers, and flung open the wardrobe doors. "Come on," he said, "or I'll be late." He ran his hands along the clothes rail, picked out a shirt and a tie and a suit, and laid them out on the bed.

"I'll drop you off at the Fairview on my way," he said as he struggled into a pair of briefs.

I watched him dress, buoyed up by his lively nature, by his energy and verve and zest, his strong physical presence.

My breath caught in my throat, and I sent out a silent prayer to my personal gods, thanking them for their blessings and my great good fortune.

Yes, it was good to be home.

CHAPTER THREE

It was supposed to be a chance to catch up with an old friend. But it hadn't gone as planned.

Nathan had dropped me off at the Fairview as promised and, once I'd waved him off and made my way out to the terrace to meet up with Karen, the morning had passed pleasantly enough.

Right up until lunchtime.

Until some bozo with an attitude had spoiled it.

And what had started, for me, as a chance to relax and take some time out had escalated into an ugly scene with an inebriated knucklehead oblivious to the spectacle he was making of himself.

He was standing by the steps leading down to the Esplanade. Loud and angry. Shouting into the face of the woman he was manhandling.

And I didn't much like guys who got physically aggressive with women.

I headed towards him.

"This ends now," I said and grabbed his arm. He was one of those city types; all capped teeth and cologne.

He twisted toward me, face red with rage, still holding on to the wrist of the woman struggling to escape his grasp.

He didn't look much of a challenge. But he was drunk and looked too far gone to know when he was on the wrong end of a bad deal. I wasn't looking to get into a brawl, but I wasn't about to back down either.

Around us, the hum of conversation died away, as other patrons, sheltering from the sun under canopied tables, waited to see how the drama would unfold.

"Let her go," I said.

Before he could respond, his victim pulled herself free, stepped away from him, and rubbed the angry red mark where his fingers had dug into her skin.

He snarled, eyes blazing, and wrenched his arm from my grip. "Not your concern, fella." His hands curled into fists.

I braced myself, muscles tensed, ready for action. "I'm making it my concern."

He was shorter than me, about five-ten, and of a stockier build with a florid fleshy face under an ivy-league hairstyle.

Swaying, he fixed me with a hard stare and seemed to consider his options as we sized each other up.

Bravado must have lost out to common sense, and he backed down, relaxing his stance.

"Just a private discussion," he said. "No big deal."

"Didn't look it from where I was standing." I turned my attention to the woman. "Are you all right?"

She nodded, continued to rub her wrist, and offered her thanks. "Just a bit shaken but I'll be okay."

She was tall for a woman, not much shorter than him, willowy with a proud erect posture. Short brown hair framed a carefully made-up face with bright red lips, long dark eyelashes over hazel almond-shaped eyes and a tan that was too even to be real. She smelled expensive.

I said, "Would you like me to call the police?"

"No." She spoke the word sharply as if it was the last thing she wanted. "It was just a silly argument that got out of hand."

"It's nothing to do with the police." City boy was getting belligerent again.

Another voice came out of nowhere. "It's everything to do with us."

From somewhere behind me, Richard Lowe appeared, announcing his presence with a sharp rebuke, the craggy features marred by a scowl.

Richard Lowe, Police Sergeant with the local force, was engaged to my close friend, Karen Dyer, owner of the Fairview, and I guessed he must have been on the premises. He had a habit of dropping by on his breaks if he was in the neighbourhood.

As he approached, he reached into the breast pocket of his uniform for a notebook. "You wish to make a complaint, madam?"

City boy looked both surprised and aggrieved but said nothing, his jaw clenched.

The woman declined to take up Lowe's offer, making light of the situation, and pleaded the need to leave for an appointment.

"I really don't want to make an issue of it," she said.

"You're free to go then," Lowe said, stepping back to let her pass.

She clattered down the steps on gravity-defying heels and made her way towards a Porsche on the far side of the Esplanade.

City boy was about to follow, but Lowe held up a restraining hand. "Not you. I'm writing this up in the incident log. I'm going to need a note of your personal details." He took a pen from his pocket. "Let's start with some ID shall we?"

I nodded a curt greeting, and left him to it, making my way back to the table I had been sharing with Karen before the disturbance had flared up.

We had been enjoying each other's company and catching up on old times during the post-lunch lull. Most of the guests - those who weren't on the terrace or propping up the bar inside - had gone out for the rest of the day and it was an opportune time for Karen to take a break before the evening rush.

As I dropped into my seat, the hum of conversation started up again, louder and more excited than before.

"You didn't tell me you were running such a disreputable dive these days," I said.

Karen pulled a face. "He's not usually that bad."

"You know him then?" I asked, turning my head to keep a wary eye on Lowe and the subject of our discussion. City boy was looking decidedly less aggressive now.

"Marcus Farrow. He works up in London during the week. A banker, I think. He's often in the bar at the weekends, but he usually holds his drink better than this."

I shifted the position of my chair slightly to keep him in my line of sight. "And the woman?"

"Ah, now." She leaned forward and looked around to make sure we were out of earshot. "Bit of gossip there."

I snorted, my gaze still fixed on Lowe and Farrow. "What is it with this town? Can't anyone keep a secret here?"

Taking part in small-town gossip was way off my agenda. Still a sore point with me. It was the local gossips that had helped drive me from here in the first place.

Karen slumped back into her chair. "Well, if you don't want to know." She ran her fingers through her flame-hued untamed hair and, with a disdainful flick of the head, swept it behind her.

Before I could respond, Lowe dismissed Farrow with a terse reminder about the need for public order and headed in our direction, sliding the notebook and pen back into his pocket.

Farrow glared back at us and headed off in the opposite direction and down the stairs as Lowe sank into the other chair at our table.

Lowe grinned and said, "You've been back - what? Two days? - and you're already getting into scrapes."

I gave him a thumbs up. "Never was one for the quiet life." Tipping my head in the direction city boy had taken, I said, "So what's the story here?"

Karen said, "So now who's gossipping?"

"This isn't gossip," I said, grinning. "This is intelligence gathering."

She snorted and raised her eyes in mock despair.

Lowe laughed and filled me in with the details. "She's Lydia Carrington, engaged to John Farrow, Marcus's father."

I did some quick mental maths and raised an eyebrow. "City boy must be fiftyish, and she's obviously much younger."

"Quite," said Karen. "Lydia's got herself a sugar daddy. He's at least thirty years her senior. And by all accounts, she's milking him for all he's worth."

Lowe interjected. "No fool like and an old fool, eh?"

Another well-worn quote came to mind. 'A fool and his money are soon parted.' And, given what I had just witnessed, I had an uneasy feeling that Marcus Farrow wasn't the type to sit around and let that happen.

Karen interrupted my thoughts. She squeezed Lowe's arm and said, "Just as well you were passing, hon. Could have been much worse otherwise."

"I can take care myself," I said.

"It's not you I was worried about."

Lowe laughed and said, "Always happy to help out. But, much as I enjoy seeing you, my love, I wasn't just passing." He leaned over and planted a kiss on Karen's forehead. "This time, I dropped by to see Mikey."

He turned back to me and said, "The Chief said you'd be here. There's a case file you wanted to check out?"

"Yes, the Chief said you wouldn't mind. Is that okay?"

As Head of the Regional Crime Squad, Nathan was Lowe's immediate superior officer, and I was always careful to use his title in conversation.

"I have it down at the station. So if you want to call by in the morning."

My heart sank. "That's great," I said, hoping I sounded more enthusiastic than I was.

So much for all my well-made plans.

I'd hoped that once I had settled in at the Fairview, Nathan and I could spend some time together, a break from routine for both of us. A chance to get close again.

But it wasn't to be.

And now an altercation had spoiled an opportunity to take some time out with Karen and relax before getting back down to some serious work. Yet another anticipated pleasure ruined.

The pressures of work over the past few weeks on top of the strain of a protracted divorce settlement were taking their toll. I needed a break. But here I was, already tasked to the hilt, a publisher's deadline long overdue, and now another case file reluctantly thrust on me.

Yet another well-known quote came to mind. 'No rest for the weary'.

CHAPTER FOUR

By the time we reached the end of the pier, Karen was flagging. Struggling for air, she bent over, hands against her thighs. "Enough," she gasped. "I need a break."

A row of wooden benches lined the edge of the pier against the railings, and she lowered herself into one of them, panting heavily.

Beneath us, the sea swelled, slapping against the wooden supports, and threw spray high into the air.

Karen drew in a deep breath and said, "I'm not as fit as I used to be."

It was the following morning, and she had jumped at the chance of joining me on my usual run but was finding it hard going.

I settled into place beside her. "Just as well I'm home then. I'll soon have you back in shape."

She pulled a face and slapped my arm.

We fell into a comfortable silence, breathing heavily, our backs against the railings.

From along the shoreline at the other end of the pier, the distant sounds of shouted conversations and bursts of laughter caught on the breeze and drifted towards us across the water.

The beach was already crowded as the first of the season's holidaymakers made the most of the hot spell.

Despite all my recent pressures, personal and professional, Elders Edge was working its magic, and I was starting to relax. I was at peace, and all was well with my world.

"Glad to be back?"

Grinning, I flipped open my water bottle and handed it to her. "You'd better believe it."

My old hometown had seemed such a dull sleepy backwater to my teenage self. A rundown seaside town, long past its best. And following the rift that had split my family apart, I had left it behind, drawn to the bright lights and golden glitter of London, city of my dreams.

But after twelve years and two ex-wives, the lights had dimmed, the glitter had worn off, and the dream had faded. The less superficial attractions of Elders Edge had drawn me back.

Karen swallowed several mouthfuls of water and passed the bottle back to me. "And the divorce?"

Taking the bottle from her, I groaned and said, "When it comes to the gentle art of squeezing blood from stones, Donna has become quite the master. Or mistress in her case." I took a generous swig of water and splashed the rest of the bottle's contents on my face.

"Sorry, I didn't mean to spoil the mood."

"I'll get over it. It's all settled now anyway bar the paperwork. But it does seem to have dragged on forever."

She adjusted the sweatband on her forehead. "And Nathan? How's that going?"

"Ask me again when I've managed to pin him down. He was supposed to stand me dinner last night but stayed over in London. Do policemen ever take time off?"

Karen snorted. "Welcome to my world."

It was my father's untimely death three months earlier that had brought me back to Elders Edge and back into Nathan's company. And it was my renewed relationship with him that would keep me here.

"But everything is working out okay?" she asked.

Her concern was understandable. My on-off relationship with Nathan hadn't been one of the easiest of rides.

"Early days," I said.

"And are you, er… are you getting any closer?"

I paused in the process of wiping my face on my sweatshirt and squinted at her through narrowed eyes. "Yes, we are having sex," I said.

"Mikey!" A sharp rebuke. "That's not what I asked."

"Yes, it is. You don't fool me any."

Before she could respond, a whistling fisherman walked into earshot, a wicker case and folding stool hanging from his shoulder, and a fishing rod in hand. We exchanged nodded greetings, and he turned aside and set up his equipment nearby.

"Let's walk," I said, pushing myself to my feet.

Karen followed my lead, and we trotted back down the pier, passing strolling holidaymakers on the way.

We jogged side by side, and I shot her a sideways glance. "You know how it is with us," I said. "I let him down big time."

"But you're past all that now aren't you?"

"We're getting there," I said, "but he's still very wary. And let's face it, he never was one for jumping into anything feet first."

"That's for sure."

"He's being cautious. And I'm okay with that. All will be well."

When my father, the local priest, found out about my relationship with Nathan all those years ago, and brought down the wrath of his vengeful God on my head before disowning me, I faced a choice. Either take control of my life and stand firm for what I wanted, or run away.

I ran away.

Dumbest thing I ever did.

I turned my back on the man I loved and left without a word. An act of cowardice that hurt us both, and not something I was proud of.

But I never forgot him.

And when fate brought us together again after all those years apart and the smouldering embers of that latent desire ignited again, we were both determined to reestablish the relationship we had once shared.

But old hurts die hard and Nathan, ever cautious, was struggling to accept my renewed commitment and was taking it slow, needing to reestablish our relationship step by step, and give us time to get to know each other again.

But at least we were moving in the right direction.

Sometimes, life gives us second chances we don't deserve. I knew I didn't. And so when it was given, I'd grabbed it with both hands and held on tight, ready to settle in for the long haul.

And so I was content.

"No chance of you moving in with him?"

"I'm not sure either of us is ready for that yet. I'm going to need some time too."

"You know you have a room at the Fairview for as long as you need it?"

"I know. And I'm grateful. But I have to find somewhere more permanent. Somewhere I can spread out and call home. I'll start looking around in a few days."

"I'm sure you're doing the right thing here."

"I hope so." I changed the subject. "And how about you and lover boy? How's that working out?"

She frowned. "His name is Richard," she said, emphasising each word to make known her displeasure at my choice of name. "And we're doing just fine, thanks."

I grinned in response. "Big changes for both of us," I said. "And for what it's worth, I think you're doing the right thing too. He's a nice guy."

Richard Lowe and Karen had announced their engagement a few months before. They'd decided on a Spring wedding the following year, and Karen was busy planning for the big day as well as running a busy time-consuming business. But she still found time to engage in and support her friends' relationships when they needed it. Which is why she was still my best friend after so many years.

I glanced down at my watch. "That reminds me, we'd best get a move on, or I'm going to be late."

"What's the hurry?"

"I have a meeting with lover boy in an hour. And I wouldn't want to keep him waiting."

I broke into a run, laughing at Karen's explosion of expletives from behind me, and raced her back to the Fairview.

CHAPTER FIVE

Lowe slid the file across the desk. "What's the deal with this?"

I pulled the manila file towards me and opened it at the first page. It was headed 'Investigation into the Murder of Candy Bayliss'. "Her brother was one of my psychology students in London."

We were in Lowe's office at the back of Elders Edge Police Station. The muggy weather pressed in around us, hot and humid, and the wall fan struggled on full power to cool the air. Outside the window in the compound beyond, the early shift prepared to set off on their morning run, and the slamming of car doors and the revving of an engine interrupted the clattering of the fan's whirring blades.

Lowe dropped into the other chair at the side of the desk. "So how'd you get involved?"

"Reluctantly."

I brought him up to speed on my conversation with Rusty. Richard Lowe was well acquainted with my profiling techniques, including crime scene analyses and suspect appraisals, procedures he was often involved with. So once I'd explained how I structured my lectures around my work with the police, he understood why Rusty might assume I'd be able to use my skills and my connections to help kick-start the investigation into his sister's death.

But the more I tried to explain, the more it sounded as if I was interfering. Lowe had become a good friend over the past few months but, friend or not, I was wary of treading on his toes. The last thing I wanted was for him to think I was questioning his competence.

Once I'd finished, I added an apology. "Just so you know, I made it absolutely clear you'd be on top of this. He knows cold cases are under constant review. I don't want you to think—"

Lowe interrupted and dismissed my apology with a wave of the hand, "You don't need to explain. We're nearly two years down the line on this and, God knows, it can't be easy on the guy. It must be hard as hell to sit on the sidelines and wait. I get that."

"Just so you know."

"No worries. And if you want me to run through it with you, I'd be happy to."

"I know the body was found in Tinkers Wood but could you show me where?" A large glass-fronted map hung on the wall adjacent to the window, a high-resolution aerial view of Elders Edge, and I nodded towards it as I spoke.

Lowe pushed himself up from his chair, crossed over to the map, and tapped it near its centre. "It was here. An old abandoned cottage, right in the middle."

I rose and went to stand next to him. The map showed Tinkers Wood to the left, a large expanse of unspoiled woodland with the town bordering it to the east and running in a partial crescent around its edge.

Lowe had his finger pressed against a spot at the heart of the woods.

"I know that place," I said. "It was the gamekeeper's cottage back when Tinkers Wood was part of a private estate. We played in the old ruins as children."

"Then you'll know how remote it is."

"And that's where she was killed?"

He nodded. "One of the worst I've seen. Barely anything left of her face. He cut off her hair too."

"Rusty told me how she died." I returned to my chair and dropped into place. "Can't say I envy you that particular spectacle."

"There are some photos in the file with the pathology report if you need to see them. But I warn you, they're not pretty." He followed me back to the desk and took his seat on the other side.

I wrinkled my nose and held up a hand between us as if to rebuff the suggestion. "I'll pass on that particular pleasure for the moment." I pushed the file away. "Something else. Something that struck me as odd. Rusty lost touch with his sister before her murder. The first he knew of it was following coverage in the media. Yet when he contacted the police, they weren't able to tell him any more than he already knew; where she'd been living, who her friends were, what sort of life she'd led."

"I picked up on that too."

"I may be wrong, but the impression I got from Rusty was that enquiries about her recent past drew a blank. It's as if her corpse just materialised out of the ether. And that puzzled me."

"And me."

"No one followed up on that?"

He shrugged. "It wasn't down to me. Baxter handled the investigation back then."

Something in his tone suggested he was less than impressed by his predecessor. "Do I detect a hint of disapproval there?"

"I had a look through the file before you arrived. And far be it from me to criticise a colleague but I would have handled it differently."

I leaned back and folded my arms. "You want to tell me about that?"

"You said it yourself. She seems to have appeared from nowhere. What does that suggest to you?"

Instead of answering directly, I said, "I'm presuming you followed all the usual procedures at local level; house-to-house, local media. Anything there?"

Lowe confirmed what I was already thinking. "Total blank."

I turned some thoughts over in my mind. And for a few moments, the only sound was the whirring of the fan.

I said, "It's not unusual for a murderer to disfigure his victim and dispose of the body far from the crime scene. An unrecognisable victim with no local connections would seriously hamper any investigation. In this case, the victim was killed here. But if she was brought here for the sole purpose of killing her far from her usual environment, the effect would be the same."

"That's the line Baxter followed."

"Given that she wasn't known locally, and the way she was disfigured and shorn of hair, it's not an unreasonable assumption to make." Another thought struck me. "How was she identified?"

"Her bag was found nearby. There was ID in it. And her fingerprints were on file. She had some form."

"Yes, Rusty told me about that. Any other identifying marks?"

"There was a hummingbird tattoo on her left shoulder. No record of it though, so it must have been fairly recent."

I drummed my fingers on the desk while I thought through the various fragments of information and tried to piece them together. "Why would her killer make sure she couldn't be recognised and yet leave some ID at the scene?"

"The bag was discovered in the undergrowth by her side against one of the walls. Seems the killer overlooked it. Just carelessness. And he probably wouldn't have known her prints were on record."

I nodded, accepting the point. "Okay, so let's recap." I tapped the file. "The approach taken by your predecessor appears to have been that Candy Bayliss was brought to or lured to the scene of her murder from outside the area. This assumption based on the failure of enquiries to establish a local connection."

"That seems to be about it."

"Now let's consider an alternative."

"That's more than my predecessor did." That disapproving tone again.

"You would have taken a different approach?"

"I don't think she wanted to be found. Why else would we hit a dead end? It should be easy enough to keep tabs on someone."

Seems we were thinking along the same lines. "And if she had wanted to disappear, a change of name and location would be the best way to do it. And maybe a change of appearance."

"So she could have been living locally after all. Under another name. And instead of following that particular line of enquiry, Baxter let it pass. A big mistake."

"It also raises the question of why."

"She could have been in some kind of trouble. Maybe hiding from someone." He snorted. "Not that it did her much good in the end."

Something else occurred to me. "Were there any missing persons reports at the time?"

"No, but then people move around all the time. Quite legitimately.

So we wouldn't necessarily know if someone had suddenly disappeared from the scene. And it's not something that was given much attention. The investigation focused solely on trying to trace Candy Bayliss. So if she was living under an assumed name with a new identity, it wouldn't have registered."

"Then why don't we start there? Get things rolling again with some house-to-house and local publicity. Only this time, we're interested in anyone who left the surrounding district at around the time of the murder. Regardless of who they are."

"I'm already way ahead of you on that. It's what we should have done in the first place. And at the very least, it should settle some of my misgivings about the initial investigation."

"In the meantime, I'll let Rusty know we're taking another look at it. That should help persuade him the investigation is still active."

I pulled the file towards me again and settled down to reading it in detail. I was energised, my earlier lack of enthusiasm dispelled. Murder and its perpetrators was my subject after all, and once I got the bit between my teeth, there was nothing I liked better than probing into the darker corners of the human psyche.

CHAPTER SIX

"Nathan?"

He came to with a start. "Sorry, what was that?"

I faced him across the table and said, "I've been talking to myself for the past few minutes."

For all the attention I was getting, I could have been talking to a brick wall.

"Sorry, what did you say?" The dark heavy brows creased into a look of concern.

We were sharing a meal at the Bar Grill on the Esplanade. This was supposed to be a chance to take some time out together and relax. But Nathan was anything but relaxed. He had returned from London earlier that day in a sombre mood and had been distracted all evening, his mind obviously on other things. And I was becoming increasingly irritated as the evening wore on.

The place was busy. It was the evening rush and most of the other tables were taken. Diners sat all around us in animated chatter. Only at our table was the conversation muted.

And, okay, so he would never be a garrulous bundle of scintillating wit, but I expected more than the occasional grunt.

I tried again, "I was asking how the conference progressed."

"Oh, you know, just the usual sort of thing."

No, I didn't know. Not that I was particularly interested in the inner workings of police procedural practises, but any conversation would have been better than this.

Before I could respond, the pimply youth behind the counter barked out our order and Nathan went over to fetch our meals, sparing me any more embarrassed silences.

On his return, he transferred the contents of the tray to the table, dropped back into place, and pushed fries around his plate while I tucked into a cheeseburger.

I said, "You don't seem to have much of an appetite."

"I'm not really hungry."

I snorted. "Since when were you never hungry?"

He snapped. "Right now for instance." He spat out the words and his lips curled.

I stiffened, the cheeseburger halfway to my mouth. I put it back on my plate. "Okay, enough."

Elbows on the table, I leaned forward. "I don't know where your head's at, Nathan, but it's not here. It hasn't been here all day. So what's up?"

He groaned and screwed his face into a show of self-reproach. "I'm really sorry, Mikey. I'm just out of sorts. It's been a shitty week and I've come back from this goddamn conference to a pile of work."

As excuses went, it was pretty lame. Nathan was the type who took everything in his stride. Always on top of his game. "This isn't like you. Something isn't right."

"I'll be fine once I've settled back into my usual routine." He shot me an apologetic smile and stabbed at his fries.

Perhaps it wasn't the best of times to remind him that my return to Elders Edge was meant to upset his usual routine. At least, I'd hoped it would. That was the point of coming back after all. And, frankly, I'd expected a more enthusiastic response to my suggestion of some time together.

Something didn't add up. The warm welcome I'd received before Nathan's trip to London had morphed into a lukewarm reception on his return. And his lacklustre attitude wasn't doing much for my self-esteem right then. How could so much have changed in so little time? Something had dampened his mood. And some half-baked excuse about pressure of work would not convince me otherwise. But he wasn't about to enlighten me so I let it be.

He picked up his bun and looked around for the sauce. His idea of the perfect burger was one hidden under a thick layer of ketchup.

There were no condiments on the table so I motioned him to stay where he was, swung myself out of my chair, and headed over to the rack by the counter. Anything to give me a break from that monotonous monosyllabic conversation. Even if only momentarily.

I helped myself to a handful of sachets of sauce, and salt and pepper, and threaded my way back towards the table.

I was almost there when an unfamiliar figure intercepted me, a slight man, mature with thinning grey hair and round metal-framed spectacles. The gaudy blue and red Hawaiian shirt and bright green shorts were at odds with his general demeanour.

He said, "It's Mr MacGregor, isn't it? Michael MacGregor?"

I had no idea who he was. But I greeted him warmly, anyway. Working in the media gave me a high public profile, and it wasn't unusual to be approached by strangers familiar with my work. My TV series about the psychological aspects of unsolved murders was particularly popular just then and earned me more than the usual amount of attention.

He held out a hand. "Graham Worth. I helped organise your last lecture tour."

"Of course," I said, feigning recognition, and shook his hand. It would be impossible to remember the many brief encounters of my working life. But it always seemed more polite to pretend otherwise.

"And how is your charming wife?" he said.

I didn't have the heart to tell him that my 'charming' wife and I were engaged in a bitter battle over our divorce settlement. With a rueful smile, I explained my current marital circumstances.

His obvious embarrassment at learning of my separation was put to rest when I explained that all was well and I was happily settling into a new relationship. "So no need to be concerned on my behalf."

"Perhaps you and your lady would care to join my wife and me for dinner this evening," he suggested.

Thrown off kilter by his presumption and unsure whether to correct him, I stammered out an excuse, pleading a prior engagement.

"I'm sure I'll find more time for socialising when my work schedule allows it," I said, sidestepping the issue.

Given we weren't likely to cross paths again, I let his mistaken assumption pass without comment, ended our conversation with a promise to find time for us all to meet up at a later date, and made my way back to the table.

Nathan was scowling. "Lady? You want to explain that?" His face had reddened.

"He took me unawares." I slid onto my chair, dropped the sachets onto the table, and picked up my fork.

"Really? And it never occurred to you to put him right?" He waited for my response, stern-faced. The square jaw clenched.

"I didn't think it was that important." I kept my head down, unable to meet his gaze, and speared a couple of fries.

"Well thanks for that, Mikey. It's good to know our relationship means so little to you."

Reacting sharply, I sat bolt upright. "How can you say that?" I stared at him, shocked by his words. "Where the hell did that come from?"

He grunted and played around with the food on his plate without looking up.

"No, you're not getting away with that." I glanced around to make sure no one was listening and leaned towards him, teeth gritted. "I don't know what the hell is going on with you right now but you're not going to make me the butt of your bad mood."

"Is that all you think this is?" His eyes burned. "You just casually brush aside our relationship without a thought. How do you think that makes me feel?"

"I didn't know what to say?"

"It's really quite simple. You could have introduced us and told him who I was."

"It's not that easy."

"Seems easy enough to me. Unless you have a problem with our relationship."

This was escalating into something serious.

"I'm here, aren't I? I gave up everything I had for this. Doesn't that count for something?"

"Oh really? You mean your failed marriage and your sad wasted life? You mean that? 'Cos I don't see much of a sacrifice there."

His words hit me like a blow and I flinched, stunned into silence.

He went back to his meal, grim-faced, and squeezed several sachets of ketchup onto his burger.

Around us, other diners carried on with their conversations. Someone laughed. The counter staff called out more orders.

We sat in a small dark pool of silence and I watched him toy with his food, head down, a scowl on his face.

And for the first time since my return, the doubts crept in. Uncertainties. Could we still make this work? Or had we grown too far apart?

He was right of course. My life had been a waste. And while he was carving out for himself a successful career as an openly gay man, I was living a lie.

I was successful and popular in all the ways that didn't matter. Alone and unhappy. Trying to conform to a lifestyle that had never suited me. And now here I was, hoping for a second chance at the only relationship that had ever mattered.

But what did I know about committed gay relationships? About the constant need to stand against discrimination and prejudice, against presumption and hetero-centric thinking, about the need for openness?

I had returned full of hope, willing to commit myself to a long-term relationship, but without the experience or the social tools to help me make it work. So many issues I hadn't thought through. I had so much to learn. But I needed Nathan's support when I got it wrong, not his criticism. Did he even understand what it was like, how difficult it was to adjust? Or was he so well integrated into his lifestyle, he couldn't see the problems? Or maybe he did see them. Maybe he had his own misgivings. Maybe that explained his present mood.

A darkness settled over me and my spirits sank.

We sat a while longer in uneasy silence, until, eventually, Nathan pushed his plate away, and said, "I'm not up to this. It's been a long day and I'm tired. We should do this another time."

I nodded without speaking.

We left the remains of our meal, and I followed him out onto the Esplanade.

Nathan's Astra was parked at the roadside and, as we reached it, he said, "You need a lift?" He said it without enthusiasm, his voice flat.

I tried a smile, a feeble attempt to make amends. "No need. It's not far."

He didn't react to the smile and, unable to face him any longer, I turned and walked away without looking back.

A cool breeze blew in from the sea. I pulled up my collar as I trundled home to the Fairview, my spirits at an all-time low.

I'd thought I was making a new start, leaving all my problems behind. I hadn't realised I was creating a whole set of new ones.

CHAPTER SEVEN

Five missed calls. Four from Nathan and one from Lowe. Nathan could wait. After the previous night's disastrous meal, I needed a couple of strong coffees and a decent breakfast inside me before I was up to talking with him.

I took the stairs down to the dining room and returned Lowe's call on the way. He had some good news.

"There's been some progress on your case. We have a potential witness on her way over. You might want to sit in on this."

Breakfast could wait.

Fifteen minutes later I pulled into the car-park at the front of Elders Edge police station.

Nathan's Astra was parked in one of the bays. There was a sinking feeling in the pit of my stomach.

I needed to clear the air between us, but I was hoping to put it off until later. I was still smarting from his jibe, and the last thing I wanted right then was another unsettling confrontation.

Inside the station, I stood in line while a lively young woman with spiky hair and a spiky attitude lambasted the desk sergeant with demands for access to her boyfriend. I kept a guarded eye out for any sign of Nathan, hoping he was safely ensconced in his office, out of the way.

Fortunately, the sergeant recognised me and waved me on my way through Reception, so I didn't need to linger any longer than necessary. My luck held, and I made it to Lowe's office without having to cope with an embarrassing encounter.

Lowe offered me a seat, waving me toward the chair at the side of his desk. I took it, and said, "I didn't know the Chief would be here this morning."

His forehead furrowed as he sank into his chair.

"I'm trying to stay out of his way. Not sure what's eating him but he's been growling at everyone since he got back from London." He raised a questioning eyebrow.

My relationship with Nathan was no secret to Lowe. And God knows, we'd had our ups and downs. But why did anyone have to presume I was responsible for his moods?

I spread my hands in a show of incomprehension. "Just for once, it has nothing to do with me." That wasn't entirely true, but I wasn't about to take the blame for the sour mood that had preceded our recent spat.

Lowe shrugged, but he didn't seem convinced. "If you say so."

I grunted and changed the subject. Nathan's unaccountable mood swing would have to wait for the moment. We had more pressing issues to deal with. "So what's with this new witness? And, more to the point, witness to what?"

Turning his attention back to the matter in hand, he brought me up to date with recent developments. "I've already briefed my men, and they've been making local enquires in anticipation of a full case review in a couple of weeks' time. We also had some coverage on the local community website which seems to have paid off; it looks like we've come up with a possible lead."

"Who? What?" I was eager for him to cut to the chase and give me the specifics.

"Abby Walsh. A shopkeeper over in Colton Drey. It's only a couple of miles away, so it's still close to town. We've not got the full story yet, but it seems one of her customers fits the description of our victim, and she supposedly moved away at about that time."

He sounded bullish and upbeat, and I hoped he wasn't going to be disappointed. I was apt to be more sceptical about these things. "Let's hope she's not a time waster. We both know the sort who likes to be centre stage in local dramas. Especially something as big as this. It could be nothing."

He glanced at his watch. "She'll be here soon so you can judge for yourself."

Reaching over the desk, he turned on the monitor. "The camera's already set up in the interview room. Miles Barber will conduct the interview."

He finished fiddling with the controls and, once satisfied, sat back in his chair. "He'll be wearing an earpiece, as usual, so anything you need to ask, just use the mic here."

While he was explaining, the phone rang. It was Reception. Barber was on his way through the station with the witness.

A few minutes later, we were watching the screen as Constable Miles Barber showed Abby Walsh into the interview room.

Abby was somewhere in her middle years, long tangled locks of dark-brown hair and overly made-up eyes in a sallow care-worn face. She accepted the proffered chair and sat with her hands folded in her lap, waiting patiently and in silence for the interview to begin.

Miles Barber, an experienced interviewer, tried to put her at ease, asking if she was comfortable or if he could offer her some refreshment. All his attempts met with terse responses. Abby Walsh was clearly not in the mood for social niceties.

"Where would you like me to start?" she asked.

As Lowe and I watched them on the screen, I said, "She strikes me as the no-nonsense type. That can't be a bad thing."

Lowe agreed.

Barber began his interview by asking what had prompted her to come forward.

Abby Walsh's story was straightforward enough. Tammy Page, an old school friend, and later a regular customer at her baker's shop, had struck up a friendship with another woman, Melony Draper, a newcomer to the area.

"Everyone presumed they were sisters; the two were very much alike. But, of course, I knew they weren't. Tammy didn't have a sister. I have to say though..." and here she wrinkled her nose to express her distaste "...there seemed to be something a little - how shall I put this - a little unnatural about their relationship. They seemed to be much more than just friends if you see what I mean."

She broke off for a moment to allow Barber to react to the full horror of her revelation. When he failed to do so, she drew in a breath and shot him a disdainful look.

I silently thanked him.

She continued, "They spent all their time together. To the point of obsession, I have to say. They even shared their clothes. And they were always swapping jewellery and makeup. It all seemed rather strange to me." She sniffed again. "Well, anyway, I lost touch with Tammy. We used to socialise now and then. At first, I thought she'd changed her routine and was spending more time with her..." another sniff, "...her new friend."

Did I detect a hint of jealousy here?

Barber said, "I presume that wasn't the case?"

Abby pulled a face. "I never saw either of them again."

"You must have been aware of the investigation into the murder of Candy Bayliss. Why did you not come forward then?"

There was a touch of truculence in her tone when she replied. "I thought they must have moved away together. It never occurred to me that one of them could have... well... that something might have happened to one of them. And besides, the name meant nothing and neither of them fitted the description. They both had short brown hair. The woman in the papers had long blonde hair. I didn't make the connection."

"So when did you make the connection?"

"It was the tattoo. Your Constable made a thing about it. A tattoo of a hummingbird on the left shoulder. I suppose because the rest of the description didn't fit, I didn't give it much thought at the time."

"So this friend of Tammy's had a similar tattoo?"

Abby Walsh blinked and faced Barber with a blank stare. "No, you don't understand," she said. "It was Tammy who had the tattoo. It was Tammy you found in the woods that day."

CHAPTER EIGHT

We sat for some time after the interview was over, arguing over the implications of what we'd learned. Abby Walsh's statement had blindsided us, raising possibilities neither of us had considered. We were having to come to terms with the unpalatable; that the original investigation had identified the wrong woman. But Lowe was having a hard time taking it in.

"We can't have got it so wrong," he said. "It doesn't make sense."

"It makes perfect sense. Both women disappeared at the same time, they both fit the general description of the victim, and Tammy and the victim shared a specific identifying feature. It has to be her."

He wasn't convinced. "She had ID. And Candy Bayliss's prints were all over the handbag."

"You heard what Abby said. They shared possessions. Something they did all the time."

"Ah, but you're forgetting something." Suddenly animated, he snatched up the file and rifled through the pages. "We had a fingerprint ID, remember?"

"I seem to remember the ID was made from personal documents and Rusty's later confirmation."

Lowe stopped at one particular page, ran his finger down it, and groaned.

"Well?" I said.

"You're right. Fingerprints were taken from the bag, not directly from the victim."

"Shouldn't that have been done as a matter of course?"

"Not if the original ID was made by other means. Prints would have been lifted from the scene as a possible means of identifying the murderer. When some of them matched those on Candy's records, they would have been considered as additional confirmation of the original ID. And then her brother's later identification would have clinched it."

We sat in silence for a while, both lost in our own thoughts.

"This is going to change everything," I said.

Lowe nodded, finally accepting the inevitable. "I'll have to take this to the Chief." He picked up the file and rose to his feet. "Might as well get it over with." He hovered over me, waiting for me to follow his lead.

"You want me there too?" I said.

"Sure I do. I want your support."

Reluctantly, I rose from my seat and followed him out into the corridor towards Nathan's office. I'd hoped not to have to face Nathan yet but I hadn't been left with much choice.

Lowe knocked on Nathan's door and stuck his head inside. "You got a moment, Chief? We have a situation here."

"Sure. Come in."

I followed Lowe into the room.

Nathan was seated behind his desk, a large mahogany affair with an inlaid green leather surface. Files and papers were arranged in neat orderly piles on the desktop, unlike Lowe's desk which always looked as if it had been thrown around in an earthquake.

A flicker of surprise crossed Nathan's face when he saw me but he said nothing. Pushing aside the file in front of him, he waved us towards a couple of chairs on the other side of his desk, leaned back, and waited for an explanation.

We seated ourselves, and Lowe handed Nathan the Bayliss file before briefing him on the recent interview.

While he listened, Nathan flipped through the file and, once Lowe had finished, he closed it and said, "Your interviewee referred to Tammy's friend as Melony Draper. How sure are we that she and Candy Bayliss are the same person?"

I said, "We've already discussed the possibility of Candy Bayliss living under an assumed identity. It would explain why there's no trace of her in the months before her death. This new information would support that theory. And Candy Bayliss's prints were on the bag. We know that the two women shared their clothing and accessories, so it seems almost certain they were one and the same."

Nathan picked up a pen and turned it over and over in his hand, his eyes focused somewhere in the distance behind us.

A side window opened onto the car park, and the muted sound of passing traffic drifted into the room while Lowe and I sat in silence, waiting for Nathan's reaction.

"Okay," he said, "here's what we do. We go public with the two names but, for the moment, the official line is that we're making enquiries in respect of the Candy Bayliss murder. No mention of a possible misidentification. For the moment, we'll keep that under wraps."

I said, "We can't keep it quiet indefinitely. It will be public knowledge soon enough. So we need to be ahead of the game. We need to tell Rusty."

Nathan agreed. "Can you deal with that, Richard?"

I butted in before Lowe could respond. "Would you mind if I spoke to him? It might be better coming from a friend."

A slight hesitation. "Okay," he said, and turning to Lowe again, "But be sure to follow it up, would you? Let's do it by the book."

He rose from his chair, indicating that the meeting was over. Lowe and I followed suit and Lowe said, "I'll get things moving." He headed for the door.

I waited for him to leave.

There was some unfinished business to deal with here and now was as good a time as any. As Lowe closed the door behind him, I turned to face Nathan and squared my shoulders.

"You were trying to get hold of me," I said.

"I wasn't sure if you'd got my calls."

"My phone was off. And then all this." I waved a desultory hand across the room.

"Yes, of course." He cleared his throat.

With so much more to say and neither of us finding the words to say it, the exchange dried to an uneasy silence.

He seemed as lost for something to say as I was and we faced each other, embarrassed, unsure how to continue.

And then a flurry of words.

"I just wanted to say how sorry—"

"I shouldn't have said—"

We both stopped and smiled. And the tension eased away. Nathan's jaw relaxed and the wide shoulders dropped.

"I'm an idiot," I said.

"Welcome to the club." He stepped around from the other side of his desk, opened his arms, and murmured, "Come here."

A moment later, I was in his embrace and this time the silence was warm and comforting.

I wrapped my arms around him and hugged him close. "I know it was a dumb thing to do and I'm sorry."

He tightened his hold around me. "Yeah, well. I could have chosen my words more carefully."

Pulling away, he held me by the arms and stared into my face, a questioning look in his eyes.

"Come sit," he said and, keeping hold of one arm, he lowered himself onto the nearby couch and pulled me down beside him. Still holding on to my arm, he said, "I know it's not been easy for you, Mikey. I know what you had to put up with back in the day. But this isn't the Dark Ages. You don't need to live a lie anymore."

"I know that up here." I tapped the side of my head with a forefinger. "It just came out wrong. This is all new to me."

He tilted his head to one side, and his forehead creased into a frown. "Am I asking too much of you?" he said.

"No more than you'd ask of any reasonable person. Not your fault you ended up with a flake."

He responded with a grin. And his cheek dimpled.

I became serious again. "I know these aren't the Dark Ages. But someone forgot to tell my parents. And I'm still learning how to deal with the fallout from that."

"You can't live in the past, Mikey. You have to move on."

"You think it's so easy?" I didn't wait for a reply. "I've lived the lie so long, it's become a part of me. I guess I'm still catching up with the rest of the world."

I tried to read his face, looking for some sign of acceptance. "And I know you're right but let's not pretend it's all plain sailing. Even in these enlightened times, there's still plenty of prejudice out there. And I'm not you. I find it difficult to deal with. Don't tell me you haven't had to face your share of prejudice along the way. Especially in your line of work."

"Sure I have. But you don't solve the problems by hiding away. I'm not pretending it's always easy. You often have to go that extra mile to prove yourself. But you get there in the end."

I nodded, accepting his point with an understanding smile. "Maybe it's you who should have settled for an accountant."

He snorted. "I'm not sure I could stand the excitement." He treated me to one of his dimple-making smiles. "So no more lurking in the closet, eh?"

"Okay," I said with a grin. "And I have to admit, it does get a bit claustrophobic in there."

"Tell you what..." He gave my arm an extra squeeze. "...let's go get some lunch." He stood up. "My treat. To make up for yesterday. We both need to unwind."

"Sounds good to me."

We left the station together, chatting aimlessly, secure again in each other's company. And whatever misgivings I'd had fell away. Sure, I was going to have to make some changes along the way; living behind a false facade wasn't an option anymore. And I was more determined than ever to make this work.

The sun was riding high in a clear blue sky, raising a shimmering heat haze from the tarmac. And as we crossed the car park, I took off my light linen jacket and slung it over my shoulder.

We reached his Astra, and Nathan changed the conversation back to the investigation. "I went through the outstanding cases when I took over at Division. Can't say I saw any problems with the way the investigation was handled." He unlocked the Astra's doors with his fob, climbed into the driver's seat, and started the engine.

I slid in beside him and threw my jacket onto the back seat. "A written account doesn't always give the full picture."

"True enough. I'll go through the file in more detail later." He slipped the Astra into gear, headed over to the car park entrance and swung out onto the main road. "But for now, let's forget about work shall we? Time enough for that later."

"Suits me." I turned on the air conditioning. "But first, I need to make that phone call." I dug into the pocket of my jeans for my mobile. "Probably best to make it while you're here. You can hear how it goes."

I called Rusty and spent several uncomfortable minutes explaining the current position with the investigation. It wasn't one of the easiest calls I'd ever made.

I finished my carefully rehearsed words and waited for a response. There was silence at the other end.

"Rusty? Are you still there?"

An audible exhalation of breath. "I don't know what to say. I'm stunned."

Hardly surprising. I figured having a dead sister come back to life after a couple of years might have that effect.

"Nothing's certain," I said. "At the moment, it's just an outside chance. But it's the sort of thing the media picks up on. I wanted you to be prepared before it hit the news."

He thanked me and I finished the call with a promise to let him know of any developments.

"That must have been one hell of a shock," said Nathan. "What's this guy like?"

"He's a good friend. The type who stands by you and looks out for you when you need it. I owe him. And I'd like to give him my support now he needs it."

Nathan grunted but said nothing.

He took a left turn and pulled over onto the forecourt of the Dog and Duck. "If we really do have a case of mistaken identity here, and if his sister is still alive, you have to wonder why she's not been in touch with him."

"If she's still alive. You hit the nail on the head." I reached over the back seat for my jacket as Nathan turned off the engine.

We climbed out of the car, and as we strolled towards the pub, he explained his thinking. "Someone may have realised their mistake and got it right the second time." He swung open the door to the lower bar and ushered me in. "So for all we know she could already be another victim."

"Could be. It would also explain why she never contacted the police. You'd think if her life was in danger, she'd want to report it."

"Depends what she was mixed up in."

The Dog and Duck wasn't too busy. We found a table over by the window and I dropped into place, draped my jacket over the arm of the adjacent chair and picked up the menu.

"I'm starving," I said. "I skipped breakfast this morning." Glancing up at him, I added, "I hope you have your appetite back."

The underlying meaning in my words wasn't lost on him. With a twinkle in his eyes, he said, "No need to get in a sweat about it. I promise I won't bite your head off."

I leaned back in my chair and grinned. "It worries me not to see you wolfing down your food."

"Then worry no more. I'm starving too."

He wasn't joking either. He ordered a triple cheese and bacon burger with fries and extras while I went for a lasagna. And when we finally got our meals, there seemed to be enough on his plate to feed a family of four for a week. I always wondered how he managed to stay in such great shape with all the food he shovelled away and guessed his gym routine must be a punishing one.

We passed the rest of the meal pleasurably enough with a lot of light-hearted banter and casual small talk, both of us much more relaxed. This was the Nathan I knew, the dependable one.

While we waited for the bill, the conversation took a more serious turn. I said, "I know I let you down, Nathan. I've not always made the best of choices and I know what a mess I made of things. But I promise you, I won't let you down again."

He stared at me blankly for a moment. And then the light went out of his eyes and he looked down at the table. When he answered, his voice took on a flat monotonous tone. "We all make mistakes, Mikey. I guess it's how we deal with them that matters."

It was only afterwards, thinking back to that pained look on his face, I wondered what mistakes he thought he'd made.

CHAPTER NINE

"The Chief's with us all the way on this," said Lowe. "He took a closer look at the file and he agrees the investigation needs to be steered in a different direction."

It was early morning, and we were in Lowe's Astra heading towards Tinkers Wood.

"Any progress on that?" I asked.

"Not yet. But my men are still out there making enquiries. Only now we're looking for anyone who had a connection to Tammy Page and Melony Draper."

"The media coverage should help with that. I guess we'll just have to wait."

A week had passed with no new developments on the investigation. But, hopefully, the publicity would bring in results.

On a personal level, life wasn't ideal either. Nathan's heavy work commitments and our living apart imposed limits on our time together. What little time we did have to ourselves was precious and pleasurable enough. But relationship? Not so sure about that. It was more like the setup he'd had with Brandon, his ex. A friendship with benefits. Casual.

But if, eventually, we were to commit to something more lasting, we needed to establish a common shared routine; my occasional stopover at Nathan's flat in Charwell wasn't going to hack it.

His desire to reestablish our relationship a step at a time was understandable. It's not as if my past behaviour had inspired much confidence. But if I could find a more permanent home for myself and persuade him to stay over for longer periods, it would be a step in the right direction.

Which is what this morning's outing was about. A possible rental. One that Lowe had learned of.

Just past the end of Old Farm Lane, he turned into Woodside Road, pulled over, and parked against the low flintstone wall running alongside the embankment to the left.

He switched off the engine and nodded towards a building on the other side of the road. "This is it."

The building was a cottage of ivy-covered yellow stone under a peg tiled roof, the type you usually see only on the cover of chocolate boxes; too good to be true. And yet here it was. In glorious isolation right on the edge of Tinkers Wood.

It crouched in a hollow by the roadside, peering over the top of a privet hedge from the far side of a garden run riot with rambling roses, hollyhocks, and a host of country flowers, and shaded by surrounding elms.

"It's perfect," I said. "How did you come across it?"

"The last tenant did a runner and took some of the landlady's furnishings with him. She called it in as a theft."

"Great. You sure she wants another tenant after that?"

"She jumped at the chance. A long-term tenant is a much safer bet."

"If you're sure."

"She's hardly likely to turn down a recommendation from the local police, is she? And I knew you were looking for somewhere. Seemed like the ideal solution for both of you."

"Well, let's go see," I said, getting out of the car.

"You're lucky to find a place during the holiday season," said Lowe as we made our way along the garden path. "The last tenant got it only because there was a last minute cancellation."

A stern-faced woman met us at the door, thin, pointed hawk-like features, grey hair scraped back in a bun. Lowe introduced her as Martha Stubbs.

This was going to need a full charm offensive.

I shot her one of my best winsome smiles, sympathised with her loss, and spent the next few minutes praising her gardening skills and asking her advice on the most suitable growing conditions for dahlias. Moments later, I was ducking through the doorway and a smiling Mrs Stubbs was showing me around an oak-beamed living room and giggling like a schoolgirl.

Lowe rolled his eyes at me behind her back. "I'm sure you don't need any help from me," he said, making no attempt to hide his sarcasm.

He took his leave of us and returned to the car while I toured the house and talked terms with Mrs Stubbs.

"I've always liked the rustic look," I said. "And this a perfect example. It's charming."

It was too. Dark varnished oak floorboards creaked underfoot as I made my way around the room, running a hand over the white stucco walls, admiring the low wooden beams, trying out the deep fabric-covered window seat on the wall facing out into the woods.

"I don't know how anyone could bear to leave here, Mrs Stubbs," I said.

"Do please call me Martha," said Mrs Stubbs, and continued, "I usually let it out short term as a holiday rent, a week or two at a time. But it's becoming too much of a chore. Especially when this sort of thing keeps happening."

I raised an eyebrow. "The theft? It's happened before?"

"You'd be surprised. Usually, it's just towels and crockery. People these days don't even think of it as stealing. But the last one went too far."

"I hope the police can help."

She waved a dismissive hand. "I shouldn't think so. He paid by post; a Bankers Draft. So I doubt they'll trace him."

"Didn't you give the police a description?"

A rueful look. "I never met him. I left the keys under the mat."

Some people are too trusting for their own good. But I wasn't going to say so. After all, it had been to my advantage.

"Not that it's much consolation," I said, "but it did me a favour. I couldn't have wished for anywhere better."

"You're happy with it then?"

"Couldn't be happier. Not sure how long I'll need it but I'm willing to pay three months up front."

Much as I loved the cottage, the furniture left something to be desired. Utilitarian at best, it was the sort of cheap make-do stuff typical of transient short-term living. I needed something more substantial, more permanent. In other words, my own furnishings.

Might as well broach the subject and see how she felt. "There is one thing. Given that it's a long-term stay, I'd feel much more comfortable with my own furniture around me. Would that be okay?"

Her expression suggested she wasn't too sure, so I hastily added, "Mine's in storage in Charwell at the moment and I'd be prepared to have yours take its place. At my expense, of course."

I held my breath while she thought it over.

Finally, with a slight tilt of the head, she smiled and said, "I'm sure it will be fine. I can't see any problems."

I breathed a sigh of relief and thanked her. "You won't regret it," I said.

For the next few minutes, we talked terms and payment and, once agreed, she said, "I'll have the cottage cleaned and have all the ornaments and bric-à-brac stored away, and then you can clear it out and move in as soon as you like."

We shook hands before saying our goodbyes and parting company, and I made my way back to the car feeling more cheerful.

Lowe didn't seem in a mood to share my good fortune. He was hurrying up the path towards me, grim determination stamped on his face. Clearly, something was amiss.

"What's wrong?" I said.

"We need to be on our way, Mikey." His face was drawn. "Just had a call from the station." He turned back towards the car.

I hastened after him and climbed in beside him as he switched on the ignition.

Something about his manner put me on alert. He was troubled, perplexed. None of the usual professional detachment. This was something different.

"Who, what, where?" My mind was awhirl with questions.

"We have a murder on our hands."

"What the...?"

I fastened my seatbelt as he swung out into the road. A moment later we were racing away around the perimeter of Tinkers Wood, emergency light flashing.

He said, "The Duty Sergeant sent a team over there. But I need to see this for myself. They found her in Tinkers Wood. In the old gamekeeper's cottage."

A slow creeping sensation spread across my chest, and my throat tightened. A sixth sense told me I was about to learn something I didn't want to hear.

"This is just getting crazy," he murmured. "It doesn't make sense any more." He was no longer talking to me. He was talking to himself as if he was trying to convince himself of something.

"What the hell is this?"

"It's Candy Bayliss. They just found Candy Bayliss."

CHAPTER TEN

Less than ten minutes later, we were in the middle of Tinkers Wood, trudging towards the crime scene.

A fetid smell rose from shallow hollows in the rocky ground where the early summer rains had settled into dirty stagnant pools. I wrinkled my nose against the stench and swatted away the cloud of midges hovering before us in the damp humid air.

The ruins of the old stone cottage lay nestled in the undergrowth ahead and as we neared them, I said, "It is definitely her? You're absolutely certain?" I still couldn't quite believe it.

"We use electronic fingerprint scanners at the scene these days. We got a match on the national database."

"No arguing with that I guess."

Struck by a sudden thought, I pulled up short. "Do you want me to speak with Rusty?"

Lowe stopped too. "You're off the hook there. This is a new investigation. So best to keep it official. I'll call him when I return to the station."

"Rather you than me."

We set off again.

"I need to get him down here anyway," said Lowe. "We'll need to re-interview him and he'll have to formally identify the victim."

Bright yellow duct-tape cordoned off the wooded area around the building's crumbling remains. A uniformed officer stood guard at the access point.

Lowe greeted him with a nod and asked for his assessment of the current situation.

"The pathologist got down here pretty sharpish, Sir. He's already finished his initial examination of the body." As he spoke, the young constable handed us both a set of disposable coveralls and overshoes. "He was waiting for your arrival before having it moved to the path lab."

We both donned the protective clothing and, as we entered the crime scene, Lowe said, "The Chief's been apprised of the situation. I understand he wanted you to see the body in situ."

It wouldn't be the first time I'd assisted the local force under Nathan's command. The first one being a case in which I was personally involved given that the victim had been my father.

"Is the Chief on his way?"

"He went up to London. I thought you knew."

I didn't. And it seemed odd he hadn't told me. But I said nothing and put it from my mind.

Lowe said, "He'll be back later today. I'll give him a full report then."

Around us, crime scene investigators went about their duties. Uniformed officers searched the ground, some on hands and knees. A photographer moved from spot to spot, taking shots from a variety of angles, and nearby, someone was sketching a map of the area.

"Okay, let's do this." I swallowed hard. Examining corpses was one of the less appetising aspects of my work. Necessary, but not something I relished all the same.

Lowe stepped forward.

I took him by the arm and brought him to a halt. "But first, I'd like to know how she died. Did you get any details?"

Lowe nodded.

"Same MO?"

It wasn't lost on either of us what we were probably dealing with here. This was a copycat killing with a difference; the possibility that the intended victim had been the same in both cases.

"Yes, she was battered to death," said Lowe. "Several blows to the head and face." He grimaced. "Sorry, I should have warned you. It's not going to be the prettiest of sights."

"Great." Mentally bracing myself, I turned toward the blue plastic awning that covered the victim's final resting place. "May as well get it over with then."

This time, it was Lowe's turn to put a restraining hand on my arm. "Before we go in there, let me have your thoughts on the crime scene itself."

These woods were part of my past. I knew them well. All about us, majestic ash trees, tall and wide-domed, filtered sunlight through to the shade-loving ferns, foxgloves and sweet-smelling honeysuckle at their bases. High above us, the raucous shriek of a jay interrupted the musical trill of a blackbird.

I said, "The Chief and I played here as children. The local kids used the old cottage as a den."

"I wasn't around these parts back then," said Lowe, "but I heard some tales about the place. Got a bit of a reputation, hasn't it?"

"We used to say it was haunted. It added to the mystique. Made it more attractive."

"The gamekeeper, wasn't it? Some sort of accident?"

"No one's really sure. It was a private estate in the old days. Sylas Gray was the gamekeeper. They found him one day next to his shotgun with his head blown off. Never did find out if it was suicide, an accident or murder."

"Looks like the old place just got itself some more ghosts. So what can you tell me about the scene itself?"

It's not as if any of this was new to me. Just part of a well-worn routine. But this was different. This was home ground, familiar territory, and it felt personal. These were old childhood haunts.

"Was she killed here?" I said.

"Forensic analysis confirms otherwise. Signs of livor mortis show she was moved, and she was covered in carpet fibres, suggesting an indoor location."

"Then presumably our murderer killed his victim somewhere that could be linked to him. His home maybe. That's the usual reason for moving a body."

I scanned the site again, taking in more detail.

The old cottage was right at the heart of Tinkers Wood, a considerable distance from the perimeter on all sides. Broken stone walls smothered with chickweed and ivy surrounded the rubble-strewn approach. Nearby, a couple of rotting car tyres lay half-buried in the mud. Most of the building's outer wall had collapsed, leaving a pile of shattered stones partially blocking the entrance.

"It's off the beaten track," I said. "Which is what you'd expect. He wouldn't want to risk dumping a body somewhere too public."

I turned in a complete circle, looking out into the woods beyond the crime scene, trying to remember the layout. "Where's the nearest vehicle access?"

"There's an old dirt road leading into the wood from the side opposite the town. But it's been overgrown for years. You can't get very far. Barely a few metres."

"And that's the point. This place is almost too remote. Too inaccessible. The killer could have left the body nearer the perimeter and still been well away from prying eyes."

"And the area around is uneven and strewn with debris. Difficult to reach."

"Which, all in all, just confirms my first thoughts. The scene was staged. As soon as I knew the location, I figured it might be a setup."

Lowe agreed with my assessment and said, "But why go to all that trouble? Why recreate the original murder?"

"That remains to be seen."

Somewhere up above, the jay shrieked out another warning.

Lowe took me by the arm. "Let's go look at the body." He guided me around the half-hidden collapsed wall and under the shade of the protective awning.

It was the smell that hit me first. The sweet sickening stench of death. I pressed a hand to my mouth and pinched my nose.

The corpse lay full length on its back, dressed in a mud-splattered beige trouser suit, arms and legs spreadeagled.

What had once been a face was now a twisted mess of bone and flesh caked in congealed blood and surrounded by a tangled and blood-clotted mass of dark brown hair. The single remaining eye stared up in a mockery of wide-eyed surprise. The mouth was a gaping hole filled with broken teeth.

The body was already decomposing, a sign that it had lain here for a few days. Three or four large flies, disturbed by our presence, buzzed around the body.

I closed my eyes. Squeezed them tight shut. And waited until my heart had stopped pounding.

Turning away, I opened my eyes and stepped back into the open air. Lowe followed behind me.

I paused for a moment. Took in a long deep breath. And exhaled slowly. Nothing would ever prepare me for sights or smells like this.

Nearby, the jay repeated its nerve-jangling shriek.

"Okay?" said Lowe.

I nodded and said, "God help the poor sod who first stumbled into this particular nightmare. Do you know who found the body?"

"An early-morning dog walker called it in. I don't think Fido will be frisking around here again any time soon."

"You know we're dealing with a psychopath?"

"What?"

"Whoever did this. He's a psychopath."

"You want to explain that?"

"A killer often moves the body after death. He'll arrange it so as to hide what he's done or to restore some dignity to the victim. It's a show of remorse, a belated attempt to make amends. Something we call 'psychic erasure' or 'restitution'."

"But not this killer?"

I shook my head. "He left her exposed in a way that drew attention to the act. Did you notice the dried mud on her clothing?"

Lowe confirmed that he had.

"It looks as if he dumped the body face down and then turned it over and staged it in a way that fully displayed the brutality of his act. He wanted the world to admire his handiwork. This is a killer who took a great deal of pleasure in what he did with no regard for the dignity of his victim."

We stood in silence for a minute or so.

I said, "Two murders in the same place. Doesn't exactly enhance the town's reputation as a must-visit holiday destination does it?"

I turned away, stared out through the trees into the past, and watched myself running, laughing, enjoying a time of childhood innocence. We'd been safe here. Despite the area's macabre past, there had been no thought of danger, not in this idyllic place, among the sun-dappled clearings and humming bees. But that had changed. Now it was a killing place again.

CHAPTER ELEVEN

The town square bustled with activity. It was market day. Locals and holiday makers alike pressed about the many rickety wooden stalls, buying their weekly groceries or browsing for other goods. A cacophony of sounds reverberated around us, echoing back from the buildings surrounding the square.

Karen and I were at the greengrocer's stand. I was helping her pack her purchases into a large folding shopping trolley.

In need of some company after the previous day's depressing events, I'd let her persuade me into helping with the shopping.

Next stop was the hardware stand at the far end of the market. We headed towards it.

The air was rich with the aroma of cooking from a variety of food stalls. As we passed the beefburger kiosk, a plume of smoke carrying the woody tang of charred meat drifted towards us, vying for olfactory attention with the yeasty smell of freshly baked bread from the nearby bakery stand.

Cloth awnings flapped in the breeze. From beneath them, vendors called out to customers, their cries mixing with the animated chatter and laughter from groups of shoppers milling around us.

At the hardware stall, Karen rifled through a rack of paint charts and kept up a constant stream of talk about the pros and cons of various colour schemes.

She had taken it into her head to turn one of the Fairview's larger storerooms into extra living space for when Richard moved in and was fussing over decorating ideas for the eventual makeover.

A can of paint stood within reach on the counter. I drummed my fingers on its lid and stared into the distance, only half listening.

The carefree atmosphere of my surroundings was in sharp contrast to the grim sombreness of the previous day's scene in Tinker's Wood. But I couldn't shake off the gloom I'd felt afterwards.

Not that it was the only thing on my mind.

"Will you stop that?"

I came to with a start.

Karen's face was pinched.

"Sorry," I said and folded my arms.

She stared at me a moment longer without speaking, and then, "You're not your usual self, Mikey. What's wrong?"

"Oh, you know. Things."

She tilted her head to one side, the way she always did when she was about to interrogate me, and fixed me with a glassy stare. "No, I don't know. What things?"

"It's probably nothing." In an attempt to change the subject, I pointed to the chart in her hand, and said, "Have you made up your mind?"

She wasn't to be deterred. Taking me by the arm, she drew me to the far end of the stall, out of earshot of the stall holder. "I'm waiting."

"You'll think I'm mad."

"For God's sake, Mikey. This is like wading through treacle. Do I have to drag it out of you?"

I sidestepped a young couple heading past us towards the centre of the market and let out a sigh of exasperation. "Nathan was up in London yesterday. I drove over to his place when he got back."

I hesitated for a moment, unsure how to say what was on my mind. "He left some receipts lying around and I happened to notice one for a restaurant in Stoke Newington."

"So?"

"Isn't that where Brandon lives?"

Karen knew of Nathan's past relationship with Brandon Barwell. They had met while Brandon was holidaying at the Fairview.

Her face set hard. And then her hand closed around the chart she was holding, and she screwed it into a tight ball in her fist.

Maybe I'd been a bit too hasty in raising my concerns.

She leaned towards me, chin thrust forward, and, raised her voice several octaves. "Are you insane?" Her tone suggested she'd already settled on an answer to that particular question.

I glanced about me. Fortunately, we were at the quieter end of the market and not too many people were around to hear Karen's dictum on the state of my mind. "See. I said you'd think I was mad."

"Well, you got that right at least."

"It just seemed a bit out of his way. He always has his meetings in the city. Presuming he had a meeting. He was even cagey about that."

"He's entitled to some downtime, for God's sake. And Stoke Newington's known for its restaurants. People go there from all over."

"I suppose," I said, not convinced.

"Listen, Mikey." Her tone was brittle. "You're way off the mark here. As far as Brandon Barwell is concerned that ship has well and truly sailed. Nathan made his choice, and that's the end of it. And if you really are that bothered, why don't you ask him?"

I wrapped a hand around one of the stall's support poles and gripped it. "I can't do that. He might think I'd been snooping."

"You were snooping."

"No, I wasn't." I was indignant.

"Right. So you just happened to see this receipt lying around. And you just happened to pick it up and read it."

"Okay, okay, I was snooping." I released my grip on the support.

"But why, Mikey? Why the doubts all of a sudden? Where's this coming from?"

"It's just a feeling I have."

"A feeling? You have a feeling?" She spat out the words as if they were tainted.

"Don't knock it. I know when something's wrong." I stretched out a hand towards her, imploring. "Look, everything was fine till his conference trip to London. But something happened. I know it. He seems to have the weight of the world on his shoulders. You must have noticed it."

I leaned back against the counter and looked for some understanding in her expression. I didn't find any. "And something he said the other day. It's been on my mind. He wanted to know if he'd asked too much of me. Coming back here. It was as if he was questioning the whole idea."

"He's bound to be concerned. It was a big change."

"That's what he said."

"Well then." She smoothed out the chart in her hand and dropped it into the bag she carried over her shoulder.

"It seemed an odd thing to say."

"You're being paranoid." She grabbed the handle of her trolley and moved away, closing the discussion and making it clear her words were the final say on the subject.

We stopped at the newspaper stand and I picked up a copy of the Charwell Echo. The stand-holder was nowhere in sight so, while Karen simmered in silence, I browsed through a rack of magazines and waited for his return.

A seagull screeched overhead as it headed towards the beach.

Nearby, an elderly man on a mobility scooter shouted obscenities at the youth who stepped into his path and earned a raised finger in response.

A young woman behind the counter of the adjacent linen stall occasionally glanced over at us from its far end.

Karen lowered her voice, and said, "Everything is okay between you and Nathan isn't it?"

"We did have a bit of a disagreement the other day but we sorted that out."

A small groan escaped her lips, and she muttered something under her breath. She gripped my arm, and said, "Look, Mikey. When you went back to London, you left giving Nathan the impression you'd soon be back. It was getting on for four months."

My throat tightened, and I swallowed hard. "There was a lot to sort out. Work commitments. The divorce. And I stayed in touch as much as I could."

The young woman at the linen stall moved towards us along the counter, folding and rearranging sheets and pillowcases as she went. She was still watching us.

Karen flashed her a smile and waited until she had moved away before resuming our exchange. She let go of my arm. "I'm not blaming you for anything here. I'm just saying how it was."

All the same, I felt a twinge of guilt. I would have given anything to come back sooner.

The news-stand stall holder spotted me from across the square and raised a hand in acknowledgement as he headed towards us, a sandwich in his other hand. I fished in my pocket for some loose change.

"The point I'm trying to make," said Karen, "is that Nathan was on tenterhooks all that time. He couldn't wait for you to get back. Brandon Barwell was the last person on his mind."

I shrugged. "Maybe I'm being dumb."

"There's no 'maybe' about it. You are being dumb. Sometimes you go out of your way to make trouble for yourself."

The news vendor reached us, apologising profusely. I paid him, dismissing his apology with a smile and a shake of the head, and we moved away.

Karen was about to launch into yet another diatribe about my faults but didn't get the chance. We were interrupted by the young woman from the linen stall.

She stepped in front of us. "You're that bloke from the telly, right?"

I halted, surprised by the sudden intrusion. "I have appeared on TV now and again, yes."

Karen interrupted. "It's Mia, isn't it?"

"Yes, ma'am." Mia dipped in a half-curtsy.

I suppressed a grin. Karen had that effect on people sometimes.

Karen offered an explanation. "Mia works for me at the Fairview when we're busy."

I acknowledged this with a nod and turned my attention back to the girl. She was short, not more than four feet tall, on the chubby side with dark brown hair scraped back from a pudgy round face. She shuffled uneasily from one foot to the other as if discomforted.

"What can I do for you, Mia?" I said.

She pointed at the newspaper in my hand. "You're mixed up in this murder, aren't you?" Once the news of the murder had broken, it had hit the Echo's headlines the following day along with all the depressing details of its connection to the first murder.

"I wouldn't put it in quite those terms," I said. "But, yes, I am part of the investigation team."

"Thing is…" Mia shuffled uneasily once more. "…I might have seen the bloke what did it."

CHAPTER TWELVE

Mia stared up at me through defiant eyes as if daring me to doubt her. A small fist twisting the top of her tabard.

"What makes you so sure?"

"I saw them arguing. I told Abby - I work with her see. A Saturday job. And it was after she told the police - but she said I was being foolish. It was a while back. A couple of years. But I should say something, shouldn't I? I still remember. I know what I saw." The words came tumbling out, tripping over themselves in a hurry to be heard.

I held up a restraining hand. "Just take it easy and tell me what you can."

She was still shuffling from foot to foot, still twisting the top of the tabard in her fist. "I do some evenings in The Partridge over in Colton Drey. And the woman who, you know..." She pointed to the newspaper again "...she was sometimes in there with that friend of hers." She hesitated. "The other one."

"We're talking here about the two murder victims?" I said.

A short rapid nod. Lips pressed in a tight line.

"It's okay," I said. "Take your time."

"They were sat in their usual place. Always came in together. And then one night, this man comes in. I'd not seen him before. He comes right up and speaks to her. To Tammy's friend. I didn't know her name. I knew Tammy of course. From the shop. She often came in. Her and Abby was good friends at one time. Though not so much lately."

Mia was gabbling again.

"Whoa." I held up my hand again. "Slow down. Tell me about this man. What makes you think he's involved?"

"It was the look on her face." Mia's eyes dimmed, and she stared out into the distance, focused on the past. "She was scared. Really scared. I'll never forget it."

A sharp complaining voice brought her back to the present. "Excuse me, Miss. Are we going to get any service over here today?"

Mia turned towards the scowling middle-aged woman waiting at the linen stall and then back to me, a pleading look in her eyes.

"Why don't you serve your customer and then come and talk to me again." I pointed to a row of metal-framed wooden benches over by a low brick wall that flanked the square's side boundary. "We'll wait for you there."

Her face relaxed, and she dipped again in a half-curtsy before scuttling over to the complainant.

Karen's took my arm as we walked away and, after a quick glance back at Mia, lowered her voice, and said, "I should warn you, Mia's a bit of a fantasist. She's the kind who can make a drama out of the smallest thing."

"She seemed genuine enough."

"I'm just saying. Don't take everything she says at face value."

We reached one of the benches and seated ourselves. Over at the linen stall, Mia was wrapping her customer's purchase and occasionally glancing our way.

I said, "Let me try something. When she comes back, say something to show you doubt what she says. Nothing confrontational. Just a gentle rebuff."

Karen wrinkled her nose. "How is that supposed to help?"

"I want to see how she reacts. It should be different depending on whether or not she's fabricating or building it up."

Before Karen could question me further, Mia was hurrying towards us. As she reached us, I stood up to greet her.

Out of breath, she pressed a hand to her chest, and said, "Sorry about that."

I offered her a seat between us, and as I reseated myself, I said, "Nothing you've said so far persuades me that this man had anything to do with our investigation."

Mia wriggled into place. "It was what I heard later. She was on the phone. In the Ladies. I heard her."

Karen interjected. "Mia, you are sure about all this, aren't you? It was a long time ago. Sometimes things get exaggerated in our minds. Are you sure this actually happened?"

Mia's hand flew to her throat and rested there. A pacifying action. An attempt to calm herself. It was a telling moment. But it was over in a trice. A momentary flicker and her hand came down again.

Hands now pressed together, and her voice an octave higher, she said, "No really, I remember it well."

Our bodies never lie. It's easy enough to spin a tale, to confound and deceive with words. But our bodies betray us every time. Learn to read a body and you learn to see the truth. It's what I did. And I did it well.

Caught in a lie, most people react in similar ways. It's usually in the hands. Twisting them together, clutching hold of something.

For women, it's often a hand covering the front of the neck or playing with a necklace or other piece of jewellery. For a man, he may play with or adjust his tie, tug at his collar, or brush some imaginary specks from his shoulder. And it is in the continuing and prolonged use of such pacifying actions that the lie is caught. It's the fear of being found out.

Not so, in Mia's case. A reaction to an unexpected challenge. Over and done with in a moment. I was sure she was telling the truth.

I tipped my head to Karen, signalling that I was satisfied, and turned back to Mia. "Tell us what you heard, Mia."

"She was saying how frightened she was. She actually said that. Something about being in danger. That was the word she used. She was talking to this Rusty bloke. She said his name."

Karen and I shot each other knowing looks.

Turning to Mia once more, I said, "Can you describe this man?"

Mia stared out in front of her, fading out of the present as her mind bore her back to the past. She described him as tall and thick-set, fair hair cropped short, and dark, deep-set eyes. But what she remembered most distinctly were two tattoos; one, a snake, green and red, coiling its way up his right arm, and a date, inked in blue on the back of his neck.

I said, "A date?"

She nodded briskly. "It was '1488'. I remembered it 'cos it reminded me of when my brother was born. 1st April 1988, see? I thought that was funny."

Somewhere in the back of my mind, an old memory stirred, conjuring up a feeling of unease. Something about that number. I pushed it aside for the moment.

"Mia, you do know the police will want to talk to you?"

"I wasn't sure. Abby said I would be wasting their time."

I assured her she wouldn't be and asked if she had something on which to write her address and phone number. Karen interrupted, explaining that she had Mia's personal details in her employment file.

"I can let you have those," she said, and, turning to Mia, added, "If that's all right with you."

Mia nodded.

After reassuring Mia her information would be taken seriously, we ended our conversation, and as Mia hurried towards her stall where a queue was already forming, Karen and I returned to the car.

As we crossed the square, I took Karen's trolley from her and handed her the keys to the Elan. "You drive," I said.

"What?" The surprise in her voice was obvious. "You're going to let me drive your precious Elan? What have I done to deserve this honour?"

The sarcasm wasn't lost on me but I ignored it. "My iPad's in the car. There's something I want to check on the way home."

While Karen started the engine, I packed her trolley in the boot and, once in the car, grabbed my iPad from under the passenger seat. I found what I was looking for as Karen drove us out onto the main road.

"Listen to this," I said, reading from the screen. "14 stands for the fourteen words quoted by the Nazi leader, David Lane, 'We must secure the existence of our people and a future for white children.' The 88 is shorthand for the eighth letter of the alphabet twice, HH, the initials of the phrase 'Heil Hitler'. This tattoo can be found anywhere on the body."

"What on earth is that?"

"I'm quoting from a site about prison tattoos. Whoever our man is, he sure as hell is no saint. A white supremacist with a prison record by the looks of it. Not someone you'd want in your circle of friends."

"No wonder Candy looked scared. Who wouldn't be?"

"And it seems Rusty knew about it. The sooner he gets here, the better. He has some explaining to do."

I needn't have worried about the timing of Rusty's return. We arrived back at the Fairview to find him and Lowe waiting for us in Reception.

I felt my face flush as we crossed towards them. Since the discovery of Candy's body, I hadn't been able to shake off the feeling that, somehow, her murder was my fault. As though by revitalising the investigation with its subsequent publicity, I had set in motion events that had ended with her death. I was embarrassed.

Maybe he sensed my discomfort. Not one to show his feelings, he had never, to my knowledge, made a public display of his emotions. But this time, he reached out and embraced me, hugging me close. "None of this is your fault, Mikey." He must have read my mind.

Karen greeted him. "Welcome back," she said. "I'm sorry the circumstances are no better."

Puzzled, I frowned. Rusty caught the look and said, "Ms Dyer and I are already acquainted," and, with a trace of sarcasm in his voice, added, "I stayed here the first time my sister was killed."

CHAPTER THIRTEEN

I checked my watch again. 8:10am.

Karen stirred her coffee. "You've plenty of time. Stop fidgeting, Mikey. He's not coming till ten."

Karen and I were sharing morning coffee in her private sitting room. Lowe was picking me up later on his way to the station in readiness for Rusty Naylor's interview.

"Any sign of him yet?" I said, tipping my head towards the door leading to the public area. I didn't need to say who.

"No. He stayed in his room after dinner last night."

"Hardly surprising. I doubt he's feeling sociable right now. Probably didn't get much sleep either."

"He should be down before you leave if you want to see him."

I shook my head. "No, I need to be objective during the interview, stay detached. Maybe later when it's over."

I drained my coffee mug and put it on the table. "I'd forgotten he'd stayed here before. I remember you telling me about the murder at the time but I never connected it to Rusty."

Karen finished her coffee too and pushed the empty mug to one side. "That's how I met Richard. He brought Rusty over to book him in."

I snorted. "Priceless. Only you could turn a murder investigation into a dating opportunity."

She glowered at me. "That's not quite how it happened."

"What sort of impression did he make on you?"

"Richard?"

"No. I think I can work that out for myself. Rusty Naylor."

She dwelt on this for a moment and pulled a face. "He didn't make much of an impression. He's the sort who keeps to himself. Not very demonstrative."

"Hmmm. That's what worries me." I drummed my fingers on the arm of the chair. "He's too undemonstrative."

"What's that supposed to mean?" She reached over for the coffee pot and filled our mugs again before settling back in her chair, mug in hand.

I picked up my coffee. "Richard is relying on me to guide the interview. It's going to be difficult."

"I don't understand."

"You remember last night? When Rusty hugged me? That's what brought it home to me. It was out of character. In all the time I've known him, he's never been one to show his feelings. We've gotten close over the months but, in all that time, he's always held back, always kept something in reserve." I drank some coffee.

"Why should it matter?"

"I need to read his body language. It's how I can tell if someone is lying or not. Doesn't matter what we say, our bodies tell the truth; the way we cross our arms, glance at the exits, wrap our legs around each other. We all have our own quirks, our own 'tells' that give us away."

"And you don't get that with Rusty."

"No. And it's knowing where those differences are that helps me direct an interview; what questions to ask, where to focus, when to probe more deeply. With someone like Rusty, I'm not sure I can give it my best."

"But surely, Rusty's interview will be straightforward. He doesn't have anything to hide, does he?"

Before answering, I took another swig of coffee. Maybe Rusty was hiding something, but instead of saying so, I avoided the issue.

"It's not my opinion that counts here. I'm just part of a team. And I have a professional duty to treat him as I would any other interviewee."

Truth be told though, Rusty's claim not to know of any motive for Candy's murder worried me. If Mia's account of that phone call was to be believed - and I'm sure it was - it cast doubt on that claim. Maybe there was a simple explanation, but it needed investigating all the same.

I said, "It needs the same rigour I'd bring to any other investigation."

"You'd think even the most reserved of people would show some emotion. Everyone has feelings."

I finished my second mug of coffee. "Yes but…"

I cut myself short as a thought burst into awareness and I stared at Karen transfixed.

Leaning towards her, I took her head between both hands and planted a kiss on her forehead.

"You're a genius," I said, and fell back into my chair.

"Recognition at last. Any particular reason for this sudden insight into my superior intellect?"

"You've just given me an idea." I put down my mug and dug into my pocket for my mobile. "Now I need to get my hands on your fiancé. Figuratively speaking that is."

She shot me an old-fashioned look and rose from her chair. "Glad to be of help." She gathered up the mugs and percolator and carried them over to the kitchen.

By the time she returned, I was talking to Lowe. I'd interrupted his breakfast. "Do you have a high-speed camera down at the station?" I asked.

They hadn't.

"We don't have much use for one," he said.

"Not to worry, I have my own. But I'll need your help setting it up." I glanced down my watch. "You can forget breakfast. I'll meet you at the station in ten minutes."

Looks like I'd found a way forward after all.

CHAPTER FOURTEEN

Lowe ran the back of his hand across a sweating brow. Perspiration stained his shirt underarm and a larger patch spread over his chest.

Occasionally, he pulled on his collar and blew down the inside of his shirt in a futile attempt to cool his skin.

We were taking a breather in the shade of the covered walkway at the front of the station. Lowe had helped me set up the camera on the wall of the interview room and the increased temperature from the continuing heatwave had made it a sticky unpleasant task.

I didn't envy his having to wear the uniform. Even in just a tee and light cotton slacks, I was uncomfortably warm. Rivulets of sweat ran down my back and chest and the sodden tee stuck to my flesh.

Nathan was crossing the car park towards us, suited and booted as usual in a lightweight grey summer two-piece. A heat haze played around his feet as he approached.

God knows how he managed to appear so cool in these temperatures.

He greeted us cordially enough. But my informal dress style earned a disapproving glance. A stickler for protocol, he expected his team to adopt the same regulation look. I mentally dared him to challenge me but he knew better than to say anything and kept quiet.

Trying to sound as casual as possible, I said, "I forgot to ask. How was your London trip?"

That seemed to throw him. As much as he was ever thrown. He stammered and said, "It was fine."

"Those bosses of yours sure like to keep you on your toes."

Lowe said, "I didn't realise it was official business. Anything I need to know?"

Brushing the question aside, Nathan said, "It was personal."

I interjected. "You never said."

Instead of responding, he changed the subject. Addressing Lowe, he said, "Miles Barber tells me you set up another camera in the interview room and moved the desk. What's that about?"

Already tetchy from the heat, I bristled at the perfunctory dismissal of my probing. It was such an obvious brush off.

No matter what Karen said, something wasn't quite right here. I wasn't so stupid I couldn't read the signs; Nathan was keeping something from me.

Lowe responded to his question. He flipped his head in my direction and said, "Mikey asked me to make some changes to help with the interview."

Nathan raised a brow and fixed me with a quizzical look. "Was there any real need for that, Mikey?"

Already irritable, I was in no mood for his heedless criticism. I snapped. "What kind of dumb question is that? You think I just worked myself up into a sweat for the fun of it?"

I groaned inwardly. Even as the words spilled out of my mouth, I regretted them. That was so wrong. Caustic comments in private might just about be acceptable, but not in front of his men. It was unprofessional. But that was me; speak first, think later.

Nathan blanched and his jaw muscles tightened. He didn't respond, but I knew I was in for an ear-battering later. He opened the door to usher us inside.

As Lowe stepped through into Reception, he raised his eyebrows and shot me a wide-eyed look but said nothing. My heart sank.

We followed him in and Lowe said, "I'd like to interview Naylor if you've no objection. Mikey's briefed me on the direction he wants to take."

Nathan grunted his agreement. "I'm sure you know best," he said, but his tone was cool. "And this girl Mikey spoke with yesterday, where are we on that?"

Lowe said, "We took a statement from her yesterday."

Nathan nodded. "Put the file on my desk when you have a moment. I'd like to look through it." He turned his attention to me. "I want a word with you in my office, please." It sounded more like a command than a request.

"I'll go wait in the interview room till Naylor arrives," said Lowe. "The monitors are set up in the small meeting room when you're ready."

Nathan nodded again, brusquely, but didn't reply. He headed towards his office. I knew what was coming, and I followed meekly behind, mentally bracing myself for a roasting. He opened the door, stood aside to let me in, and closed it behind him.

Gesturing over to the couch, he barked out an emphatic, "Sit."

I knew better than to object and sank onto the couch as ordered.

Holding up my hands in surrender, I said, "I know what you're going to say and I'm sorry. I was out of order."

"You're going to hear it, anyway." He stood over me, and said, "I don't appreciate being spoken to like that in front of my men, Mikey. And if you don't have the wit to work it out for yourself, we need to reach some agreement about how we communicate on a professional level."

His rebuke was justified. Suitably chastened, I apologised. "I'm sorry. You're right. I shouldn't have snapped."

I spread my hands out to him, a gesture of appeasement, and said, "In my defence, I had just spent an uncomfortable hour wiring up and bracketing that camera to the wall. I mean, come on, questioning my professional judgement about its use wasn't likely to improve my mood any." I raised my eyebrows and tried a smile. "Okay?"

That wasn't the main reason for my bad mood but it came a close second.

The hard line of his jaw slowly relaxed, and he nodded. "Okay. I could have been more diplomatic. But no more, okay?"

I bit my lip and nodded briskly.

He seated himself beside me and squeezed my thigh. "There's nothing else troubling you is there?"

Had he already sensed my deeper concerns? Maybe realised I knew something was wrong? And just how was I supposed to respond, anyway? I could hardly voice my worries based on some nebulous unfounded feelings. And the last thing I needed was to alienate him even more.

And so I tried a different tack instead. "I've not seen much of you these last few days."

He opened his mouth to speak and paused as if weighing his words. And then, "I'm under a lot of pressure at the moment. But I promise you, it's not always like this." He added, "It doesn't help living so far apart."

Well, he'd got that right at least. Of course, there was a simple solution to that particular problem, but it was one he would have to work out for himself.

"And this goddamn investigation takes up so much time too," he said.

Not to mention dining out with ex-lovers in Stoke Newington. Or maybe not so ex. Or was I really just being paranoid? I pushed the thought aside and tried to stay positive.

"Having the new place should make life easier," I said. "Maybe you can stay over sometimes."

He squeezed my arm. "I'm sure I can." He glanced at his watch. "Come on, Naylor will be here soon. We'd best get in place."

I followed him out of the door towards the meeting room. For the moment, it seemed we were at stalemate again.

CHAPTER FIFTEEN

"So why two monitors?" Nathan dropped into one of the chairs in front of the desk.

I followed suit and said, "I was concerned about Rusty's behaviour patterns. Some people are hard to read, Rusty being a typical example. They're very good at keeping their feelings under control with few if any visual cues. It makes it difficult to read their body language."

"So how does the second monitor help?"

Both monitors were powered up and showed images of the interview room from different angles. I tapped the screen on the left. "This just displays the usual mid-range view of the room so I can observe Rusty's overall body language.

"But this one..." I tapped the other screen. "This one is connected to a high-speed camera that allows me to focus directly on his facial expressions." I leaned over to the control panel in front of the monitor. "Watch." Using the joystick on the panel, I zoomed in to show how the camera could be manipulated to close in at a specific location.

"I'm still not sure how that helps."

As he spoke, the door of the interview room opened and images on both screens showed Rusty Naylor follow Lowe into the room.

"It'll be easier to explain later when the interview is over." As both men seated themselves and faced each other, I used the joystick to zoom in with the camera until Rusty's face filled the screen. At my request, the table had been removed, so I had an uninterrupted view of Rusty on the first monitor.

A microphone in front of the monitors connected to Lowe's earpiece, and I pulled it toward me, ready to direct his questions if need be.

Nathan and I sat in silence as Lowe ran through the usual procedures, advising Rusty of his rights and stating the time date and place. Lowe conducted the interview much as I'd asked.

When he raised the issue of the phone call, Rusty looked puzzled. "I'm not saying Candy didn't call now and again but I don't recall such a conversation." He paused as if casting his mind back and shook his head. "No, it doesn't mean a thing."

Lowe pushed the point. "Our witness was certain about what she heard."

"Candy could be a bit of a drama queen at times. It's possible she was exaggerating about something and I didn't take it seriously. Your witness could have beefed it up as well. These things happen."

I said, "Did you see that? Did you see how Rusty reacted?"

Nathan rubbed his chin. "I didn't see a reaction."

"Exactly."

He wrinkled his brow. "Am I missing something here?"

Keeping an eye on the screen, I said, "Lowe challenged him. Even from someone with nothing to hide that should have got some sort of reaction."

I leaned toward the microphone, switched it on, and said, "Richard, ask him if he knows of anyone who might want to cause harm to his sister. Keep pushing it and see if we get a response."

Lowe asked the question but got a negative response and no reaction.

Lowe drummed his fingers on his thigh. "Your sister is overheard telling you she's in some kind of danger and then both she and her friend are murdered. And you're telling me you don't remember the conversation and you have no idea who she could have been talking about?"

"I only wish I did." Rusty Naylor stayed calm and composed, his hands resting in his lap.

"You can't think of anyone who could have been a threat?"

"As far as I know, she didn't have any enemies."

Lowe tried a different approach and described the tattooed man Mia had seen in the bar. "You don't know anyone who fits that description?"

As impassive as ever, Rusty answered in the negative.

I switched off the mic and said, "Not a flicker. You see how calm he is?"

In front of me on the table was a remote recording device, part of the camera configuration I'd helped set up. And each time Lowe asked a pertinent question, I recorded the response.

Nathan rapped a knuckle against the second screen. "There's no change in his facial expression either."

"You'd be surprised."

He glanced towards me, brows knitted into a frown.

"I'll show you later." I turned my attention back to the two screens.

Lowe continued the interview but, learning nothing of any consequence, eventually brought it to a close. After formally concluding the interview, asking Naylor to make himself available for future interviews, and escorting him out of the station, he joined Nathan and me in the smaller of the two meeting rooms.

"That was a waste of time," he said.

"Don't be so sure. We'll know more when I've checked the recording."

"That shouldn't take long," said Nathan. "You recorded only a few seconds each time."

"It's not that simple," I said. "These cameras are capable of 1,000 frames a second and I need to check each frame. I reduced the speed for this interview but it will still take me a while to check through the recording."

Nathan said, "That could take a while. I hope you have something to show for it."

"I'll let you know."

The two of them left me to it, returning to their own offices and other duties. It took me the rest of the morning to trawl through the camera footage, stopping briefly to grab a sandwich and coffee from the mini-mart next door. No offence to Rusty but by the time I'd finished, I was heartily sick of the sight of his face. But at least the exercise had been worth it. And when I summoned Nathan and Richard back to the meeting room after lunch, I had some interesting images to show them.

They were impressed.

Lowe said, "That's amazing."

Nathan grunted his agreement.

We all three sat around the screen displaying Rusty's image as I flipped from one frame to the next and back again. The first image showed Rusty's usual inscrutable expression. But the second frame showed something completely different.

"He looks scared," said Lowe.

"I'd call that an understatement," said Nathan.

"I don't understand," said Lowe. "How can his expression change so quickly? And why didn't we notice it before?"

I'd already marked the frames I wanted them to see, and I flipped through to the next one. It showed Rusty's response to Lowe's description of the tattooed man. "Welcome to the world of micro-expressions."

They both stared at me, incomprehension showing on their faces.

I leaned back in my chair. "Let's suppose you're off duty for the weekend," I said, tipping my head in Lowe's direction, "and you're looking forward to watching the Charwell FC game on Saturday."

"I'd be a damned sight more enthusiastic if they weren't doing so badly in the league."

I chortled. "Even so. Now let's say the Chief here cancelled your leave." I hooked a thumb towards Nathan. "Said he needed you to work. How would you react?"

Lowe squirmed in his seat, embarrassed. "Well, I'd have to work of course. I wouldn't have a choice."

"Yes, but how would you feel?"

"I guess I'd be disappointed."

"I put it to you, you'd be more than disappointed. You'd be angry."

Lowe protested. "I wouldn't go that far."

"You may not even be consciously aware of it. But it would happen all the same. Human nature. Of course, you wouldn't want it to be known so you would make sure you didn't display that anger."

"No, of course not." Lowe sounded dubious.

"And that's how micro-expressions occur. When you deliberately try to suppress your feelings. You see, no matter how much you tried to hide that anger, for that one split second before you got your emotions under control, it would show on your face, an involuntary reflex action."

Nathan said, "Too fast to be seen?"

"There are seven main common universal expressions encoded by micro-expressions." I checked each one off on my fingers. "Disgust, anger, fear, sadness, happiness, contempt and surprise. And each one is expressed for no more than a fraction of a second. Which is why we can see them only when recorded on a high-speed camera."

"So Naylor was deliberately trying to hide something from us?" said Nathan.

Lowe interjected. "But what does it mean? Frightened of what? Of being caught out? Frightened of whoever threatened his sister?"

Nathan again. "That's something we need to find out. Looks like we'll have to pull him in again."

"Maybe not," I said. "I suspect he's not the type to be easily pressured.

"It's not as if we have a choice," said Lowe.

"I've got a better idea," I said. "I'll still be at the Fairview for a couple of days until the new place is ready. So why don't I invite him to join me for a drink? Try the soft approach."

Nathan was reluctant, but I set out to persuade him that my approach was probably best. And in the end he acquiesced. "Very well. I suppose it's worth a shot."

CHAPTER SIXTEEN

Rusty was waiting for me, already seated at the bar, slumped over his beer. He gazed down at the half-empty glass, a picture of despondency.

It was early evening and most of the Fairview's patrons were in the restaurant next door, the muted background hum of their conversation making its way out to us. The only other drinkers were a middle-aged couple at the table over by the window, he reading the evening paper and she concentrating on the screen of her mobile. A bored-looking barman leaned against the wall behind the counter, half-heartedly towelling a glass. He looked almost pleased to see me as I entered from Reception. He must have been having a slow shift.

Rusty turned at my approach, tried a smile, and held out a hand in greeting.

I took it in mine, shook it warmly, and slid onto the stool next to him. After ordering myself a vodka and tonic, I apologised for not having had a chance to talk with him earlier. "I was hoping we might get together after your interview this morning."

"You were there, of course?"

"Whatever I can do to help."

"And the high-speed camera would have been your idea." He looked me straight in the eye, challenging me. When I didn't respond immediately, he said, "There were two cameras in that room. It was obvious why."

There seemed little point in either denying it or apologising for it.

Not that I needed to. I passed it off with a smile. "I always said you were one of my better students. I bet you learned all my techniques by heart."

"Wondered why you felt the need is all."

"You must know it's not personal, Rusty. I have a responsibility to the police, my employers, to use whatever techniques I feel are appropriate."

He finished his beer and put the empty glass on the counter. "And when was it you knew I was lying?"

So much for my intended softly softly approach. But if this was how he wanted to play it, then so be it. I wasn't about to let him throw me off track with his directness.

I drained my glass and signalled the barman to let us have another round of drinks. "You know how this works as well as I do. So you know when it was. The moment you lied about that phone call. You knew who threatened Candy. And you told me you'd lost touch with her. Another lie."

"That much was true. That call came out of the blue. And she wouldn't tell me where she was or what she was doing. She told me she was too scared."

Our drinks appeared in front of us. Rusty picked up his beer and raised his glass to me. "I guess I have some explaining to do."

Raising my glass to him in return, I said, "I guess you do."

He grimaced and nodded in agreement. "I'm not who you think I am."

"None of us are."

He snorted. "Spoken like a true psychologist."

"So who are you?"

He slid off his stool still holding his drink. "Let's take a turn outside. The walls are closing in on me. They always do when I think back to the old days."

I followed him out onto the terrace, drink in hand, and we leaned against the balustrade looking out over the waves. The blood-red sun was already on its slow descent behind us, colouring the sky over the sea with its crimson glow.

He said, "You didn't know I'd done time, did you?"

"So that's why the walls were closing in?"

"I remember telling you my sister hadn't led a blameless life. But we're from the same stock. I had my moments too. It's in the blood I guess."

Blaming our genes or our upbringing or our circumstances were all too common as excuses for our misdeeds. Understandable, of course. Human nature dictates that we seek to justify our actions, no matter how bad, by looking elsewhere for the cause. It would be too painful to accept responsibility ourselves. But I didn't contradict him.

He said, "It happened bit by bit; petty theft, street crime. I did some stretches inside. And then I got into the big time. Smash and grab and store robbery with one of the local gangs. I was the getaway driver."

Before continuing, he drew in a deep breath as if to ready himself. "And then it all went belly up. The owner of a late-night convenience store fought back. He was shot. Died on the spot."

He shifted his stance. The boards beneath him groaned.

"I turned Queen's evidence. Shopped 'em." He twisted around to face me, gripping the rail with his free hand. "That must seem strange to you. After the kind of life I'd led."

"Not really. We all set our own moral codes, the standards by which we live. And somewhere within that set of values, we all draw a line. You're no different from anyone else."

He told me of the consequences of that decision. A reduced two-year sentence. And anonymity. But something went wrong. After his release, his complicity in the eventual arrest of the other gang members was leaked. And, by his reasoning, from inside police ranks. As he spoke, he finished the rest of his beer and left the empty glass on the balustrade rail.

"Is that why you never reported the threat made against Candy?"

"I didn't think they meant her any harm. Not for a moment. It was just their way of trying to get to me. I was lying low. Trying to hide. I told her she was safe." He leaned against the balustrade, arms on the rail and looked over to the ground below. "What a mistake that was."

I downed the rest of my drink in one go, my mouth suddenly dry. "And afterwards?"

Rusty straightened up again.

"The deed was done. It's not like I could bring her back. So why make it hard on myself? I've been living under a false name, see. If I'd come clean about who I really was, about why she was killed, I'd be a sitting target. Which is what they wanted, right? I still think I was stitched up by the bizzies. So I wouldn't be doing myself any favours 'fessing up to the ones who'd dropped me in it to start with."

The tables on the terrace were filling up as diners finished their meals and came out into the sun to finish their drinks or to enjoy the warm weather.

I put my empty glass on a nearby table and said, "Let's walk down to the front. It's more private there."

We made our way down the steps to the Esplanade and as we crossed the road towards the beach, I questioned him some more. Why had he chosen to stay silent after learning that the first victim wasn't his sister? Why hadn't he given the full circumstances to the police?

A family of holidaymakers trekked towards us, the father laden with deck chairs, the mother chastising an exuberant over-excited child trying to pull free of her controlling grip. We leaned up against the sea wall and waited for them to pass before continuing our conversation.

Once they were out of the way, I said, "I don't understand why you said nothing."

"I didn't believe it. I didn't believe it was her. It didn't make sense. I was sure the first victim was Candy. If she was still alive, why had she never contacted me?"

"Maybe she was still too frightened?"

"Maybe. But I wish she'd got in touch all the same."

"And the tattooed man? Do you know him?"

"No. But I recognised the description of the prison tattoo on his neck and put two and two together. It had to be someone tied to my old gang."

"So what now?"

He turned to face me. "I guess I'm going to have to come clean after all. Perhaps it's something I should have done long ago."

I agreed. Glancing at my watch, I said, "I have to make a call to my publisher shortly but why don't I drive you down to the station later?"

He declined the offer. "Might as well head on over there now and get it over with." Pushing himself away from the wall, he added, "Why don't you phone your Sergeant friend and tell him I'm on my way."

As he moved off, he called back, "Wish me luck."

In the circumstances, there was little else he could do. But even so, it would have occurred to both of us that he was about to put himself back in the limelight, into the full glare of publicity.

And back into danger.

CHAPTER SEVENTEEN

Rusty reached out from the back of the Movano low loader and took the wooden dining chair from me.

"That's the lot," I said.

He gripped the toprail in one beefy hand, swung the chair around as if it were made of matchwood, and stored it inside with the rest of Martha Stubbs' furniture.

He had an upper body strength that made me feel inadequate by comparison and, despite the evidence of a sweat-sodden shirt clinging to his muscular frame, he had made our morning's task seem a snap.

He jumped down from the back of the van. "I'll secure this lot," he said, "and we can be on our way."

"Thanks for this, Rusty. You're a star."

He beamed, a wide open grin, and wiped his hand across his brow, brushing aside the damp hair that stuck to his forehead. "Always happy to help out," he said.

It was moving day. My new home awaited. And Nathan, the one I had relied on to help with what, after all, was a significant event, had let me down, pleading a heavy workload.

I'd complained to Karen at the Fairview reception desk, looking for a sympathetic ear. Not that I got one. Just the usual blah about the pressure policemen were under and how I should be more supportive. Lowe's brainwashing techniques had obviously been a resounding success.

Rusty, on his way to breakfast, had overheard us and offered to help. I'd jumped at the chance. Not only did his offer get me out of a hole, but it also gave me an opportunity to find out how he'd fared down at the station the previous day.

He took the wheel, and on the drive over to the storage centre at Charwell, I asked him about the interview. It seemed Lowe hadn't been best pleased about what he'd termed 'a failure to disclose significant information'. After reading Rusty the Riot Act, he'd warned him of the penalties for non-disclosure. But he had, at least, understood the reasons and so Rusty was off the hook. I made a mental note to call Lowe later for a briefing. Rusty was more concerned about my attitude towards him once he's confessed his lawless past.

"I'm surprised you'd even want to speak to me again. You and me being on opposite sides of the fence an' all."

"Not any more we're not. Seems to me that once you'd drawn that line, you made all the right choices. Left that past behind."

"I wasn't going back there."

"I'd rather be a friend to someone who learns from his mistakes than an idiot who never does."

"Sure, but if I hadn't been such a dumb-ass back then, Candy wouldn't be lying in a morgue right now. It's not like we were close any more, we had our own lives to lead, but she was my sister after all, and what happened was down to me."

We forget sometimes that our past mistakes can have future consequences. Something I knew only too well. In his case, however, the consequences could be life or death. I shot him an anxious glance. "You need to be careful." I didn't need to spell it out.

"Yes." He understood well enough.

We dropped the subject and drove on in silence for a while.

On the Charwell Road, we pulled into the National Service Station to fill up with petrol. While Rusty busied himself at the pump, I got out of the van to stretch my legs.

Job done, Rusty took a loo break, and I went to the shop to pay for the purchase and buy some drinks and snacks. I had already grabbed a six-pack of beer from the cooler and was browsing through the confectionery display when I heard my name called from the other side of the counter.

"Good afternoon, Mr MacGregor."

I looked up, a couple of chocolate bars and beer in hand, and caught the gaze of the smiling young man who'd addressed me. The face seemed familiar, but I couldn't place it. I stared at him blankly and tried to recall where I'd seen him before.

My lack of recognition must have been apparent. "Andy Burns? Bartender at The Fairview?" He grinned.

And then I remembered. "Of course. I'm sorry." I returned his grin. "If you'd given me a shot of vodka, I would have recognised you instantly." I gave him some cash for the purchases.

He laughed at that, rang up the sale on his till and handed me my change.

"This must be less demanding than bar work," I said. "Not so many drunks to deal with."

"I'm full time here. I do a few evenings at The Fairview to make up my wages." He pulled a face. "Expensive girlfriend."

I was about to tell him that maybe a change of girlfriend might help his finances when I was interrupted from behind.

"You ready, Mikey?"

Rusty was waiting in the doorway.

I gave a thumbs up to Adam, followed Rusty out to the forecourt, and handed him a chocolate bar as we got back into the van.

We stuck to more mundane topics for the remainder of the journey and didn't find much time to talk during the changeover of furniture at the storage depot.

Rusty drove back with the furniture while I returned in the Elan which I'd earlier left at the facility when picking up the low loader.

We'd left Martha Stubbs back at the cottage, and she opened the door to us on our return, duster in hand. I followed her inside, and a moment later Rusty joined us.

Relieved of most of the clutter, the rooms seemed larger. In my mind, I was already arranging the furniture, working out where it would all go, making myself at home.

Martha Stubbs fussed around us, insisted on opening every cupboard to show me how much storage space there was, and thrust into my hand a manila folder stuffed with instruction manuals for the cooker, washing machine, dishwasher, and every other household gadget she'd left behind.

"I've already stored all the smaller objects up in the loft," she said. "The ornaments and such like. I'm sure you prefer to have your own pieces around you but feel free to use what you want. I just wish I'd had time to give the place a more thorough clean."

I assured her she'd made a good job of it. She left us to get on with our work, and we laboured through the afternoon, carrying in and placing furniture.

I'd either disposed of or left behind the accumulated bric-à-brac of my previous life, all those small personal possessions that made a house a home, so the rooms looked spartan. But I was satisfied with the overall effect.

By mid-afternoon, we were exhausted but finished, and badly in need of a drink. I fetched the six-pack from the car, and we slumped on the couch and pulled some tabs.

Rusty downed his first can in several audible gulps, crushed it in his fist, and discarded it on the coffee table in front of him.

Thirst quenched and now more relaxed, he settled back in his seat and began what appeared to be an interrogation.

"So now you know what I left behind. How about you? What are you running from?"

Rusty sure couldn't be accused of talking around a subject. "Why would I be running from anything?"

"Come on, Mikey, I'm not dumb." He spread his hands wide, embracing the space around us. "New home, new start, new life. I asked if you had someone back home, remember? Well, I sure as hell don't see any sign of it. So that leaves us with the other option. You're running from something."

What was I supposed to say? Did I tell him the truth? And if I did, how would he react? Would he be angry because I'd not come clean about my sexuality? Would he be hostile? Just how accepting of my lifestyle would he be? How did I deal with this?

"You must have left something behind," he said.

I grimaced. "I left a wife behind."

"You're married?" He sounded surprised.

"Not for much longer. Big mistake."

He let out a long low whistle. "Well, there's a turn up to be sure.

Why'd you never say?"

"I'm not the only one who keeps secrets, am I?"

"You got me there." He grinned.

I leaned back. Studied his face. Wondered why he needed to make such a big issue of it. "It was over a long time ago. Not part of my life anymore. And not something I wanted to be reminded of."

"There was someone else?"

"Yes."

"Another woman?"

I hesitated. For the briefest of moments. But it was enough to give me away. And in that moment, he learned the truth.

"It was another man, wasn't it?"

The heat rose in my face, and I stammered.

An even bigger grin spread across his face. "Thought as much." He seemed to enjoy my embarrassment. "I wondered about that."

So that was it. He knew more about me than I'd cared to admit to. "Does it matter?"

"Yes, it matters."

"Why?" I was on the defensive.

He locked eyes with mine. "It might have made a difference to us."

I stammered again.

He said, "You never thought I might want to be more than friends?" He inched closer, pressed his leg against mine, and ran a slow hand over my thigh. "A lot more." His eyes brimmed with desire.

I jerked back as my whole body stiffened in shock and an involuntary cry escaped my lips. My hand spasmed, and I dropped the can I was holding. It clattered on the wooden boards and spread its contents across the floor at our feet.

"Shit." I reached down and grabbed it and, sitting up, turned to face him and stammered again, at a loss for words. I eased away from him, pressed up against the arm of the couch.

He raised his hands, fingers spread, and drew back. A look of concern on his face. "Am I reading this all wrong?"

"No. I mean, yes. I mean, no." I was stuttering.

He was smiling again. "You're not sure?"

I put my half-empty can on the table, wiped my wet hand on my jeans, and paused to get my breathing under control. "I had no idea.

I'm sorry."

"Gaydar not working?" Now he was openly amused.

"Maybe I'm out of practice."

"I spent some time inside, remember? You must know how it is in there."

"Different circumstances."

"Don't get me wrong. I like my women. But inside, you learn a few things about yourself. And I won't deny I enjoyed what I found."

My mind raced as I tried to gather my thoughts together.

I was struggling here. Out of my depth. My emotions a roiling mix. I couldn't deny his physical attractiveness; that powerful body, the strong defined face and deep dark eyes that hid secrets. How could I not find him attractive? But that was as far as it went. I'd never considered our relationship as anything but platonic. And now this was no longer the Rusty I knew. The friend. I didn't know how to react to him.

"I don't know what I'm supposed to say, what I'm supposed to do." That sounded so lame.

"Then let me decide for you." He leaned towards me and pressed his lips to mine.

Only for a moment did my body object, stiffening at his touch. And then I melted into his kiss, savouring the taste of him, his musky scent, enjoying the pressure of his lips against mine, the soft feel of his tongue as it found its way into my mouth.

The rational part of my mind screamed at me to stop, fought against the burning desire that flared up inside and set my flesh on fire. I pressed my free hand to his chest, held it there while my mind fought for control, and then, almost reluctantly, I pushed him away.

"No," I murmured.

Out of the corner of my eye, I caught a movement, and with the sudden shock of recognition, I pulled back and sat upright.

Nathan was standing in the open doorway, staring down at us, his eyes hard and cold, his mouth a tight line, compressed in anger.

"Nathan." His name dropped from my lips like a dead weight. I didn't know what else to say.

"I came over to see if you needed any help," he said, his voice caustic, "but I see you have it covered so I'll leave you to it." He turned away and closed the door behind him. Gravel crunched beneath his boots as he headed away down the path.

"Nathan." This time, I shouted out his name, leapt to my feet, and chased after him. I wrenched open the door and hurried towards his retreating figure.

I reached him as he opened the door of his Astra and caught him by the shoulder. He stiffened at my touch, and froze where he stood, but said nothing.

My heart raced, but I tried to stay calm. "Whatever it is you thought you saw just then, you're wrong."

Shrugging my hand from his shoulder, he half turned towards me, his hand grasping the top of the open door. He looked me up and down his breathing laboured, and said, "And what was it I saw?" His voice was icy.

I looked him in the eyes, and said, "What just happened came out of nowhere. I didn't encourage it, and it was uninvited."

His gaze moved around my face as though he was searching for something in my expression.

Pressing home my case, I said, "Rusty took me by surprise. I didn't even know he had a gay side. He's always been just a friend and nothing more."

I waited for a response. Nathan still didn't seem convinced. "He wasn't even totally sure about me," I continued. "He took his chances." I added, "And he didn't know about us."

This time, he faced me fully, letting go of the car door, and repeated my words, emphasising each one. "He didn't know about us." He shook his head slowly. "And not for one moment does it occur to you why that may be the problem here?"

I didn't respond.

He turned and climbed into the Astra.

"You do believe me?"

"I don't think he's the sort of person you should be associating with," he said, and slammed the door.

I wasn't sure how much of an answer that was to my question but it was the only one I was getting.

He drove away and disappeared into the distant heat haze.

I was shaking as I made my way back to the house.

Rusty was still in place on the couch. He held a hand out towards me, palm up, questioning. "What was that about?"

"You asked me what I was running from," I said. "Well, you got it wrong. I came back to Elders Edge because I'd stopped running."

His blank stare turned to one of enlightenment as my words sank in. "DCI Quarryman?"

I bit my lip and nodded.

A mixture of surprise and disbelief flitted across his face before fading to an expression of grim concern. Throwing up his hands, he leaned back, his forehead creased. "I messed up, Mikey. I'm so sorry."

"Not your fault."

The pool of liquid by his feet where I'd dropped my beer can had spread over the floor. I headed to the kitchen and came back with a roll of paper towel.

"I hope I haven't messed things up," he said.

"I'm the one who messed up," I said, as I mopped up the spilled beer. I grabbed Rusty's discarded can from the coffee table and took it back to the kitchen. "I should have told you." I threw the can into the trash can along with the wet towel.

"So why didn't you?" he called back to me.

"Because I'm an idiot," I murmured to myself. I slung the paper towel roll onto the kitchen top and returned to the living room. "I guess I've always been worried about how people will react."

"For fuck's sake, Mikey. Screw what anyone else thinks. It's your life. You do what you want with it."

"So I'm beginning to realise." I dropped back into place beside him and picked up my half-empty can of beer.

"Look, I overstepped the mark here. I'm sorry. I screwed up."

"No, you didn't." I gulped down the remains of my beer. "I screwed up. I'm always screwing up. It's what I do best. So don't worry about it."

"The last thing I want to do is spoil our friendship."

"Not going to happen."

As he continued to plead his case, blaming himself for what had just happened, I responded on automatic, trying to reassure him, but only half listening. While my life was slowly unravelling, my relationship with Rusty was the least of my worries.

CHAPTER EIGHTEEN

Maybe it was just me. Just the mood I was in. But the living room that had seemed so bright and cheery the day before, looked drab, all muddy browns and dark corners, reflecting my own dark mood.

Martha Stubbs had dropped by earlier with a shag pile rug, a replacement for one stolen by her previous tenant - obviously, the more sophisticated light-fingered tourist had progressed from towels and toilet rolls. Its brightly coloured swirls of red and yellow stood out in sharp contrast to the rest of the furnishings, making them seem even drabber by comparison.

That morning, I'd tried to settle down to some work at my desk, surrounded by scattered scribbled notes, my laptop open before me, it's empty screen waiting patiently for the rattle of my fingers on its keys.

But I couldn't concentrate.

I pushed the laptop away. Yet another treatise on the abnormal psychology of yet another psychopath would have to wait.

My mind was elsewhere, trying to figure out what had happened yesterday.

Trust.

We were back to that old bugbear again. Was it always going to be an issue? Would I always need to watch every move I made in case it was misinterpreted?

A serious heart-to-heart conversation with Nathan was long overdue. But I needed to figure it out first. Settle the arguments in my mind.

In the meantime, I needed a distraction. I'd already taken my early morning run along the seafront but I was still edgy, unsettled, and needed something physical to expend my energy on.

Martha Stubbs had said something about storing all the ornaments and other decorative objects in the loft. Maybe I could find a few items to brighten the place up. And if not, it would keep my mind off the more depressing aspects of my disorganised life.

An hour later, sweating from the effort of carrying heavily laden boxes up and down the ladder to the loft, a pile of suitably decorous objects lined the upper landing; a matching set of faux-Chinese pottery made up of a large bowl and a matching lidded jar, both glazed in bright blue with splashes of red; a wood-framed wall print, an abstract representation of colourful seaside cottages tumbling down into a sparkling azure sea - not my usual taste, but bright and cheerful all the same; a cheap and cheerful wall clock depicting a row of highly coloured beach huts; a hand-carved wooden trinket box, decorated with a Celtic design, a more tasteful item among the rest that would serve as a bedside small-change box; and several other colourful objects that could be placed around the cottage.

I busied myself through the morning, distributing these various objects around the house, adding some colour where needed. With everything else finally placed to my satisfaction, I took the wooden box into the bedroom and put it on the bedside cabinet. It was stuffed with old receipts and other scraps of paper, and I'd just emptied them out into the wastepaper basket when the doorbell rang.

Nathan?

I grabbed some scraps that had overspilled the basket onto the floor, dropped them in with the other rubbish, and hurried downstairs to answer the door.

It was Rusty.

I hoped the disappointment didn't show on my face. I feigned a welcoming smile and invited him in.

He stepped through the door, guardedly, his eyes troubled and downcast, his whole demeanour more reserved than usual. "I came to apologise." His voice had lost its upbeat lilt.

Only then did my incipient anger at his previous unwanted attention swim up into awareness, and just as quickly ebb away. "I'm not sure you're the one who should be apologising." I could hardly blame him for fancying his chances. And it's not as if I'd been upfront with him about my circumstances.

I stepped back to let him into the room. "Go grab yourself a can from the fridge and chill out."

"If you're sure?"

"Sure I'm sure. I could use the company." As he went over to the kitchen, I called out to him. "Get me one too."

He returned with a couple of frosted cans and handed me one. I rolled it against my forehead, enjoying the ice-cold feel of it against my sweating brow and then pulled the tab, letting its contents foam and run over my fingers.

"Let's take them outside." I headed for the back door. "I need some air. I've been stuck in all morning."

Outside, we sheltered from the blistering sun in the dappled shade of a spreading beech that hugged the wall at the end of the garden. I arched my back and rubbed the back of my neck, easing the tension that had built up over the morning, grateful for another diversion from my brooding.

"So. You and the Chief, eh? That came out of left field."

"We go back a long way. We grew up together."

"Why didn't you tell me? I thought we were mates."

"I guess I'm still feeling my way, Rusty. It's a big change for me. I'm still not sure how to handle it."

"Jeez, Mikey. What planet are you from? It really shouldn't be a problem."

"So Nathan tells me."

"So it's not going too well?" He raised an eyebrow.

What was I supposed to say? Did I really want to get into all the reasons why my relationship wasn't working?

I didn't go out of my way to seek publicity. But my status as a minor celebrity - unwanted though it was - sometimes drew unwelcome attention. And so when the news of my divorce was made public, it also led to speculation about the reasons; about the numerous affairs, the sexual encounters with other men, reasons well-known to Nathan. Any wonder that he found it so hard to trust me?

That particular media storm had been short-lived and had

eventually given way to more pressing concerns, and, hopefully, had faded from the memories of those who drew delight from the misfortunes of public figures. But its aftermath was still all too fresh in the minds of those who knew me well. And still a source of pain.

Fortunately, I was saved from having to delve any further into the ramifications of my troubled relationship by the incessant ringing of my mobile. It was the ring-tone I'd set for calls from Nathan. I made my excuses and answered the call.

Rusty said, "Should I leave you to it?"

I shook my head.

Nathan said, "Is someone with you?"

For the briefest of moments, I considered lying. But why should I? I had nothing to hide. "Rusty's here."

A long silence.

I waited for him to continue.

His tone was curt. "We've had some developments."

I listened while he filled me in on the details.

"A local businessman filed a missing persons report. His fiancée."

He explained how the description had fitted that of the murder victim, and how the man had later identified the victim as the missing woman.

"And we have a possible suspect in custody," he continued. "The man's son was known to have made threats against her on several occasions."

"You want me to come down to the station?"

"Of course." He was brusque. "You're still on the team aren't you?"

I wasn't sure if it was a statement or a question.

CHAPTER NINETEEN

"So how is Rusty?" There was an acerbic edge to Nathan's tone.

Of course, he wasn't really asking after Rusty's welfare. What he really wanted to know was why Rusty was over at the cottage. And, no doubt, he'd already drawn his own conclusions about that.

We were in Nathan's office waiting for Lowe to set up the interview with his suspect. This was meant to be a briefing, but I got the feeling Nathan was trying to turn it into an interrogation.

He sat behind his desk and I faced him from the safety of the couch at the other end of the room. The wayward frond of a potted palm at the side of the couch poked me in the face as if urging me to confess. I pushed it aside. "He's fine. He came round to apologise."

"Apologise?"

"For what happened yesterday. He was embarrassed. He thought he might have offended me and wanted to say sorry."

Nathan grunted. A non-committal response. I couldn't tell if he was acknowledging my answer or refuting it. But his eyes were full of doubt.

Whatever irritation I'd felt at his brusqueness melted away in the face of his uncertainty. A rush of tenderness and sorrow swept through me. How could I blame him for being so unsure?

I moved over to the desk, dropped into the chair on the other side of him and leaned toward him, my hands on the desktop, clasped together. "I love you, you idiot. Why would I want to spoil what we have?" To push home the point, I added, "Rusty got it wrong, okay?"

He reached across the desk and took both my hands in his. "And why do you suppose that was?"

I pulled a face, looked down at the desk, and nodded. "Okay, I get it. I should have told him about us." Head still lowered, I raised my eyes, meeting his gaze from under furrowed brows. "But did you really think there was something between us?"

"Well, I didn't think you were discussing the weather." He let out a long slow sigh, and said, "You told me what happened and I accept your explanation. There's no point to this if we can't learn to trust each other. But if you hadn't put yourself in that position in the first place, we wouldn't be having this conversation now, would we?"

"Okay, my bad."

He continued, "Let's forget it and move on, shall we? We both get things wrong at times."

I laughed, and said, "I think it's fair to say your track record is better than mine."

I pulled one of my hands free and pressed it to his. And for a moment we sat together, hands entwined, and made silent peace with each other.

Sometimes, the past had a way of reminding us it hadn't yet finished with us, that we still have a way to go before we can shake it off.

To allay any lingering doubts, I said, "Rusty was a good friend when I needed one. And now it's my turn to be a good friend to him. But that's all he is. A good friend."

The telephone interrupted us before he could reply. Its sharp rebuke brought us both back to the present, reminding us we had work to do.

Nathan groaned, let go of my hands, and leaned back in his chair as he took the call. And then, "Keep him in holding till we're ready for him."

Dropping the receiver into its cradle, he said, "I'd best fill you in on where we are with this before the interview."

He looked around for the file, and as he reached towards it, I placed a restraining hand on his arm. He paused and looked up.

"Are we okay?" I said.

His eyes crinkled to match his smile, and he said, "We're okay."

He pulled the file towards him, flipped it open and ran his finger down the first page. A moment later, he was running through the details, bringing me up to speed on the investigation.

Listening to him reminded me of how much I enjoyed watching him at work. His professionalism, the way he focused on the task at hand, his confidence, the sure and certain way he commanded his team, his coolness under pressure. And how much more ashamed I was for the way I had treated him, dented his confidence, made his so unsure of himself. I still had a lot of making up to do.

He was explaining the victim's circumstances, and I pushed all other thoughts to one side and focused on his words.

He said, "She's been living locally all this time. Under an assumed name. Lydia Carrington."

I snorted. "Nice choice. Sounds like someone from a soap opera." A sudden remembrance. "I'm sure I've heard that name before."

"You should have. She was your damsel in distress."

It came back to me. "Of course. The terrace at the Fairview. Some jerk was getting physical with her."

"Lowe filled me in on the details."

"Is he the suspect?"

"Yes." He checked the file. "Marcus Farrow. She was engaged to his father, John Farrow. It was the father who reported her missing."

"So what are the circumstances?"

"She was supposed to be taking the train to London, visiting a friend and should have been back the following day. That was the last he saw of her. Her Porsche was still in the station car park."

"And the friend?"

Nathan shrugged and closed the file. "Who knows? Farrow had no idea who it was. She never said. And, anyway, she obviously never made it."

I drummed my fingers on the desktop while I thought it through. "And Marcus Farrow? What's the evidence against him?"

Nathan leaned back and clasped his hands behind his head. "Circumstantial so far. It seems the altercation you witnessed wasn't the first public spat they'd had. And we have a text message."

That sounded more promising.

Nathan checked the file again. "Her mobile was in the car. There was a message from Marcus Farrow." He jabbed at a spot on the file.

"Here it is." He read it out. "Say a word and you're fucking dead."

"Short and to the point," I said. "Though his prose style could use a little work."

Nathan grunted. His usual response to one of my quips.

I said, "It's still all circumstantial. Do we have anything more substantial?"

Nathan rose from his desk. "Let's go find out shall we?"

CHAPTER TWENTY

The wall fan above Lowe's desk stirred the papers on the desktop as it swept back and forth on its spindle, but did little to cool the heat-laden air.

Lowe was already seated at the desk, twiddling the brightness control on the monitor. Nathan gently squeezed my arm before we dropped into place on either side of him. Lowe leaned back, arms folded, and we sat in silence, all eyes on the monitor as an image of Miles Barber with Marcus Farrow in tow appeared on the screen. Another uniformed officer followed them into the interview room and took up a position in the corner as Farrow and Barber seated themselves facing each other.

Farrow was agitated, a nervous mess, pulling at his collar every few seconds, crossing and uncrossing his legs. Reading his body language wasn't going to be a problem.

Miles Barber ran through the usual preliminaries for the sake of the recording and launched into his questioning by asking for details of Farrow's movements around the time of the murder.

Farrow tugged at his collar. "Well obviously, I'm in my office in London, during the day." Sweating profusely, he pulled a handkerchief from his trouser pocket and wiped his forehead. "I've always been a creature of habit. I get back on the same train every evening and I'm back home by seven." He dabbed at his forehead again. "I'm sure my family can confirm that."

"And your employers?" said Barber. He glanced down at the file in his lap, "That would be The Brightside Building Society." He looked up again. "They can account for your time during office hours?"

Farrow stiffened. "It surely won't be necessary to involve my employers?"

"We need to verify your whereabouts at all times."

Farrow, pulled at his shirt cuffs, each in turn, and pressed a hand to his brow. "Let me think. I might have got it wrong. So easy to get the days mixed up." A short sharp laugh. "I may have taken a few days off." He wriggled in his chair.

"You may have? You're not sure?"

"Yes, I did take some time off. I just can't remember when." He squirmed. "It could have been over the last few days." He swallowed hard. "Yes, now I think of it. It was."

"We're talking about the last week. You surely must know what you were doing during that time?"

"Yes, of course. I was getting confused."

And so it continued. Like a drowning man, Farrow sank deeper and deeper into a churning sea of deceit and prevarication and evasion, thrashing around for something to grab hold of, and finding nothing that wouldn't pull him down further.

I groaned. "You really don't need me to tell you how this is going."

"Looks like we've got our man," said Lowe.

Nothing could be further from the truth but I let it pass for the moment.

Leaning towards the microphone on the desk, I said, "Miles, it's Mikey. Could we pass on this pitiful display and go for motive? Find out what he and the victim were arguing about."

Barber touched his earpiece, nodded imperceptibly and said to Farrow, "You didn't much like her, did you?"

That simple question opened a floodgate of vitriolic abuse. Farrow seemed to be on firmer ground here. To say he disliked her would be an understatement. We were regaled with a list of the many reasons Candy Bayliss deserved his undying hatred. Top of the list was what Marcus deemed to be her sociopathic manipulation of his father, driven by insatiable greed, followed by the lesser sins of spite, vindictiveness, and a total disregard for the needs of others, all in no particular order of priority.

It was safe to say daddy's fiancée would never have made it onto his party list.

Under Miles Barber's questioning a broader picture of Farrow's circumstances and relationships became clearer; his own dire financial situation following near-bankruptcy brought about by a gambling addiction that had left him near destitute. His skin had been saved by his father's financial support which included moving back into the family home with his wife after losing their own home.

Candy Bayliss's arrival into the family nest must have been a serious blow to his dreams of finally inheriting the family fortune and getting out from under the yoke of what he described as his father's oppressive control.

The poisonous atmosphere that must have built up in that particular family unit was hard to imagine.

Miles Barber finally brought the interview to a close after advising Farrow he was being released on police bail pending further investigation and reminding him, much to Farrow's annoyance, that he would have to return for more questioning at a later date.

Lowe was overjoyed. He punched the air. "Result."

"Think again," I said.

Nathan knitted his brows, waiting for an explanation.

Lowe lowered his arm and faced me, eyes narrowed. "You knew he was lying. It couldn't have been more obvious. You made that clear yourself."

"And that's how I know he didn't kill Candy Bayliss."

Lowe said, "I don't get it."

Nathan grunted.

"Have a good think about our guy. He's a mature intelligent man in a profession that calls for a sharp agile mind. And yet he was left floundering."

Lowe said, "That was obvious."

Nathan nodded.

"Do you seriously suppose our killer wouldn't have come up with a decent alibi by now? This guy was all over the place. You don't need me to point out the obvious."

"He was lying all the same," said Lowe.

"Sure, but not about this. And that's what you'll be getting in my report," I said, bringing any further dissent to an end.

Nathan said, "We'll have to follow the usual procedures all the same." To Lowe, he said, "Get a warrant to search the house and then talk to his employers."

Lowe looked glum. "Looks like we're back to square one." He leaned over and turned off the monitor. The image faded to black.

"Not necessarily," I said. "Forget about alibi and think about motive in the context of what Farrow told us."

"His opinion of Candy Bayliss is clear enough," said Lowe, "but given that she may well benefit financially from her relationship with the father at Farrow's expense, he's almost certain to have a negative view of her." He picked up a pen, flipped open the file in front of his and scribbled some notes on the inside cover.

Nathan added, "It is a subjective opinion."

I said, "Our opinions of others are always subjective. That doesn't make them wrong. And my interpretation of Farrow's body language tells me he firmly believed his own assessment." As an afterthought, I added, "And if he had killed her, he'd be more likely to play down his feelings. He wouldn't want to give us the chance to make a case against him."

"So we need to assume that Farrow's opinion of Candy's character is correct and see where it leads us."

"Exactly," I said.

Lowe tapped the desktop with his pen while he thought about this. "If Farrow's father had realised he was being taken for a ride, that would give him a motive for murder. He wouldn't take kindly to being conned."

Nathan added, "And Farrow wouldn't be the only one to lose out financially. So would his wife. That gives her a motive too."

Lowe sounded more cheerful. "Looks like the whole family had something to gain from her death."

I didn't share his mood. I was much more concerned about Rusty's feelings. If Farrow's assessment of his sister's character was correct, carrying with it the implication that it was her own behaviour that led to her murder, the news would hit Rusty hard.

Nathan said, "I've arranged a press conference for tomorrow. Naylor will be attending along with John Farrow and his family. So if you could make yourself available, Mikey."

I agreed to be there, but my spirits sank. Rusty was about to face the inevitable barrage of abuse heaped on his sister. And nothing could be done to spare him the ordeal.

CHAPTER TWENTY-ONE

Time on the road was time to think. And I had plenty to think about.

Foot to the floor, wind in my face, the Elan tearing up the road beneath me, I sped on my way, eyes protected from the dazzling sun by wraparound mirror shades, mind in confusion.

Ten days since my return, six days on from the murder, it was the day of the press conference, and I was on my way back to London, my mind focused on more pressing matters. More pressing to me that is.

I'm in a new relationship now. The last thing I need are these sort of complications.

The phrases kept spinning around in my head.

I hadn't meant to listen in. Just bad timing I guess. Or maybe not. Maybe there were a few things I needed to know before I got in any deeper.

That morning, my analysis of Farrow's interview typed and ready, I'd driven over to the station to hand it in to Nathan, and to let him know some urgent personal business had cropped up and I wouldn't be around for the press conference. But, hearing him on the phone, not wanting to interrupt, I had waited outside his office door until he'd finished his call.

And what a call.

The last thing I need are these sort of complications.

I had no doubts about who he was talking to. And despite Karen's protestations at my suspicions about Nathan's possible oversight in forgetting to end one relationship before starting another, I wasn't

104

convinced that all was well with my world.

No sooner did my relationship with Nathan seem to be back on track than something threw it off kilter again. And I needed to put those suspicions to rest, once and for all, one way or the other, no matter what the outcome.

There were two reasons for my return to London. The first, the one I had originally planned for, was to view an apartment, something I needed as a stopover when work brought me to the Capital.

The second, the more covert reason, was to confirm my suspicions. Or otherwise, as the case may be. And that was the purpose of my first call.

Before long, I was in Stoke Newington. One of London's more fashionable suburbs, famous for its range of good eateries.

I turned off the High Street into Stoke Newington Church Street and pulled up outside The Gastronomica which, despite its pretentious name, was a popular French restaurant. It was the restaurant for which I'd seen Nathan's receipt a few days before.

In my mind, I went over the ploy I had rehearsed one last time, took a few deep breaths, and headed over.

The proprietor, a Monsieur Gaston, was a thin man, neat and crisp like a newly sharpened pencil, and eager to assist.

"I hope you can help," I said. "A friend of mine dined here some days ago and thinks he may have left his notebook behind."

He was even more eager to help when I gave him the name of my 'friend'.

"DCI Quarryman used to be a regular here," he said. "I know him well. But I'm sure he didn't leave anything behind."

"Maybe one of his guests picked it up," I offered. "Would you know who he dined with that night?

I readied myself to hear the worst.

So eager to help was the poor man, he seemed almost devastated when he wasn't able to. "DCI Quarryman had only one guest that night. And I'm afraid I don't know the young woman's name."

Young woman?

My chest tightened, and I cut short a sudden intake of breath.

Recovering myself, I feigned a more relaxed attitude, made my excuses with a smile, telling Monsieur Gaston that I had an idea who the woman was and would contact her direct, and left hurriedly.

Sitting in the car afterwards, my heart racing, I felt ashamed and stupid. Ashamed at having stooped so low as to put myself through that pitiful charade. And stupid for having gotten it so wrong.

My cheeks burned with embarrassment, and the busy street sounds around me were an indistinct background hum, muffled by the pounding in my ears.

What was I thinking of? How could I demand Nathan's trust if I wasn't prepared to trust him in return? And what sort of basis was my deceitful behaviour for a stable relationship?

In my usual foolhardy manner, I hadn't thought through the implications of my actions. What if Nathan was to find out? There was every possibility he might. How would I explain what I'd done?

Dejected and subdued, I switched on the ignition, put the Elan into gear, and made my way to my second destination.

My agent, Jerry Martin, was already in the middle of negotiations when I arrived.

Still dispirited following my stupid behaviour, I stayed out of the way, leaving Jerry to haggle with the harassed young man from the rental agency while I took an initial cursory look around the apartment.

At five feet seven, Jerry was way under average height but in terms of sheer strength of character, he filled a room. And he was more than capable of hammering the bespectacled salesman into verbal submission over the rental payments.

He was already on the offensive in response to a tentative offer from the young man. "Nonsense," he said, with a dismissive wave of the hand. "This apartment would have been snapped up weeks ago if you hadn't overvalued it."

The salesman stammered out an objection but failed to dent Jerry's stubborn resolve.

I left them to get on with it, my back turned, and stared out of the window.

As the proprietor of Martin Media Enterprises, it was Jerry's job to manage and promote my career, a role that included taking care of my finances, planning interviews, and negotiating contracts for my media work. But like the sterling agent he was, he also managed my personal affairs and, I knew I could trust him to get me the best deal.

It was rush hour and, down below, the Islington streets were at their busiest as city workers made their ways home. Every so often, Angel Underground Station would disgorge another mass of commuters from its gaping maw, and they would swarm out onto the already crowded pavements. The occasional blare of a horn cut through the constant hum of traffic competing with the intermittent wail of a siren.

I had always loved this city. But it was time to move on, and put the past, and my stupid mistakes, behind me.

"Mikey?"

The sound of my name pulled me out of my reverie and I turned to face the two men. They stood side by side, like Tweedledum and Tweedledee, waiting for a response to some unheard question.

"Sorry," I said. "I was miles away."

Jerry scowled. "I said, we've agreed a reasonable rent. Now it's up to you."

The rental guy, name of David, said, "It is a bit on the small side. If you're looking for a family home, we do have some larger properties."

No doubt he was looking for an increased rental and a bigger bonus.

I said, "There's no family. Just me and my partner. And our primary home is outside London, anyway."

"Will she need to view the property?" said David.

I opened my mouth to speak, stuttered, closed it again and, after the briefest of pauses, said, "He. My partner is a 'he'."

I'd made enough mistakes for one day. And now was as good a time as any to start making amends.

The salesman flushed and said, "I'm sorry. That was presumptuous of me."

I brushed his apology aside with a smile. "Easy enough mistake to make."

And that was it. Over and done with. Nothing had changed. The sky hadn't fallen in. Why had I ever thought it was such a big deal?

To the salesman, Jerry said, "Mr MacGregor and I would like to look around before making a final decision."

"Of course."

David blinked several times under Jerry's unceasing gaze until, finally taking the hint, he said, "Take your time. I'll be waiting down in the lobby." He made his excuses and left.

Once we were alone, I said, "I think this will do nicely."

Jerry said nothing. Just fixed me with his famous stare. The one he used to beat others into submission.

"What?"

"This is going to be a major change for you, isn't it?"

"Elders Edge isn't that far away," I said. "London's only a two hour drive."

"We're not talking geography here."

There was a trace of censure in his tone. Worry lines creased his forehead.

Jerry had been my agent for many years and I knew him well enough to know that beneath the brashness and bluster, and despite his feigned truculence, he had a big heart, and cared about my well-being. He had become as much a friend as an agent. I was touched by his concern.

"All will be well, Jerry."

"I hope so."

"Let's face it, I've made one hell of a mess of my life so far. I made all the wrong choices. This is my chance to put things right."

He didn't look convinced.

"There's nothing left to keep me here," I said. "What have I got to lose?"

He appeared to consider this for a moment and then said, "You should bring Nathan over some time. I'd like to meet him."

I snorted. "That would be interesting. Cops are used to giving third degrees. I'm not sure how he'd feel about being on the receiving end of one."

Jerry's mouth quirked into a half-smile. "All part of the service. I wouldn't be doing my job if I didn't look after your interests now would I?"

"You always do that, Jerry."

I reached out and squeezed his shoulder. "Come on, let's go put that harassed young man out of his misery and do the deed."

"The sooner the better. You'll be needing the use of this place sooner than you think." He had that supercilious I-know-something-you-don't look on his face.

I narrowed my eyes. "What are you up to?"

He grinned, enjoying the moment. "You've been nominated for the Broadcast Awards. Best factual programme. Did I not mention it?"

My jaw dropped, and I stared at him open-mouthed. And then, "I think I would have remembered."

"Good news all round, eh? Bigger fees for you. More commission for me."

"I'm just grateful for the nomination. I'm flabbergasted."

"Fine by me. You take the acclaim, I'll take the money. Seems a fair deal."

I shook my head, grinning from ear to ear. "Only you."

"Come on," he said. "Let's go do that deal. I'll fill you in on the details later."

I followed Jerry out of the room and turned in the doorway to take one last look around, still grinning.

It wasn't much of a place. A poky studio flat with separate bathroom and kitchen, neither of which was much bigger than a broom cupboard. But it was good enough for my needs. It was never going to be home. London was never going to be home. Not anymore.

My future lay elsewhere. Back in Elders Edge. And now I was more determined than ever to settle down to the life I had always wanted and start making plans.

Unfortunately, the good mood that buoyed me up on the journey home wasn't to last. By the time I got back, all hell had broken loose.

CHAPTER TWENTY-TWO

Even before I reached the door, I heard the ruckus from inside. Rusty, Karen and Mia were grouped around the Fairview's reception desk. Rusty was banging his fist on the counter, agitated and loud. Karen, it appeared, was trying to placate him, confronting him face on, flinty-eyed, and holding up a restraining hand. Mia was snivelling.

Karen turned to me as I approached. Her face was pinched and the usual welcoming smile was absent.

I'd dropped by on the way home to share the good news about the award with Karen, but I'd got more than I'd bargained for.

"What the hell is going on?" I said.

"This," said Rusty, waving a small white envelope under my nose. "This is what's going on." His voice boomed out around the reception.

A middle-aged man and his bespectacled female companion stopped on their way between the foot of the stairs and the restaurant to see what the commotion was about. The woman glared at Rusty over the top of her specs and hurried her companion away. A younger woman seated in the lounge area turned at the sound and, craning her neck, peered at us over the back of the couch.

I took hold of Rusty's arm, less concerned with the cause of his tantrum than the behaviour itself, and said, "Come on, let's sort this out somewhere else."

I caught Karen's eye and tilted my head towards the door of her private apartment behind the desk, eyebrows raised. She caught the look and nodded briefly.

Rusty trembled as I guided him through the door into Karen's sitting room. I seated myself on the couch and drew him down onto the other side of it. Karen pushed a still sobbing Mia into the room and they made use of the facing chairs.

"So is someone going to clue me in on what this is about?" I said.

"This." Rusty held out the palm of his free hand and tipped the contents of the envelope into it.

A bullet.

I stared down at it, initially uncomprehending, and finally realising its significance. I looked up at him.

Comprehension must have shown in my eyes. He nodded briefly. "Yes, that's right. A threat."

"How and when?"

Holding the offending object as if it was contaminated, Rusty dropped the bullet back into the envelope. "That's what I was trying to find out."

Karen said, "You're not going to get very far by shouting at my staff." The tone of voice made her displeasure clear. "And I won't have them abused."

Her words had the desired effect. Rusty dropped his gaze and flushed. Suitably chastened, he said, "Sorry, I was out of order."

He looked over to Mia on the chair opposite and said, "I'm sorry I shouted. It was a shock. I was upset."

Still sniffing, Mia said, "That's okay," and wiped her nose on the sleeve of her cotton shirt.

"So?" I said, still waiting for a response.

"It was in a plain envelope with just my name on it," explained Rusty, "so I supposed it must have been brought in. I was trying to find out who delivered it."

"Has anyone called the police?" I asked.

Karen said, "I called Richard as soon as I found out. He's on his way over."

I turned my attention to Mia. "So where did it come from?"

In between sobs and sniffles, Mia managed to piece together an explanation. The bullet, contained within the envelope bearing Rusty's name had arrived in the usual morning post in a larger brown envelope addressed to the Fairview. She had opened it and left the contents in Rusty's pigeonhole for his later retrieval. The original envelope, that would have been postmarked with its origin, had been discarded with the rest of that morning's waste.

Karen confirmed that the garbage had been collected as usual earlier in the day and so there was no chance of recovering the original envelope. Not that it was likely to be of much benefit, anyway.

While Karen was still trying to console a sniffling Mia, assuring her she had done nothing wrong, Lowe arrived, letting himself into Karen's apartment.

He took control.

"Okay, people, nice and easy does it." He stood over us and held the open palms of his hands towards us in a calming gesture. "Let's take it from the beginning shall we?" He tilted his head towards Rusty. "You first."

Rusty, now more composed, handed the envelope up to him. "You'd best take this. You'll be needing it."

Lowe checked the contents, eyed Rusty with a look of concern and slipped the envelope into his breast pocket. "Okay, let's have it," he said and took out his notebook.

Rusty went over the events of that morning.

Lowe listened intently and scribbled down the details. Once finished, he went back through his notes and had Rusty confirm them. Satisfied he had it all down, he sent Mia on her way, impressing on her the need for confidentiality, and warning her not to discuss the matter with anyone. After crossing her heart and hoping to die, she scampered off, obviously delighted to be out of the firing line.

Pocketing his notebook, Lowe said, "Now, we need to get down to practicalities." Addressing Rusty, he said,

"Looks to me like this is down to one of your former colleagues. Agreed?"

Rusty agreed and slumped back on the couch.

Lowe continued, "In which case, we have to consider security. We're already trying to trace members of your old gang - not the easiest of tasks - but in the meantime, we need to take precautions. These people aren't likely to leave it at threats."

Again, Rusty agreed, looking even more dejected.

"We can step up our patrols and look out for any suspicious activity in the area," said Lowe, "but first, we should move you out of the Fairview. Too public. Might be best if we found you a safe house."

Rusty intervened. "Maybe I could stay at your place, Mikey?"

My heart jumped.

That came from nowhere.

I licked my lips and swallowed hard. It would have seemed churlish to refuse, but I needed to think about what I would be letting myself in for.

Before I could respond, Karen said, "Are you sure that's a good idea?" She sounded dubious. "Wouldn't that put Mikey at risk too?"

My thoughts exactly.

There was an uncomfortable silence while they waited for my response. I groaned inwardly. How could I refuse?

"I can look after myself," I said, "and it does seem like the best solution. My place is out in the open, nothing else around. It would be difficult for anyone to approach without being seen."

Lowe agreed. "I know your cottage backs onto the woods but you'd soon spot someone coming from that direction too. And we can always make sure we keep an eye on the place. Regular patrols."

Personal safety wasn't my only concern of course, important though it was. It also put paid to any hopes of spending more quality time with Nathan. Somehow, I couldn't imagine the three of us sharing cosy tête-à-tête evenings together.

"Then it's settled." I rose to my feet, signalling the end of the discussion, and hoping my reluctance didn't show.

The rest of the group rose too and Lowe said, "I'll get back to the station and put things in motion."

So that was it. A done deal. I just hoped it wasn't going to be at my expense.

CHAPTER TWENTY-THREE

Rusty wasn't up to talking much. Not surprising in the circumstances. And yet here was Karen chattering away ten to the dozen, seemingly oblivious to his mood, as if all was well with the world.

She'd driven him over from the Fairview that morning, the day after I'd agreed to his moving in - no doubt bending the poor guy's ear all the way - and was helping me get him settled in at Woodside Cottage. I'm sure she was trying to stay upbeat and cheer him up, but it clearly wasn't working; Rusty had hardly said a word since he arrived. He wandered about the lower floor as if in a daze as Karen and I busied ourselves around him.

Karen had brought over some badly needed bedding, towels and household necessities. While I distributed this assortment of items to their allotted places, she occupied herself in the kitchen, making tea and arranging biscuits on a serving plate, ready for elevenses when we took a break.

We occasionally caught each other's eye and pulled wry faces after a quick glance in Rusty's direction but, on the whole, we left him to mooch around the place while we pretended not to notice his dismal mood.

He stood with his back to us, staring out of the window into the sun-dappled garden beyond, while Karen and I kept up a running stream of small talk. Eventually, he turned, half smiling, and made his excuses, telling us he was going to take a walk outside. He was probably tired of listening to our inane gabbling.

Once he was out of the way, Karen flopped onto the couch, exhaled loudly, and said, "Dear God, he's hard work at the moment."

I watched Rusty amble down the path, shoulders slumped, until he reached the far end of the garden, and then I fell into place at Karen's side. "Understandable. He's had a hell of a shock."

"The press conference didn't help much either."

"Oh, shit yes. I'd forgotten about that. How did it go?"

"Not good." Karen pushed herself up and crossed over to the kitchen. She called back, "Richard says they tore his sister to shreds. The press lapped it up."

"Ouch."

The clatter of crockery from the kitchen was interrupted by the insistent whistle of a kettle which slowly died away. A few minutes later, Karen returned with a tea tray laden with cups and saucers, a steaming teapot, and a plate of shortbread biscuits.

"Should I call Rusty," she said. She placed the tray on the coffee table in front of the couch.

"Best leave him be." I reached over to the table, grabbed a piece of shortbread and munched it as Karen poured the tea. "I doubt he's quite ready yet for polite chit-chat over a cup of tea."

Teacup in one hand, Karen patted my thigh with her free hand, a doleful expression on her face. "Might be a good idea to talk it through with him later. I think he could use a friend right now."

I helped myself to another piece of shortbread and nodded.

"In fact..." She returned her cup to the saucer on the tray and rose to her feet. "...I'll leave you to it." She grabbed her linen bag from the chair by the door. "I don't like the idea of him sitting out there brooding." She nodded towards the garden window. "He needs someone to talk to."

Despite my protestations, she took her leave, pleading the need to get back to the Fairview to help with the lunchtime trade.

After waving her off, I took a long deep breath, mentally braced myself, and went to join Rusty in the garden.

He was leaning up against the stone wall beside the gate, staring out into the woods beyond.

I got straight to the point. "I hear the press conference didn't go too well?"

His reaction was all the answer I needed. He balled his hand and hit the wall with the side of his fist, his mouth pressed into a hard tight line. His voice strained, he said, "The things they said about Candy. She's barely cold in her grave, and they talked about her like she was a piece of garbage." He leaned forward and rested his forehead against the wall. "A back-street whore would have gotten a better send off."

I cringed at his words and squeezed his arm. "I know it's hard. God knows the press have given me some knocks in the past, but don't let them get to you."

From bitter experience, I knew of the emotional damage inflicted by an irresponsible press baying for blood. I knew how painful this could be.

"It's that bastard, Farrow. He did this."

So that was it; the cause of his uncommunicative mood. A silent seething anger for the man he held responsible. I hoped he had the strength of character to bear up under the strain. It's not as if his ordeal was about to end any time soon.

"I'm here for you," I said. "I hope you know that."

A brief nod, and he slow-punched my arm.

"Come on," I said, "Let's get you settled in. We can talk some more inside."

We left the shade of the large beech and made our way back along the gravel path towards the house. Before we were halfway there, someone stepped out of the open doorway.

It was Nathan.

He raised a hand to shield his eyes from the sun. "The front door was open. Not very clever in the circumstances." He sounded annoyed.

As he made his way down the path towards us, he said, "There's no point Rusty moving in if you're not going to take security more seriously, is there?"

"I'm sorry," I said, "I wasn't thinking."

"You got that right." He pushed past us and made his way to the bottom of the garden where he stopped, ran his gaze around the stone walls, and rattled the gate.

He made his way back to us. "Those walls are high enough, but I'll have some anti-climb guards fitted as an extra precaution, and that gate will need to be padlocked."

Rusty said, "I'm sorry to cause all this trouble."

Nathan ignored him. "And I'll have a sensor alarm fitted to the back of the house. The cottage is too open to the woods for my liking."

As he turned back towards the house, he dropped his voice and said, "We need to talk, Mikey." He clearly didn't want Rusty involved in the conversation. "Walk back to the car with me, would you?"

Raising his voice again, he said to Rusty, "Sgt Lowe is arranging to have one of our patrol cars keep an eye on the place. So I suggest you stick to the house as much as possible."

It was the first time he had acknowledged Rusty's presence.

I followed Nathan out to the Astra. "You have some news?"

Opening the Astra's doors with the remote as he rounded the car to the driver's side, he said, "Get in."

I slid in beside him as he climbed in from the other side and we closed the doors. "Sorry, I wasn't around yesterday", I said. Why was I always apologising?

"It might have been better if you'd rearranged your schedule." A disapproving tone. "I would have liked you in on the interviews and the press conference."

"It wasn't something I could put off."

He grunted and changed the subject. "I've just been through the latest report on Marcus Farrow. His employers dismissed him some months ago. Seems he has a drink problem. It was interfering with his work."

"Hardly surprising he didn't want them involved then."

"He's been keeping up the pretence of travelling to work every day so his family wouldn't find out."

I snorted. "Dumb idea. They were bound to find out, eventually."

"He was hoping to find a new post before they did."

"Does he have an alibi?"

"There's an Internet café he's been using to search for work. They vouched for him. He's been spending his days there."

"That's one suspect accounted for then. What about the rest of his family?"

"As you've already pointed out, they both have motives, but their stories stand up so far. I'll let you have the files. See what you make of them. We can call them back in if need be."

"It's beginning to look as if Rusty's old crew might be involved after all. Anything there?"

"We're making enquiries in that direction. But nothing yet."

Our conversation so far had been professional and to the point. Nothing unusual there. Nathan always adopted a businesslike tone when discussing work. But why did I get the impression I was being given the cold shoulder? I hoped this had nothing to do with Rusty.

I said, "You are okay with Rusty staying here?"

"Your choice." He switched on the ignition, ready to leave, signalling the end of our conversation.

"I couldn't really turn him down could I?"

"If you say so."

My temper was fraying. His curt responses were a clear sign of his displeasure. And there was only one reason I could think of for that.

"I thought we'd settled this?"

No response

Enough was enough. I made no attempt to hide my annoyance. "I'm getting tired of being on the defensive all the time." I opened the door and got out. "If you still can't trust me, that's your problem." I slammed the door shut and stepped away from the car.

He leaned over, wound down the window, and glared up at me. "You're the one with the problem here, Mikey. You need to get over yourself."

"What's that supposed to mean?"

"Your relationship with Rusty is the least of my worries. Does it not occur to you I might be concerned for your safety?"

He didn't wait for a reply, just wound up the window, stepped on the gas, and drove away.

I watched after him as he headed towards town, and a knot formed in my stomach.

Was that it? Had I misjudged him? It wasn't his lack of trust that was the problem here. It was my guilty conscience. I hadn't yet learned to accept his trust.

He was right. I needed to get over myself.

CHAPTER TWENTY-FOUR

Nathan answered on the third ring with a brisk 'hello'.

I stopped pacing the room and steeled myself. "Was I being a bit of a jerk earlier?"

"Yes," he said, "but I'm used to it." Direct as ever. But the icy tone had thawed to something warmer.

"How do you put up with me?"

He chuckled. "I guess you're an acquired taste."

Now more at ease, I slumped down onto the couch.

"I got it wrong. I'm sorry."

"It's okay. I know it's not easy."

"Tell you what. Why don't you come over this evening and I'll make it up to you? We both need to chill out. And it would be nice to get you to myself."

A pause. "I'm not sure I feel comfortable being around Naylor right now. He is part of our investigation after all."

I glanced up at the ceiling. The sound of Rusty's heavy tread on the bathroom tiles announced his presence overhead. "He won't be here. He's going out for the evening."

"Is that wise?" A hint of frost was back in his tone. "It does rather defeat the point of installing security measures if he's not going to be there."

"Oh, come on. You can't expect him to stay indoors all the time. He'd go stir crazy. And it's not as if he can't look after himself."

I got a grunt in response.

"And let's face it," I continued, "his moving in here was as much about protecting public safety at the Fairview as anything else."

Begrudgingly, he conceded the point. "Even so, I don't like the idea of you being on your own right now."

"All the more reason for you to come over. You can keep me company."

"I have to admit, I could use some downtime. We've not had much time together since this goddamn case blew open."

"No argument from me there."

"Okay, you win. I'll come over later and pick up some pizzas on the way."

"Great. We can make an evening of it."

"Best if I don't stay over though if Naylor is going to be around later."

My heart sank at that, but I had expected it, and understood his reasons. "Just seeing you would be good."

He promised to come straight over from the local station as soon as he'd finished work for the day and arranged a time before ringing off.

Now we'd cleared the air, I felt able to concentrate on my work. I sat at my desk, ready, once again, to rattle out my thoughts on the dark and dangerous world of the serial killer. It wasn't exactly my idea of light relief but my improved mood made it a less sombre task.

Even Rusty sounded more cheerful. As I pulled the laptop towards me, his tuneful whistling filtered through from above. And when he finally came downstairs, he seemed a more jaunty self.

He'd hired himself a Mercedes Cabriolet from a local car dealer and, after promising to heed my warning about being extra vigilant while he was away from the house, he made his way out to the car and, a few minutes later, the sound of the engine faded into the distance as he headed towards town.

Left to myself, I found it easier to concentrate on the task in hand and by the time Nathan arrived that evening, I had drafted out another chapter and, satisfied with the result, was feeling more buoyant and upbeat, ready for a break. And hungry as hell.

Nathan had what was euphemistically known as a 'healthy' appetite and he brought with him not only two large barbecue meatfest pizzas but a couple of garlic loaves and side orders of penne pasta dressed with olive oil.

Not that I was complaining; I'd been so wrapped up in my work, I'd forgotten to eat, and I was ravenous.

"I'm looking forward to this," he said, dropping the boxes onto the coffee table and himself onto the couch. He tore open the boxes as I settled down at his side.

"Hey," I said and, once I had his attention, added, "Good evening."

"Oh, sorry." He leaned over, planted a perfunctory kiss on my lips, and turned his attention back to the food.

I suppressed a smile. They say the way to a man's heart is through his stomach. In Nathan's case, there were times the journey never quite made it the whole way.

"I'd best grab myself some of that before you demolish it all." I helped myself to a slice of pizza. "And while you're wolfing it down, you can fill me in on the Farrow family interviews."

"Drop by the station in the morning and you can check the files for yourself."

I finished off the slice of pizza on my way over to the drinks cabinet by the window and, over my shoulder, said, "Just your initial thoughts." I came back with a bottle of Chablis and a couple of glasses.

In between mouthfuls of food, Nathan brought me up to speed.

He gobbled down some bread and said, "John Farrow's interview was painful to watch. Poor guy was besotted with her. Can do no wrong as far as he's concerned. If he's our guy, he's making one hell of a good job of hiding it."

"It's always possible." I put the glasses on the table and uncorked the Chablis. "How about Carol Farrow?" I poured a large measure of wine into each glass before seating myself again.

Nathan ignored the wine and went for the pasta. "She's a different matter. Cool and calm." He picked up one of the plastic forks that came with the pasta and tucked in. "She's an ex-cop herself so she knows the score. Worked with the Met for some years."

I took up a glass of wine and leaned back. "That would make her harder to read." I sipped some wine and helped myself to more pizza. "She'd be more likely to keep her head under pressure."

"We did catch her out in a lie though."

"Oh?" I chewed my pizza and washed it down with a mouthful of wine.

"One thing I can say for Carol Farrow is that she's fiercely protective of her husband. At least she was until she found out he'd been living a lie for the past few months." He stopped eating briefly, reached for his glass, and sampled the wine.

"You told her? Was that a good idea?"

"We didn't have a choice. She claimed she phoned her husband daily on the bank's landline and that's how she knew he'd been in London on the days in question."

I refilled my glass and grabbed some garlic bread while Nathan polished off more of the food. I chewed slowly as I thought through the implications of this piece of information. "Clearly she has no qualms about lying to protect her husband. But if they had colluded, she would have known about his dismissal."

"My thinking exactly."

I topped up my glass again. "So, ironically, her lie puts them in the clear."

"It probably puts him in the clear. But she could be involved in Candy Bayliss's murder and still want to provide an alibi for her clueless husband."

I half-drained my glass. "Does she have an alibi?"

"Neither she nor John Farrow have alibis that can be verified for the whole period in question. But there's nothing to tie either of them to the murder." He picked up his wine glass. "Still, it's early days."

I went to the drinks cabinet and fetched another bottle of Chablis.

"Hey, be careful with that. You had most of the last bottle."

"That's okay." I uncorked the bottle. "You had most of the food, so we're quits." I poured myself a large glass.

I offered Nathan a refill, but he put his hand over his glass and shook his head.

"I'll come down to the station tomorrow," I said, "and look through the files."

"In that case, let's forget about work. We're supposed to be taking a break." He raised his glass.

"I'm not complaining." I chinked his glass with my own and took a swig before putting it down and grabbing the music centre remote from the coffee table.

"Might as well make myself comfortable," I said, and swung around, slung my legs over the arm of the couch and lay back with my head in Nathan's lap.

"Much better," I said, beaming up at him. I pointed the remote at the music centre and hit the play button. A moment later, the dancing melodies and melancholic chords of Tonbieger's 'Strandgut' filled the room.

Nathan grinned down at me and the left side of his cheek dimpled. "I'm glad we had a chance to do this. It's been a bit strained recently. Pressure of work I guess."

And the pressure of having a quick-tempered and obtuse partner who didn't always stop to think before he opened his mouth. But I kept that to myself. I reached up and stroked his rough stubbled cheek and gazed into those molten green eyes. A rush of emotion swept through me, a surge of elation.

"I know I can be a pain at times," I said, "but I do love you. Truly. I know how lucky I am to have found you again."

His eyes clouded over and for a moment he seemed to be somewhere else. And then, "It was always you. You were always going to be the right choice."

The right choice? Had he ever considered an alternative? There was still so much I didn't know about him. All those missing years. Those missing wasted years. It was all too easy now to dwell on those happy early days when we still had our lives spread out before us and forget that, once we had parted ways, we had taken such vastly different paths through life, made different choices and lived through experiences that would never be part of our shared memories. And how I regretted it.

As I gazed into his eyes, he leaned down and pressed his lips to mine. I responded eagerly, returning his kiss, searching his mouth with my tongue, my body aflame.

He pulled away, breathing hard. "When is Rusty due back?"

I didn't need to ask what was on his mind. It was signalled plainly enough in his rapidly beating heart, in the glow of sweat on his forehead, in his husky uneven voice.

Groaning, I sat up again, turned to face him and pressed a hand to his chest. "Sorry to disappoint you but he didn't say. He could be back anytime."

Nathan matched my groan with one of his own.

"I could always come back to Charwell with you," I said, more in hope than expectation. He was still being evasive about my spending time at his place on a regular basis. I suspected he saw it as a step on the way to our living together. And he still wasn't ready for that.

He grinned. "That does rather take the spontaneity out of it. And besides, I'll probably be tired by the time we get back. And I have to be up at the crack of dawn if I'm to get through my work schedule."

Excuses all. But I was prepared to let it go.

"In that case, I'll have to make do with the wine." I reached for the bottle and topped my glass up to the brim.

"Easy with that." He covered his own glass with a hand to signal he'd had enough.

"I'm not the one who has to drive home," I countered.

We passed the rest of the evening pleasantly enough, filling the time with gossip about local happenings and finishing off the wine. I was already feeling woozy from the effects of drink but, what the hell, I opened another bottle anyway. Might as well make a night of it. I'd hoped Nathan might say something that explained the mysterious phone call I'd overhead, but he didn't, and I had no intention of raising the subject myself. I had to learn to trust him.

At ten-thirty, he glanced down at his watch. Rusty still hadn't returned, but the hour was late and Nathan pleaded the need to set off for home.

I rose when he did but my head swam and I fell back onto the couch. "Oops, I seem to have overdone the wine." I laughed.

"I did tell you not to open another bottle but when do you ever listen to me?" He hooked a hand under my arm and helped me to my feet. "Bed for you I think."

I laughed again and, swaying slightly, steadied myself against him, my hand on his shoulder. Trying unsuccessfully not to slur, I said, "I suspect I'm going to have a hangover tomorrow."

He grunted his disapproval and, taking me by the arm, guided me in the direction of the stairs. "I'll make sure you get upstairs safely before I leave."

"I'm sure I can manage," I said, falling back against him.

"Yeah, right."

With one hand under my arm and the other against my back, he manhandled me up the upstairs to the bedroom and dropped me with very little ceremony onto the bed. The room was moving around me.

"And when you wake up in the morning feeling like crap, don't say I didn't warn you."

I answered with a groan and tried to concentrate on his features as they swam in and out of focus.

He glared down at me and, as he turned to go, paused, bent down, and picked something up from the floor. I screwed up my eyes to get a good look at it. A small yellow plastic card.

He turned it over in his hand. "You dropped one of your cards," he said, scanning it. "It was under the edge of the bed. A store card for ..." He stopped abruptly, stared at it intently, and then looked down at me, his jaw set firm, his lips pressed into a hard line. Finally, "It's made out to Rusty Naylor."

"What?" I pushed myself up to a sitting position and tried to focus. "He must have dropped it."

"In your bedroom?"

I shook my head, tried to clear my mind. "I must have picked it up by accident thinking it was mine."

He nodded briskly and dropped the card onto the top of the bedside cabinet.

Drunk I might be but I wasn't so far gone I couldn't understand how this might look. I stared directly into his face, forced my eyes to focus, and said as slowly and clearly as I could, "Rusty has never been in my bedroom."

He stared down at me without speaking for several moments and then he leaned down and brushed my lips with his. "Okay," he said. And then, "I'll leave you to get some sleep." And he was gone.

I flopped back down onto the bed and let the room spin around me.

If I had been anyone else, Nathan finding that card would have been no big deal, my explanation accepted for what it was, a reasonable account of what happened. But I wasn't anyone else. I was me, the man who had betrayed his lover, who had let him down, whose dissolute past had caught up with him and had lost him the trust of the man he loved.

And no matter how many times he told me we had to trust each other, and no matter his seemingly ready acceptance of my explanation, I still couldn't shake of those feelings of guilt or convince myself that he had learned to trust me. One thing was for sure, if I wanted to make this relationship work, I still had a long way to go.

CHAPTER TWENTY-FIVE

The raucous banter of a couple of electricians and the incessant whine of a power drill were the last things I needed first thing in the morning. This morning in particular. My head hurt, and each step down the stairs set my brain to thumping against the sides of my skull.

No sympathy from Rusty either.

"You look like shit," he said with a cheery grin. "Good night was it?"

Unlike me, he looked hale and hearty and ready to face the world, already groomed and dressed for another hot summer's day in shorts and a light cotton shirt.

I glowered at him, pulled my dressing gown around me, and shuffled across the living room floor. "Whose idea was it to let the chuckle brothers in?"

Out of earshot, on the far side of the room, one of the two electricians, his back to me, was pinning cable around the frame of the door leading out to the garden. He was whistling a merry tune that set my head spinning. The other, an older man with grey hair, and a ponytail that would have looked better on the pony, poked his head around the door from outside and turned off his drill long enough to shout, "Any chance of another brew?" Catching sight of me, he added, "I hope that's a hangover you have there, pal. I'd hate to think you look like that every day."

His colleague joined in the general laughter.

I groaned and shuffled my way into the kitchen. Rusty followed me in and leaned against the table, a mug of tea in his hand and a wide-open smile on his face. "Your guy was the one who wanted a security system putting in. Blame him."

The sound of the drill started up again, and I winced. "Well, you can attend to their needs. I'm not sure I'm up to service with a smile this morning." I glanced over at him, puzzled by his sudden rise in spirits. "You're in a better mood today. Did you win the lottery or what?"

"Much better than that." Still grinning, he threw the dregs of his tea into the sink and, after dropping his mug into the washing-up bowl, filled the electric kettle and put it on to boil while he set out four clean mugs. "I'll make you one too. You look like you could use a good brew."

I nodded. "So? What's better than winning the lottery?" I propped myself up against the worktop and folded my arms.

He opened the caddy and spooned some tea into the pot. "I found me some entertaining company last night." The grin widened even more.

Great. So while he was out being 'entertained', I had foregone that particular pleasure for fear of being interrupted by his imminent return.

"We really must compare schedules in future."

"What?" He poured boiling water into the teapot and stirred it.

"Never mind." I crossed over to him as he filled the mugs with tea, helped myself to one of them, and took up my position by the worktop again. "I just hope she gave you a good time." And as an afterthought, "Or was it a he?"

He laughed as he took up two of the remaining mugs. "This time it was a she. Though it's nice to have the choice of course."

He carried the mugs through to the sparkies and, much to my joy, the sound of the drilling stopped. A moment later he was back.

I dug into the pocket of my dressing gown, produced his store card, and handed it to him. "This is yours," I said.

He took it from me and stared down at it, his brows knitted in puzzlement. "Where did you find it?"

"I picked it up by mistake."

"That's a stroke of luck," he said, "I thought I'd lost it some time ago."

A stroke of luck. That was a laugh. The only luck it had brought me was to stir up doubts and misgivings about my relationship with Nathan once more.

I groaned inwardly, suddenly reminded I had promised to meet him down at the station that morning to review the recent interviews. Given my current delicate constitution, I didn't much relish leaving the house that day, but I guessed I'd just have to grit my teeth and get on with it.

I excused myself to Rusty and headed back towards the stairs, tea in hand. "I'll leave you to deal with the gruesome twosome," I said. "I need to go out." I made my way, as slowly as possible, to the bathroom.

Once I was showered, shaved and dressed, I checked my reflection in the bathroom mirror and, satisfied that I could just about pass as human, I headed out to the Elan. By the time I reached the station, the hammering in my head had subsided to a dull ache, a sign I was probably going to live after all. I ignored the desk sergeant's pitying look as he called through to Lowe, and was soon seated at a desk in Lowe's office, a pile of files, a monitor screen, and a glass of fizzing Alka-Seltzer in front of me.

Learning of my over-indulgence of the night before, Lowe added to the growing list of wisecracks. "I know a good cure for hangovers," he said. "Stay drunk." And chortling at his own feeble joke, he headed on out for his morning patrol.

I groaned and drained the glass, pushed it to one side, pushed the files to the other side, and turned on the monitor.

Soon, despite the troublesome headache, I was engrossed in the visual display of John Farrow's emotional turmoil.

He was a rake of a man, all bone and skin with a long narrow face and tufts of wispy grey hair scattered around his balding pate. Despite the summer heat of the previous few days, he had chosen to wear a dark grey suit with a plain white shirt and sober dark-blue tie. Whatever it was Candy Bayliss had seen in him to mark him out as a potential husband, it certainly wasn't his charismatic appeal.

What did stand out, however, was his posture. He sat straight, rigid and almost inflexible. It was the posture you would see in an ex-serviceman. But no matter his outward appearance, the emotional rage inside was betrayed by the many small movements that gave him away. The constant clenching and unclenching of his fists when he spoke of his loss, the way he gripped the arms of his chair when explaining how much she meant to him, the many times he tugged at his collar. The more I watched and listened, the more I understood that this was a man struggling to suppress his grief.

So too, when he spoke of his relationship with his son, the way his voice hardened when he told of the enmity between son and fiancée, the way he pushed hard against the back of his chair, jaw set firm, when he derided his son for the failure he thought him to be.

This was a family where bitterness and hate and disappointment ran deep.

In contrast, Carol Farrow's interview was a more relaxed affair. Under questioning, she appeared confident and assured, no doubt the result of familiarity with police procedures. As an ex-policewoman, she had the advantage of knowing what to expect and would feel more at home in these surroundings, albeit on the other side of an interview.

She was attractive in a no-nonsense down-to-earth sort of way; natural auburn hair, sprinkled with grey, cut in a practical bob; minimal makeup and a simple gold chain around her neck matched by a pair of gold earrings with inset amber stones. She wore a simple cornflower-yellow shift tied at the waist with a plaited rope belt in a darker ochre shade, and open sandals.

This was not a woman to be easily fazed or caught off guard. I noted the giveaways in the body language when she calmly lied about calling her husband at work, the fiddling with the earrings at the precise moment of the lie, the subsequent pacifying action when she pressed a hand to her throat. But, other than that, there was nothing in either her statement or her demeanour to suggest she was lying about her own movements over the past few days. What did strike me was how loyal she was to her husband. Not someone I would have thought warranted such loyalty. But then there's no accounting for taste.

I was getting towards the end of Carol's interview when the door opened behind me. I turned, expecting to see Lowe returned from his patrol. It was Nathan.

The stony reception I'd expected wasn't forthcoming. Instead, his usual stern expression melted into one of compassionate concern, and he said, "Are you okay? You look like—"

I cut him off. "You don't need to say it. I feel like it too."

He crossed over to the desk and dropped into the chair at my side, the look of concern still etched on his face. "We can always leave this till later if you like."

"It's okay," I said. "I'm done here. I was just about to drive home."

"You didn't drive over?" His tone had hardened.

"Sure I did."

"That wasn't very clever, Mikey. There's probably still enough alcohol in your blood to put you over the limit."

"I'll be fine."

"No, you won't. And you're not driving back." He rose from his seat. "Come on. I'll give you a lift."

I tried to protest, but he was having none of it. In the end, I dutifully followed him out of the door.

"You can give me your thoughts on the interviews on the way back," he said as we reached the car park.

"And do me a favour," I said. "Next time I try to open a third bottle of wine, take it off me and give me a good slapping instead."

He snorted. "If I'd thought that was ever going to work, I'd have done it a long time ago." He opened the doors of the Astra.

I answered with a grin as we both climbed into the car. Instead of the morose distant Nathan I'd expected to greet me after the excesses of the previous night and his less than enthusiastic acceptance of my denial of Rusty's presence in my bedroom, he was in a surprisingly affable mood. Looks like I'd misjudged him after all. Something I was grateful for.

Not that my good mood was to last long. The call that came through on the radio as we pulled out of the car park soon put paid to that.

Nathan answered the call, dropped the receiver back in its cradle, and swung the Astra around. "Here we go again," he said.

CHAPTER TWENTY-SIX

Marcus Farrow, it seemed, had never learned to leave well enough alone. Here he was, yet again, the centre of a public debacle at the Fairview. This time in the bar, with Rusty.

By the time we reached them, the argument was going full throttle. Rusty was backed up against the bar, a younger woman, blonde and buxom, seated on the bar stool at his side, cowering. Marcus Farrow, standing toe to toe with him, chin thrust forward, was shouting into his face, with Carol Farrow standing behind her husband, a restraining hand on his shoulder.

Several people hurried from the bar as we arrived, eager to get away. Those that remained watched the scene with grim fascination from a safe distance, seated at surrounding tables.

Karen stood a few strides away from the group at the centre of the spectacle, in the company of her barman, and turned towards us as we approached, her face a picture of exasperation.

Nathan marched towards the group and was soon calling the shots. "Enough." He pointed a warning finger at Marcus Farrow who seemed to be having a problem standing up. "All of you, outside now."

Even Marcus Farrow, drunk as he was, could see that Nathan wasn't to be argued with, and preceded him out of the bar, still scowling, Carol's hand clutching his arm, and with Rusty and his companion, arms linked, behind them. Karen and I followed on, trailing them at a distance.

A hubbub of voices rose up behind us as we left the bar, and other patrons in Reception watched in silence as we made our way out onto the street.

"What the hell was that all about?" I whispered to Karen.

"My fault," she said. "I was stupid enough to let that idiot back in after the last episode. But never again."

"He started it then?"

"Oh believe me. The moment he saw Rusty at the bar, he went straight in for the kill."

"What was it about?"

She didn't have time to go into detail before we reached the rest of the group, gathered around Nathan at the side of his car. "Later," she said.

Nathan addressed the group as a whole. Marcus Farrow wore his belligerent expression and swayed slightly. "Someone like to explain what's going on here?" He looked around from face to face, waiting for an explanation.

Rusty's companion, tearful, dabbing at her eyes with the back of her hand, said, "We were just having a quiet drink, and this madman came out of nowhere, started shouting and calling names."

Rusty slipped an arm around her waist and gave her a gentle squeeze.

I took a closer look at her. Presumably, this was Rusty's 'entertaining company' of the night before. A bleached blonde with dark roots, she wore tennis whites, shorts and t-shirt, now worn and faded. A pair of large cheap-looking pendant earrings of blue glass that matched the blue eyeshadow on her overly made-up face offset the plain style.

Carol Farrow was quick to jump to her husband's defence. "Watch who you're calling names." Her lip curled. "When we need the opinion of some cheap trash, I'll let you know."

"That's enough." Nathan raised his voice, cutting off any possible rejoinder from Rusty's date. "Another word from you, and you'll be joining your husband down at the station."

Rusty's companion gasped and clung to his arm, her face a picture of misery. Rusty tightened his grip around her waist and gave her another reassuring hug but said nothing.

While Nathan was still trying to calm the situation, a police patrol car came into view from around the corner and pulled over to the curb by Nathan's Astra. Lowe climbed out and shot Karen a worried glance, his brows knitted, as he made his way towards us. She answered his look with a tilt of the head and a smile, signalling that she was okay.

Nathan and Lowe exchanged brief nods of acknowledgement before Nathan turned his attention back to the group. Focusing on Rusty, he said, "Let's hear it from you."

Rusty seemed unfazed by the situation. Staying calm, he explained how he and his companion, Jenna, had met for a drink in the bar. Within a few minutes, Marcus Farrow, already drunk, had entered with his wife and, on recognising Rusty, presumably following his depiction in the local media, had launched into what Rusty described as a 'foul-mouthed tirade' about his sister, claiming Rusty was the same sort of 'low life scum' that she was.

Carol Farrow interrupted. "You have no right to claim my husband was drunk without positive proof."

Nathan pointed a finger at her to silence her. "This isn't a court of law. Most of us can recognise a drunk when we see one." He shot Marcus Farrow a scathing look.

Now it was Marcus Farrow's turn. "I don't need to be sober to know scum when I see it." He pulled free of his wife's restraining hand and lunged toward Rusty but lost his balance in the act and was grabbed and held in place by Lowe.

"It was this scumbag's sister got me kicked out of my home." He was ranting now. "I'll get even with you."

Lowe intervened. "You want me to book him, Chief?"

"I've heard enough to know how it went down. Take him to the station and charge him with public affray."

Carol Farrow objected. "That's a bit harsh. It's usually just a caution for a first offence. I know the form."

"But what you don't know," said Nathan, "is that it's not his first offence." He nodded to Lowe. "Take him away."

A sharp intake of breath, and Carol Farrow, momentarily taken aback, glared at her husband.

To Karen, Nathan said, "Okay, to use your office?" and when she answered in the affirmative, continued, "Inside the rest of you."

We all followed behind as he led the way back into the building and across the Reception area to Karen's office behind the desk.

Inside, Nathan leaned against Karen's desk and directed the rest of us to a couch and chair against the wall. Carol Farrow made it to the chair while Rusty and Jenna took up positions on the couch. I stayed over by the door and Karen hovered by the desk.

Nathan folded his arms, crossed one leg over the other and, after running his gaze over each of the three people seated in front of him, said, "Now I'd like some sensible answers. What's this about?"

Carol Farrow took up the challenge. "Marcus is in a very bad place right now. He's not himself." she cast a quick glance at the two seated on the couch. "But I'm not sure it's appropriate to discuss our personal problems in public."

Nathan accepted the point with a nod. "Then you're free to go for the moment. But you should make yourself available in case we need to speak with you again."

She rose to leave without answering, more subdued than she had been, and I stood to one side and opened the door for her.

Karen said, "Please tell your husband he's no longer welcome at the Fairview."

Carol hesitated, stared at Karen for a moment, and then swept out of the room without answering or acknowledging any of us further. I closed the door behind her.

A collective sigh of relief went around the room but it seemed Nathan hadn't finished yet. To Rusty, he said, "It might help if you kept a low profile."

His tone was accusatory as if he were blaming Rusty for the situation he'd found himself in. For the first time, I realised how much he disliked Rusty.

Rusty fixed him with a cold stare and said, "I'm not the one at fault here."

They held each other's gaze, the enmity between them almost tangible.

Nathan turned to Karen and said, "Everything okay here?" She confirmed that it was, and he said, "I'll leave you to it then." To me, he said, "I need to go back to the station. Can you make your own way from here?"

I told him I was okay with that and he went on his way.

I sank into the chair vacated by Carol Farrow and said to Rusty, "I have to say, you handled that very well. I wish we could all stay that cool in the heat of a fight."

He grimaced and said, "When you have a past like mine, especially a criminal record, it's not a good idea to upset the status quo. The past has a habit of catching up with you."

I snorted. If anyone knew how true that was, I did.

CHAPTER TWENTY-SEVEN

"He's still in bed?" Nathan glanced down at his watch. "It's eleven-thirty."

The incredulity in his voice didn't surprise me. Nathan had never understood why anyone wouldn't choose to leap out of bed, ready and raring to go, the moment the sun climbed over the horizon. Well, not unless there was good reason to stay in bed. And there was one good reason I could think of that was fast becoming a distant memory. I sighed inwardly and tried not to think about my own carnal needs.

It was the day after the fracas at the Fairview and Nathan had called round to bring us up to date.

"Jenna stayed over," I said.

"What?"

He didn't sound too pleased at that. I hoped because it was a reminder of what he was missing.

"You were the one who told him to keep a low profile. I guess this is his way of following your advice."

He grunted. "I need to speak to him but first I'd like to hear your assessment of the interviews you looked at yesterday." He glanced up at the ceiling. "Can we talk outside?" He headed towards the back door.

"Wait." I grabbed his arm. "The alarm." I scooped up my keyring from the coffee table and used the attached remote to turn off the alarm by the door.

"Is that working okay?"

"Yep. And your guys are patrolling regularly out front. So we're all safe and snug in our little nest."

Another grunt, and he led the way out into the garden. I followed him down the path to the large overarching beech tree, and we settled ourselves into the rattan chairs in its shade.

High above a flock of starlings passed by in formation, a stark black wing streaking across a clear blue sky, and nearby a bumblebee ceased its droning long enough to settle into the head of a foxglove before taking off again with its prize of gathered pollen.

It should have been a time to relax and enjoy the many pleasures of the season. But here we were, settling down in a garden full of summer's heady scents and sultry sounds to discuss the details of a brutal murder. An ironic setting for such a depressing task.

"We should be enjoying each other's company on a day like this," I said. "Not dwelling on the macabre."

"Work first, I'm afraid." And then a doleful look. "Maybe that Accountant would have been a better bet after all."

"I don't think so. I know when I'm well off."

"I know this isn't what you expected to return to. Neither of us did. Sometimes the world gets in the way." There was a faraway look in his eyes. One I'd seen before. And once again, I wondered what was on his mind.

"Everything okay?" I asked.

He came back to the present. "It will all work out in the end. But for now…" He straightened up and adopted a more positive tone. "…we need to concentrate on the present. So what do you have for me?"

"Sorry to disappoint you, but I don't."

I talked him through my observations, pointed out the lack of anything to help progress the case, and confirmed my character analysis of both interviewees; John Farrow's enmity towards his son, and Carol Farrow's unquestioning support of him.

"What about you?" I asked. "Any further developments?"

"That's why I'm here. We've had some feedback from the recent press report. Mia's tattooed man. We have a more recent sighting."

"You have a description?"

"A witness claims to have seen that tattoo."

I wasn't impressed. "Lots of men sport similar tattoos. Women too

138

for that matter."

"Maybe. But this tattoo is particularly distinctive. A large red and green serpent running up the right arm. But more importantly, the guy was seen talking to Candy Bayliss not long before she was killed. Seems too much of a coincidence for it not to be the same man."

A sudden thought struck me. "You think he's still around?"

"I'm sure he is. My theory is that the renewed publicity drew him back when he realised he'd killed the wrong woman, and he tracked her down again. And just like before, his intention was to flush out Naylor. And after all the recent publicity, the killer knows his strategy worked and Rusty is back here too. That bullet was more than just an empty threat."

I let this sink in while I considered the implications. "So Rusty could be in even more danger than we thought?"

"Exactly. Which is why I need to speak to him. To impress on him the need to be extra cautious. You both need to be on your guard while Rusty's staying here." He glanced at his watch again. "I really would like to speak to him, Mikey. Do you think you could rouse him?"

"I suspect Jenna has already taken care of that. But I'll see what I can do to get him out of bed."

Nathan tutted and raised his eyes heavenward as I rose from my chair. I grinned down at him and headed back up the path to the house. I got the distinct impression he didn't appreciate my sense of humour. Nathan followed on behind and I left him standing in the living room while I went upstairs and knocked on Rusty's bedroom door.

Sounds of movement from inside and then the door opened a few inches and Rusty's bleary-eyed countenance peered out at me through the gap.

"Sorry to interrupt your morning exercise," I said, "but the Chief is downstairs. He needs to speak with you."

Rusty groaned. "Be right there," he said, and closed the door.

A few minutes later, the three of us were seated around the coffee table in the living room, and Nathan filled us in on the details of the witness statement. Rusty was pale and drawn. Though I couldn't tell if it was a reaction to what he was hearing or overenthusiastic lovemaking.

Rusty said, "Did your witness get a good description of this guy."

Reluctantly, Nathan confirmed they hadn't. "He was wearing a grey sports jacket with the hood up. Given how hot it's been over the past few weeks, that in itself is a good indication that our man didn't want to be recognised. Fortunately, his sleeves were rolled up and that distinctive snake tattoo was on display. The description of it matched the one we got from Mia Ludlow."

"Not very clever of him," murmured Rusty.

"Quite so," said Nathan. "Lucky for us he's not too bright."

I said, "What were the circumstances?"

"Our witness took particular note because she knew Candy - or rather, Lydia Carrington - by sight and saw her being confronted by our man in what she described as an aggressive manner."

"Where was this?" I asked.

"In the High Street. It looks as if he interrupted Candy during a shopping trip."

I said, "I presume he was trying to get her to open up about Rusty's whereabouts."

"That's the theory we're working on. And then later killed her to draw Rusty his way."

"And it obviously worked," I said.

Rusty said, "So what now?"

"We're stepping up surveillance and we'll be on the lookout for any suspicious activity but I'm sure you'll appreciate that this being the holiday season, we have a lot of strangers in town. So I'm just asking you to be extra vigilant, take care of yourself."

There was a gasp from the direction of the stairs and we all turned in unison towards the sound.

Jenna stood at the bottom of the stairs, ashen-faced and trembling. I'm not sure how long she had stood there or what she had heard, but she must be wondering what the hell she'd gotten herself into.

CHAPTER TWENTY-EIGHT

Barely able to keep a grip on the large wooden crate I was carrying, I staggered out of the storeroom, and just managed to reach the door of the adjoining room before it slipped from my grasp and fell to the floor with a dull thud. The flimsy sheathing shuddered within its frame, and a cloud of dust rose up around it.

I leaned against the wall, suppressed a sneeze as I wafted away the dust, and gulped in some air.

It was later that day, and I'd been summoned to the Fairview to help Karen with what she'd referred to as a 'helping hand'. A forklift truck might have been a better bet.

Once I'd caught my breath, I called back to her, "Remind me again why I'm doing this?"

"Because you're a good and faithful friend." She appeared in the doorway of the larger room next door, her hair tied back and tucked into a pair of brand-new dark-blue coveralls that matched my own, and carrying a dirty Hessian sack tied at the neck with thick cord.

"Nice try," I said, "but shouldn't you be training your future husband to do the grunt work?"

The Fairview's annexe at the back of the main building was a later extension, comprised of two rooms, and currently used for storage. The room I'd just stumbled from was the larger of the two, the one Karen had designated as additional living space for her and Richard.

In a feeble attempt to wriggle out of another bout of heavy lifting, I'd argued that her present quarters, small and cosy as they were, would be much more romantic. But no luck there. Stubborn as ever, she was having none of it. And so here we were, heaving crates and other assorted containers from one room to the other. It was the sort of work no sane person would consider doing in the middle of a heatwave. But far be it from me to point out the obvious.

Karen said, "It can't have escaped your notice that our men are busy right now. Otherwise, I'm sure Richard would be only too happy to help."

Fair comment. Both Richard and Nathan were conspicuous by their absence at the moment. "Can't say you didn't warn me about policemen. I'll listen to you next time."

"That'll be the day." She dropped the sack at my feet. It hit the floor with a jangle and raised more dust. She returned to the larger room, leaving me to do the storing.

"At least we have each other for company while they're playing cops and robbers," I called after her. "Not sure it's what I signed up for though."

I picked up the sack, dropped it on top of the crate and, with my foot against the crate's side, pushed the whole lot through the doorway.

This room was a smaller version of the one next door. It was also dingy, damp, and with a tiny barred window that let in little light.

Containers of all shapes and sizes were already packed within its narrow confines. But with some judicious planning, we would just about manage to pack the rest of the crates and sacks into this smaller space.

Karen called back, "It's a bit more than cops and robbers. But I share your sentiment. And besides," she added, "you were the one who started this whole thing off."

I made my way to her, wiping my sweaty hands on my overalls. "If I'd known the consequences, I might have had second thoughts."

Karen had her back to me, hands on hips, surveying her surrounding. The odour of damp clung to everything and what light found its way in through the grimy windows, drew attention to the dust-laden air and dirt-smeared walls. Even so, the room was large and, admittedly, had potential as a living space.

"This won't look so bad once we've cleaned it up and given it a fresh coat of paint," she said.

"We?" I emphasised the word.

She ignored the question and changed the subject. "Talking of consequences, Carol Farrow dropped by earlier. She asked me to reconsider the ban on her husband. She promised to keep him out of trouble in future."

"I hope you said 'no'. The man's a liability."

"At first, but I felt sorry for her. In the end, I relented." She picked up two of the remaining sacks and handed them to me. "And she talked her father-in-law into letting them stay with him. After all, if he kicked out his son, she would suffer too. She can be very persuasive when she puts her mind to it."

She gathered up the last of the sacks in both arms, a more substantial one that bulged at the seams, and brushed past me into the corridor.

I came on behind and followed her into the other room. "You have to wonder why she supports him. Anyone else would have given up long ago."

"When I told Carol I wasn't happy about having a belligerent drunk on the premises, she asked me if I felt any better about having a killer around, meaning Rusty. Is that what he is?"

"That's not quite how it went down."

I dropped my two sacks onto the crate with the one I'd placed there earlier, crossed to the far side of the room where we'd already stacked several containers, and moved them around to make space for the larger one.

As I worked, I told her what I had learned from Rusty. How the proprietor of a convenience store had taken it on himself to be a have-a-go hero and had paid for his valour with a bullet through the chest at point-blank range.

"Rusty hadn't been prepared for that. A step outside the bounds of his moral code I guess. He turned them in and got a reduced sentence."

Karen said, "Carol seemed to know a lot about the case."

"She was in the Met at the time." I reached around to the other side of the large crate, stepped in front of it and, with some effort, managed to push it across the floor towards the space I had just created by the wall.

"Does Jenna know about Rusty's past?" asked Karen.

As I pushed the cumbersome object into place, I told her about Nathan's call at Woodside Cottage that morning and Jenna's reaction on overhearing our conversation. "If she didn't know before, I'm sure she does now." I turned towards her, rubbing my aching back with both hands. "Why do you ask?"

Karen said, "They were in the bar earlier. And they didn't seem to be getting on too well."

I shrugged and said, "Sounds like the end of a budding romance. Can't say I'm surprised. She didn't look too happy this morning." As an afterthought, I added, "What's she like?"

Handing me her sack, Karen said, "I only know what I've heard secondhand. She's long time divorced and shares a flat over the florist's in the High Street. I don't know much about her as a person though."

I took the sack from her and added it to the steadily growing pile in the far corner. "I just wondered how Rusty met her," I said.

"Not sure where they met. But they've been in the bar a couple of times."

I grabbed the remaining sacks from the top of the crate, placed them with the others, and then returned to the crate and sank onto it, in need of a breather. "Was she a regular?" I asked.

"Not recently. But she's been here in the past. I'd always thought she and the Farrows were friends, or at least acquainted. I'm sure I've seen her talking with Marcus."

"Really? There was no sign of it during the recent confrontation between Marcus and Rusty."

"No, I know. And Carol was positively hostile. I guess I could be wrong though. It's not as if I really know any of them. They're just customers."

She shrugged, turned on her heel, and headed for the door again. "Come on. No time to rest. One more trip and we're done."

Groaning, I pushed myself to my feet and followed her to the other room.

I picked up two more boxes, small cardboard cartons, and carried them back to the storage space. Karen followed behind with the last of them. Back in the smaller room, I dumped my cartons against the wall and took Karen's from her.

As she handed it over, she said, "I bumped into Martha Stubbs the other day. She tells me she's thinking of selling Woodside Cottage."

"I paid three months' rent up front so I've got some time yet."

"Any progress with Nathan?"

"He's too involved in this Goddamn investigation to think of anything else right now."

I placed the final carton on top of the others and, job completed, fell back into place on the larger crate.

"He works too hard," said Karen. "Which is why I'm planning a surprise for him." She sank down at my side and pushed me over to make room for us both.

"What are you up to now?" I said.

"I'm arranging a small party for his birthday next week. Just the four of us."

I snorted. "Good luck with that. If you can pin him down, you're a better man than I am. And he hates having a fuss made of his birthday."

"Tough. If I say he's having a party, he's having a party. He wouldn't dare refuse."

I believed her. Once she'd her mind made up about something, there was no denying her. And Nathan knew that as well as I did.

"I'll get Richard to find out what his work schedule is like and we'll work around it. It doesn't have to be on the actual day but he's going to have a party whether he likes it or not. He needs a break. He's not been his usual self lately."

"You've noticed that too have you?"

"I'm sure it's just this case. You know how focused he is when he's working."

"Unfortunately, yes."

"Looks as if we'll both have to bite the bullet for a while. And a night out will be a much needed treat for all of us."

I wasn't going to argue with that.

Now that was settled, Karen moved on to her current favourite subject and regaled me with details of her wedding plans. The wedding was nearly a year away, but I knew this was going to be a major topic for months to come. Not that I minded. I was happy for her. Her previous marriage had ended in disaster and it was a pleasure to see her so well settled now and with a better life to look forward to.

I only wished I could be as certain about my own relationship.

CHAPTER TWENTY-NINE

By the time Karen and I had cleaned up and shared a bite to eat, the day was drawing to a close. I was on foot and, eager to be home before nightfall, set off towards Tinkers Wood at a hurried pace, only to have my progress unexpectedly hindered as I rounded the corner into the High Street.

Two police cars and an ambulance, lights flashing, were parked by the path leading into Tinkers Wood. A couple of paramedics stood by the open doors of the ambulance.

A small crowd of onlookers had already formed at the roadside and their numbers swelled as more and more people hurried across the road to join them. A uniformed police officer was urging them back, away from whatever scene of carnage they were gathered around. Another constable was securing the area, setting up a taped perimeter. Further back in the woods, there were signs of activity as several officers, plainclothes and uniforms, moved among the trees.

It never ceased to amaze me how quickly a serious traffic accident drew a crowd. It's as if they materialised out of thin air within minutes of a major incident. And always eager to take a ghoulish pleasure from someone else's misfortune.

As the emergency services had a difficult enough job to do in such circumstances without having to deal with rubberneckers, I made my way though the growing number of gawkers without stopping, preferring not to add to their numbers.

The patrol car parked outside Woodside Cottage was a more welcome sight. Nathan had already arranged for his men to keep an eye on the place, so I was glad to see them. It was only as I drew nearer and realised the car was empty, I became concerned. Visitors at this time of day? New developments maybe?

The cottage's entrance door opened directly into the living room, and as I entered, Lowe, seated in one of the armchairs, turned to face me. He was the last person I expected to see. Rusty was seated on the couch, facing the floor, head in hands.

Lowe bit his lip and shook his head. His expression was grim. I didn't need to ask to know that something was badly wrong.

I looked from one to the other, waiting for an explanation.

Lowe said, "It's not good, Mikey."

Rusty looked up. His eyes were red. "They just found Jenna."

Found her? What was that supposed to mean? "Found her where?"

"She was on her way here," Rusty said.

Lowe interjected. "Tinkers Wood. Near the path from the High Street."

"I just passed that way. There was some sort of incident."

"I thought she must be running late." Rusty's voice was flat, expressionless. He seemed to be struggling to take it in.

"The ambulance? Was that...? Is she okay?"

Lowe said, "It was too late. There was nothing they could do."

A tightness spread across my chest, making it hard to breath. I stared at him, not fully comprehending, and then sank into the other chair, my gaze fixed on his face. "You don't mean...?" My mouth dried and I couldn't finish the question.

I swallowed hard and said, "Jenna's dead?" Stupid question really. But I needed to ask it anyway. Just to convince myself that what I was hearing was true.

Lowe confirmed my fears.

"This is my fault," said Rusty. He rubbed his eyes. "I should never have got involved with her."

"What happened?" I said to Lowe.

"Looks like we have another murder on our hands."

Rusty cried out and balled his hands into a fist. "They did this to get at me. I just know it. They used her to get at me."

I rose, crossed over to the drinks cabinet and poured out two large shots of whiskey. I drained one of the glasses where I stood and then came back, handed the other glass to Rusty, and sank onto the couch beside him. Following my example, Rusty threw back his head, swallowed the whole shot in one go, dropped his glass onto the coffee table, and stared out in front of him with unseeing eyes.

I placed a hand on his shoulder and squeezed it. Turning back to Lowe, I said, "What happened?"

"She was stabbed. Several times. She didn't have a chance." He tilted his head towards Rusty. "I wanted to let Rusty know as soon as possible before it was made public. One of my men has gone round to tell her flatmate."

"Any witnesses? Who found her? Any possible suspects?" The questions came tumbling out.

Lowe held up a restraining hand. "Hey, one at a time. First off, the only thing we know for sure is that there were two assailants."

I caught my breath and said, "So there was a witness?"

Lowe said, "No witness. She was still alive when she was found. Barely. She managed to say a few words before she died."

"Who found her?" I said.

Before Lowe had a chance to reply, Rusty said, "What did she say?"

The restraining hand again. "A local woman heard her calling out as she crawled towards the edge of the wood. She tried to speak but she was coughing up blood and choking on her words. The only phrase that stood out was 'There were two of them'. She died before the paramedics got to the scene. So that was it. Nothing else."

We all lapsed into silence again as Rusty and I took this in.

I said. "So what happens now?"

"We'll be going through the usual procedures," said Lowe. "The crime scene will be out of bounds while we carry out a thorough search. And there'll be the usual house to house enquiries. We're also going through hotel and boarding house registers to check on new arrivals to the town. But of course, this being the holiday season, it's difficult to monitor all visitors."

Turning his attention to Rusty, he continued, "What I would like to do, if you're up to it, is take you on a tour around the town. See if there's anyone you recognise. I'm sure whoever did this is lying low, and it's a bit of a long shot, but it's worth a try."

Rusty assented. "I'll do whatever I can to help."

To both of us, Lowe said, "She doesn't have any close family. But obviously, we'll be interviewing close friends and acquaintances."

I had no doubt that Lowe and his team were doing all they could to track down the killer. But I couldn't help feeling they were heading in the wrong direction.

CHAPTER THIRTY

"This is a pleasant surprise." Still early morning and Nathan was on my doorstep.

He wore faded jeans and a white sweatshirt, a clear sign he was off-duty. He also wore his smiley face. Another good sign.

A warm glow spread through me. I returned his smile and stood back to let him in. After a miserable start to the day, it was a pleasure to see him. Rusty was still suffering the emotional after-effects of the previous day's shock news, and the morning had been a cheerless one for both of us.

"To what do I owe this honour?" I said.

"I thought you could use some company after yesterday. I didn't like to think of you on your own." He looked around as he stepped into the living room. "Naylor left already?"

"Richard picked him up earlier."

Lowe had dropped by that morning to take Rusty on his promised tour of the town. I was sure it would prove a fruitless exercise but at least it would keep Rusty occupied and stop him dwelling too much on Jenna. He still blamed himself for her death and felt impotent and useless hanging around the house.

I turned from the door as he closed it behind him, but before I could move away a pair of strong arms wrapped themselves around my waist and pulled me back.

Nathan's breath was warm against my neck. "And I had an urge to see my man."

I twisted around to face him, still smiling. The molten green eyes gleamed, full of fire and mischief.

My day was getting better by the moment.

"I'm always happy to indulge your urges." I cupped the back of his head in my hand, leaned against him, cheek to cheek, and inhaled him. He smelled of pine and sea air.

My skin tingled and there was a stirring in my loins. "As it happens, I have a few urges of my own."

He chortled, and I felt the rumble of laughter as his chest rose and fell against mine.

"Hot weather stirring your blood?" he said.

My voice trembled when I answered. "Believe me, I don't need any help from the weather."

I sought his lips and pressed mine hard against his, pushed my tongue into his mouth and explored the moist warm taste of him. He slid his hand into the back of my joggers and squeezed my ass. A raging burning need swept through me and my flesh caught fire.

I pulled away from him to catch my breath and gulped in air. "Did you have anything particular in mind?" My heart raced.

His faced creased into a grin and his left cheek dimpled. "I thought maybe a day on the beach," he teased. But his breathing was harsh and ragged and gave the lie to his words.

"Great idea." I grabbed him by the hand and pulled him towards the stairs. "We must do that sometime."

He didn't argue or try to stop me. Just slapped my ass as we climbed the stairs, chortling all the way. "You obviously have more pressing needs."

"Rusty won't be back for hours. So no excuses this time. You're not leaving till my carnal needs have been well and truly satisfied."

I steered him through the bedroom door, turned towards him, and pressed my body to his. He hardened against me. I groaned, and said, "Do I sense a reciprocal need." My heart pounded now.

When he spoke again, his breathing was laboured. "I guess I have some catching up to do."

"I guess we both do." My hands were already all over him, pulling his sweatshirt out of his jeans and struggling with his belt.

He swept my hands away, pushed me back onto the bed and

finished the task for me, ripping off his shirt and jeans as I struggled out of my joggers and vest. And then he was on top of me, his naked body hot and hard against mine, the thick mat of chest hair scraping my flesh, his rampant cock pressed against my own swollen member.

A long drawn-out moan, and I locked my legs around his back, grinding my hips, pushing against him, my need as powerful and urgent as his. "Fuck me, please. Just fuck me. You have no idea how horny I am."

"Oh, yes I do." He wrenched himself free and stretched over to the bedside cabinet. "In here?" he gasped. He pulled open the drawer and rummaged inside until he found the tube of lube and a packet of condoms.

"Best check the label on those rubbers," I gasped, "in case they've passed their use-by date."

"Oh very funny. It's not been that long."

"Too long. I was beginning to wonder."

A moment later, he was slowly inserting first one, and then two, lube-slick fingers into me, and all thoughts of chiding him further melted away in a fiery blaze of carnal need. I cried out, head thrown back, and spread my legs, pushing up to meet his urgent probing as he pressed in deeper, twisting his fingers inside me.

"Please, please." I moaned.

He pulled his fingers free, grabbed a condom and tore it out of its packet. His breathing quickened and each laboured intake of breath was exhaled as a rumble from deep in his throat as, with trembling fingers, he struggled to roll the condom onto his thick shaft. Soon, he was lowering himself into position, guiding his swollen cock and pushing into me. And then he was buried to the hilt inside me, the full weight of his body bearing down on me as he slowly increased his rhythm and speed, moaning louder and longer each time he drove into me.

I matched his rhythm with my own, my legs wrapped around that hard muscular back, meeting each thrust, my desire matching his. This was no slow easy lovemaking. This was hard rampant lust, a desperate wanton need that demanded satisfaction.

When he finally ejaculated, slamming hard into me with one final thrust, open-mouthed and roaring, my own release was not far behind. As he pulled himself free, I wrapped a fist around my shaft and, in a few quick strokes, brought myself off, pumping a thick stream of ejaculate onto my chest.

He leaned back on his haunches, reached down and smeared the semen down my chest. I groaned. Every nerve in my body was on fire and his hand burned my flesh. Slowly, the fire subsided, and I rolled over onto my side. He laid himself down beside me, his body, warm and damp with sweat, pressed against mine.

We stayed there without moving or speaking for several minutes, with just the sound of our breathing and the beat of his heart against my back, his arms wrapped around me.

Finally, I turned over, and folded an arm around his chest. "See what you've been missing?"

He pressed his lips to my forehead. "It was well worth the wait."

I hesitated, and then, "We are okay aren't we?"

A long audible sigh. "Why do you need to ask that?"

"I don't know. After all that happened - you know - I suppose I'm still feeling insecure."

"I told you we needed to find a way to make this work. I haven't changed my mind."

"I hear you. I just need to convince myself."

"Well try harder." There was warmth in his voice.

Why did I still doubt him? Why couldn't I believe him?

"It's just that you've been so preoccupied since I got back and I wasn't sure why."

He drew in a deep breath, paused before answering, and then, "There really is nothing for you to worry about, okay? It's all good."

Before he could say any more, he was cut off by the harsh insistent jangle of his mobile. He groaned, rolled over, and stretched down to pick up his jeans from where he discarded them at the side of the bed. He retrieved his mobile from the pocket, sat up, and said, "Sorry, I have to take this. It's from the station."

There was a long silence punctuated by his occasional grunt down the phone and then, "I was in the neighbourhood anyway. I... I had some business in town." He looked down at me and winked, a wide grin on his face. "I should be with you in about fifteen minutes."

Grumbling, I said, "I thought this was supposed to be your day off."

He finished his call, leaned down and brushed his lips against mine.

"Policemen don't get days off."

He reached down and picked up his briefs from the floor. "And neither do you," he said, "so get dressed. Jenna's flatmate's on her way to the station. And she's pointing the finger at Marcus Farrow for Jenna's murder. We need to be on our way."

I rolled out of bed and gathered my clothes from the floor. "Just as well you had some business in town then, wasn't it?"

CHAPTER THIRTY-ONE

"I don't get it. Why did she say nothing before?"

We were on our way to the station in Nathan's Astra, and I was trying to understand why new information implicating Marcus Farrow in Jenna's murder had only just come to light.

Nathan took the turn from Woodside into the High Street and headed towards the station at the far end. "Jenna's flatmate was out of town. We weren't able to track her down until now - her name's Umaru Yaradua, by the way. She's a Nurse at Charwell General - so it's the earliest chance we've had to interview her."

"And what does Marcus Farrow have to do with this?" I was bewildered. I'd formed my own theory about what was happening and Marcus Farrow's involvement didn't fit well with my ideas.

"Farrow called on Jenna the day before she was killed. They had a violent argument. Umaru heard it from the next room."

"What was that all about?"

Nathan turned into the station car park and pulled over into his bay. "That's what we're going to find out." He was out of the car and heading towards the station door before I could interrogate him further. I hurried after him and followed him through to Lowe's office.

Greetings out of the way, we settled down in front of the monitor.

Miles Barber was already in place facing a nervous-looking woman on the other side of the desk. Umaru Yaradua was slender, probably in her mid-thirties, dressed in a plain sandy-coloured shift which accentuated her dark skin. The muted tones of her outfit were in sharp contrast to the brightly coloured curtain of beads woven into her black tightly braided hair.

Miles Barber was an experienced interviewer but, despite his best efforts to put her at ease, she sat stiffly upright in her chair, clutching a grey leather shoulder bag in her lap, and answering all his attempts at small-talk with tight-lipped monosyllabic responses.

Once the interview was underway, he switched on the recorder that sat between them on the desk, explained the procedure to her and guided her around to her statement. "You told me earlier," he said, "that you witnessed an altercation between Jenna and Marcus Farrow. For the record, would you state where and when that took place, and how you were personally involved."

Umaru clutched her bag even more tightly and shuffled uneasily in her seat. "I don't want to get into trouble. That man isn't the sort to get on the wrong side of."

"As long as you give a full and accurate description of what happened, you have nothing to worry about."

Umaru appeared to consider this for a moment and said, "They were having an affair." She blurted out the words in a sudden rush and relaxed back into her chair as though a heavy load had been lifted from her mind. "I was the only other one who knew."

Constable Barber acknowledged this disclosure and said, "So if you could go through the events of..." He ran a finger down the open file in front of him and looked up again. "...the evening of the 15th. That would be two days ago."

Umaru placed her bag on the floor at her side and ran a smoothing hand down her lap. "He came round after dinner. I was in my bedroom packing a case. I was staying with friends overnight and getting ready to leave. Jenna let him in."

"You're referring here to Marcus Farrow?"

Umaru nodded. "He was in a bad mood." She explained how, on hearing raised voices, she had eavesdropped on the exchange between Farrow and her flatmate. Farrow had warned Jenna not to say anything about them. "He threatened her. Said it would be the worse for her if she told anyone."

"How long had they been in this relationship?"

She snorted. "I wouldn't have called it a relationship exactly. To him, she was just a convenience. Someone to use for his own gratification when it suited him." Umaru was becoming increasingly more confident, more willing to pass comment on her friend's affair. "It was already over though. She kept hoping he'd leave his wife for her. But any fool could see that was never going to happen. She finally got wise to him and finished it."

"Is that what the row was about? Because she brought the relationship to an end?"

Umaru shook her head. "No. I didn't really understand what he was saying. Something about losing his home if it got out about them." She related how the argument had finally ended when Farrow stormed out the flat, leaving Jenna in tears.

Barber questioned her some more about specific points of interest such as when the relationship had ended, how Farrow had taken it, and if they were in the habit of arguing, before bringing the interview to a close.

Lowe reached over his desk and turned off the monitor. Leaning back, he said, "I can understand Farrow wanting to keep his affair private. But murder? It doesn't make sense."

I said, "There's a very good reason. One that's especially pertinent at the present time."

Nathan and Lowe waited in silence for an explanation. I continued, "It was something Carol Farrow said to Karen the other day. She'd managed to persuade her father-in-law to give Marcus a second chance. Otherwise, if John Farrow kicked his son out, and cut him off without a penny, she would suffer too.

"Always presuming she intended to stay with her husband," Lowe said.

Nathan responded. "For all his faults, she seems to be sticking by him. God knows why." He nodded towards me. "I see where you're going with this."

I continued. "If Carol Farrow found out about the affair, it may well have been the final straw, the end of their marriage."

Nathan interrupted. "And John Farrow would no longer have a reason to support his son in order to protect his daughter-in-law."

Lowe said, "And that would be a good enough reason to kill Jenna." That seemed to clinch it for him; Marcus Farrow was a murderer. "And we already know he threatened Candy Bayliss. Seems pretty conclusive to me." He leaned back and clasped his hands behind his head, a look of grim satisfaction on his face. "We'll bring him in for questioning."

Sometimes, the obvious answer prevents us from seeking other solutions. And Lowe had a habit of going for the obvious to the exclusion of anything else.

"I'm still not so sure he's your man," I said. "Yes, he's belligerent and aggressive, but he's also weak and spineless. Everything I've seen about this guy, tells me he's all mouth, not capable of this kind of act."

Nathan took my reservations on board but said, "Even so, we'll have to bring him in again. He has some explaining to do."

I couldn't argue with that but I still held to my own theory about the murders. Before I said anything, though, I needed to check out some of the details.

Later, Nathan drove me back to Woodside Cottage. He must have sensed my mind was elsewhere. "You're very quiet?" he said, "Something wrong?"

"I was just mulling over some possibilities. Other motives for the murders."

"Let's hear it then."

By now we'd reached the cottage. He pulled over to the kerb and switched off the engine.

As I unclipped my seatbelt, I said, "Marcus Farrow isn't the only one connected to both victims. So is Rusty. And it occurs to me that someone else has a good reason to kill anyone connected to him."

"Go on, I'm listening."

"The shooting at the convenience store. The victim would probably have had close friends or family. Suppose one of them is taking their revenge."

"How would that work?"

"An eye for an eye. If the killer had lost someone close, he may be targeting anyone close to Rusty."

Nathan drummed his fingers on the steering wheel as he thought this over.

"And besides," I continued, "the very first murder, Tammy Page, seems to have been mistaken identity. Which means it would be someone who didn't know Candy Bayliss. So that would put Farrow in the clear."

He accepted the point and made a note to check the details of the store robbery and make some enquiries of the victim of the shooting. "I'll let you know how it goes," he said.

"And I'd like to check through the files on the current investigation again. See if there's anything I'm missing."

Nathan reminded me that Marcus Farrow was being brought in for questioning again and suggested I come down to the station the next day to sit in on the interview and check through the files at the same time. We said our goodbyes, agreeing to meet up the following day.

I opened the car door and was about to step out when Nathan clasped a restraining hand on my arm. "I'm going to step up the patrols here, just to be on the safe side."

"I'm sure Rusty can look after himself," I said.

"It's not him I'm worried about." He sounded concerned. "Candy and Jenna weren't the only ones close to Rusty. If your theory is correct - and I'm hoping it isn't - you're a target too."

CHAPTER THIRTY-TWO

I kept a wary eye on Rusty the following morning, trying to judge his mood.

If I was to pursue my theory about the murders, I would need details about the robbery shooting; more specifically about the victim and his background and relationships. And one of the best sources might well be Rusty. But I didn't want to burden him while he was still feeling raw about Jenna's murder.

Rusty had an appetite to match Nathan's, so I cooked us both a hearty fried breakfast of bacon, eggs and sausages with all the usual trimmings of beans, mushrooms and fried bread. How those two could put away the mountains of food they did and stay in shape was one of those eternal mysteries of the universe.

I slid an overburdened plate before him on the table and was pleased to see him attack it with gusto. One thing was for sure, he hadn't lost his appetite.

From my seat at the other side of the table, I asked about the previous day's tour of the town and how they had fared.

He swallowed a piece of bacon, shrugged, and said, "We didn't have any luck. Never thought we would. I was just glad of something to do so I didn't feel useless."

That was a good sign. It encouraged me to ask for his help. While I toyed with the food in front of me, I talked him through my suppositions about the murders and asked him for details about the victim.

He chewed thoughtfully for a few moments, and said, "I wasn't part of it, remember? Not directly. I was outside in the getaway car when it happened."

"Sure, but details must have come out during the investigation."

Rusty put down his knife and fork and stared at his plate in silence. He looked up again and said, "To be honest, I tried not to think about it. About the guy, I mean. It's like the more I thought about it, the more real it seemed."

I nodded. "I get that. You were trying to depersonalise him, distance yourself from what happened."

"He was getting on a bit. I know that. A widower, I think. But that's all I know for sure. The papers were full of it, so you shouldn't have a problem getting what you want."

He picked up his cutlery again and was about to carve up a sausage when a small gasp escaped his lips. He stared up at me, wide eyed and said, "If you're right, won't that make you a target?"

"The Chief has already pointed out that depressing fact to me."

He dropped the cutlery onto his plate where it fell with a clatter and swung his chair away from the table. "This is not good, Mikey."

His breathing was heavy and laboured. "It didn't seem so bad when I thought I was the only target. But not this." He ran a hand through his hair. "I think it might be best if I moved out."

"That's just dumb. We're both well protected here. We just have to be careful."

"I'm not sure we should risk it, Mikey. I don't want any more deaths on my conscience."

I set out to persuade him that moving out wouldn't solve anything. But only after a protracted heated exchange did I get him to accept my arguments, albeit begrudgingly. He still had his misgivings but, for the moment, he was prepared to go along with the status quo.

Although I did my best to downplay his concerns, I wasn't totally blasé about the possible consequences of being Rusty's friend. I'd taken to being extra vigilant when out and about, keeping watch for any suspicious activity. And so, when later I left for my meeting with Nathan, I scanned the neighbourhood from the doorstep.

Facing the cottage was a low stone wall bordering a sharp drop on the other side to an old abandoned railway siding. So there was little likelihood of a threat from that direction. And the road in both directions was long and straight with clear views into the distance.

As I crossed over to the Elan, a police patrol car cruised slowly past, and I waved to the constable at the wheel, grateful for the added protection.

At the station, I had to stand up to pressure from Nathan to move out of Woodside Cottage. He had the same concerns as Rusty and must have been fretting about it overnight.

He'd met me at the door and it was the first subject he raised as we made our way through the station to Lowe's office.

I protested that it was unnecessary, but he was insistent. "It would make more sense to move into my place. It's much too isolated where you are now."

"It makes no sense at all. You spend most of your days here at the moment and at least I have protection where I am."

"Why do you have to be so difficult?"

"Look, the only viable threat at the cottage is from the woods behind the house. And it's protected by a high wall and an alarm system. It's much safer. Stop worrying, will you?"

"Of course I'm going to worry." He muttered something unintelligible under his breath as we entered Lowe's office.

"Your resources are stretched enough as it is. So long as Rusty and I are in the same place, you can keep surveillance on both of us at the same time." I shot him a sideways glance. "Unless you'd like Rusty to move into your place too?"

His expression told me all I needed to know. "Thought as much."

He dropped the subject and turned his attention to Lowe. "Let me know when Farrow gets here." He left without another word.

Lowe watched him go and, once he'd closed the door behind him and was out of earshot, said, "So what's with you two? Lovers' tiff?" He grinned.

I snorted and told him about our disagreement.

Lowe said, "Maybe he has a point."

Exasperated, I exhaled loudly.

He took the hint, changed the subject, and pointed to the other desk, still grinning. "The files you wanted are over there," he said and turned back to the report he'd been writing before Nathan and I had interrupted him.

I settled myself at the desk and we both worked in silence. I was soon absorbed in my task, reading through the various reports and statements. But I was having a hard time accepting some of the findings. They didn't ring true. At least, not to me.

Interrupting Lowe, I said, "Something here doesn't add up."

He put down his pen. "Go on. I'm all ears."

"I just went back through the forensics report. We originally presumed the victim was killed indoors and then moved. Right?"

"Because of the carpet fibres, yes. But that's all it was. A presumption. And given what we now know about Candy's movements, it seems unlikely. And forensics didn't find anything at the Farrow residence."

"But it was a reasonable presumption to make. Those carpet fibres are much more suggestive of an indoor location. The body was covered in them."

"Sure, but that doesn't make it proof positive. It's more reasonable to presume something happened to her on the way to the station."

"Look, Candy was supposed to be travelling to London by train to visit a friend, right? But John Farrow tells us here in his statement that she was vague about exactly where she was going and who she was visiting."

Lowe swivelled his chair toward me and folded his arms. "Where are you going with this?"

"According to the report, she never made it to the station." I tapped the file. "The only CCTV in the area is on the platform itself, and there was no sign of her. And she never bought a ticket."

"That just means someone got to her while she was still in the car park."

"So why no witnesses? We're talking here about a wide open public space overlooked on three sides by houses. And yet nobody's come forward despite all the publicity. Surely, if anything amiss had happened there, someone would have seen it?"

Lowe swivelled back and forth in his chair as he considered this. "So what do you think happened?"

"I think she may have been lying. That she never intended to go to London. I think she may have been meeting someone here she didn't want John Farrow to know about."

He stopped swivelling. "What are you suggesting? She was having an affair? Playing away from home?"

I shrugged. "Who knows? But it has to be a possibility. There could be any number of reasons. I'm just saying we shouldn't presume she was telling the truth about that trip."

"That doesn't explain the other murders. And don't forget, Jenna was attacked by two assailants."

"Agreed. All I'm saying is we may need to dig deeper. Not take anything we've learned so far at face value. It's easy to make assumptions."

Before either of us could pursue this line of thought, we were interrupted by Nathan's return. "They're just bringing Farrow through to the interview room," he said.

Something about the way he spoke caught my attention. He spoke sharply, and there was still a tenseness in his voice.

"Everything okay?" I said. I couldn't believe he was still fretting about my refusal to move out of Woodside Cottage.

Jaw clenched, he stared at me without speaking, his mouth compressed in a tight line.

He was still annoyed.

He turned away. "Let's get on with this, shall we?"

Lowe reached towards the monitor on his desk and switched it on.

I shot Nathan a last guarded look before turning my attention to the screen. Whatever argument was in the offing would have to wait.

CHAPTER THIRTY-THREE

Like Marcus Farrow's previous interview, this was more of the same; a bitter tirade against the unjustness of his situation, how he was just a victim of circumstance. The three of us, Nathan, Lowe and I, sat around the monitor and watched him shuffle in his chair and whine at Miles Barber's every attempt to elicit information from him. Even Barber, an experienced interviewer, was losing his cool.

Faced with another of Farrow's rants about the dire consequences the police would face for their continued harassment of innocent people, Barber finally lost it and slammed his fist down on the table. "If you'd been more forthcoming in the first place, you wouldn't be in this position now."

Farrow flinched and choked on his words.

Taking advantage of the sudden silence, Barber leaned towards Farrow, his expression set hard, and said, "Perhaps this would be a good time to spell out the consequences of wasting police time."

Deflated, Farrow slumped in his chair. "Have you any idea what this has done to me? I'm ruined."

"May I suggest that your current problems result from your own actions, not ours." Barber reigned in his temper and in a more even voice said, "Now, let's get back to the purpose of this interview, shall we? You can start by telling me about your relationship with Jenna Lawson."

"What's to tell?" Farrow's tone was petulant. "We were having an affair. You already know that."

"And how long had it been going on?"

"About a year. But it was over. She finished it weeks ago."

"Is that what the row was about?"

Farrow squirmed and tugged at each of his shirt cuffs in turn. "I didn't want it getting out about us. This new guy she was seeing. Candy's brother. She knew he didn't like me. If he found out, he could have caused trouble."

"And so you threatened her?"

Gripping the edge of the table, Farrow pushed himself upright. "I did no such thing. I may have been a bit forceful, but no more than that."

Barber glanced down at his notes. "You seem to have a reputation for threatening women. Candy Bayliss for example; a violent argument, a threatening text message."

"She found out about my affair and threatened to tell my wife. She was a real bitch."

"Two women you had violent arguments with. And both of them murdered. Bit of a coincidence, isn't it?"

"And that's all it is. You're not going to pin them on me."

Barber ran an eye down his notes again. "We have it on record that your father was about to disinherit you and throw you out of the family home. And he only relented to protect your wife's interests." He looked up again and stared Farrow in the eyes. "If your affair had caused a split with your wife, your father may well have changed his mind, wouldn't he? With dire consequences for you."

Farrow stayed silent.

Barber pressed Farrow some more. "Sounds to me like a good enough reason for murder."

Sputtering, Farrow said, "I was at home all day with my wife when Jenna was killed. She'll confirm that."

"I wonder if she'll be quite as willing to give you an alibi when she finds out about your affair?"

The interview carried on in this vein for a while longer. Barber's approach was a well-practised one; keep prodding away at your interviewee, goad him into losing his temper, and all too often he would slip up, blurt out something without stopping to think about it, and give himself away. Always presuming, of course, there was something to give away. In Farrow's case, I still wasn't convinced and was glad when Barber eventually brought the interview to a close.

Nothing I had seen or heard persuaded me that Farrow was involved in either murder.

Lowe didn't share my opinion. During the post-interview briefing, he made it clear he still regarded Farrow as a prime suspect. "I just don't buy it," he said. "He has to be involved."

I tried to cut in, but he dismissed my interruption with a wave of the hand.

"I know what you think, Mikey. But it's too much of a coincidence; both women murdered after he threatened them." He tapped his pen on the desk to stress his words.

"And that's all you have," I said. "Coincidence."

Nathan was unusually silent, leaving Lowe and me to argue between ourselves. Lowe said, "For your sake, I hope you're wrong."

"Why me?"

"Because if I'm wrong, and your theory is right, you're the one who's at risk. Maybe you should reconsider the Chief's offer."

Nathan's only response was to snort and rise to his feet, signalling the end of the meeting. To Lowe, he said, "Check on those alibis and keep me up to speed on developments, will you?" At the door, he said, "In my office when you're through, Mikey." And he was gone.

We waited until the sound of his footsteps had faded away, and Lowe said, "What's eating the Chief?"

"Looks like he's still pissed at me for refusing to move out of Woodside Cottage."

Lowe shook his head, a look of sympathetic understanding on his face. "Well, you know what I think. But for the moment, I'm increasing surveillance on the cottage. That should help."

I was eager to get away and finish my argument with Nathan but needed to push home my point. "There is something you're overlooking," I said. "Jenna was attacked by two assailants. So the murders may be unrelated. Which means my well-being isn't something that need concern you."

He didn't seem convinced. "Until we have more information, we have no way of knowing if they were connected or not. I'm hoping forensics can help us there."

"So what now?"

"We'll check Farrow's alibi of course. But we know from experience that Carol Farrow isn't above lying on her husband's behalf. If she's the only one in a position to verify his whereabouts, we may not be able to rely on her word."

"As Miles pointed out, she may be less inclined to defend him when she hears about his affair."

"We can but hope."

We finished our discussion on that note and I said my goodbyes. "I'd best go see the Chief and get it over with. Wish me luck."

"I've a feeling you might need it," he said as I closed the door behind me.

Nathan was sat behind his desk, the same hard expression on his face.

I dropped onto the couch and launched into a prepared defence before he had time to speak. "I don't see any point in going over this again. I still say I'm better off where I am. It makes no—"

He interrupted me. "Did you find my notebook?"

The question came out of nowhere. It took a moment or two for it to sink in. And when it did, the blood drained from my face.

"At the Gastronomica. It was you, wasn't it?"

I tried to speak, but the words stuck in my throat. I swallowed hard and gripped the arm of the couch.

"I'm waiting," he said.

CHAPTER THIRTY-FOUR

It was as if my mind had stopped working. All I could do was stare into his angry reddened face, unable to speak or move. I tried to gather my thoughts, struggling to find the right words, but finding none.

"I thought... I wanted..."

Unable to face him, I dropped my gaze. I tightened my grip on the arm of the couch, trying to stop the trembling in my hand.

"I'm sorry. I'm so sorry." I blurted out the words.

"Not good enough." He shouted out the words, sprang to his feet, and rounded his desk, coming towards me with his fists clenched. "'Sorry' doesn't cut it, Mikey. Not this time. This time, you've gone too far."

I cowered away from him. "Please don't say that."

"What the hell do you expect me to say?" He was leaning over me, shouting into my face. "What did you do? Follow me? And just what did you expect to find?" He was raging, his anger barely in control.

I raised an arm between us to ward him off. "I found your receipt. It was Stoke Newington. And I heard your call."

"Call?" He spat the word at me.

"On the phone. About a new relationship. And complications. I thought—"

"You thought it was Brandon. You thought I was cheating on you."

"I didn't know what to think." I scrambled away from him along the couch and rose to face him. "I was looking for answers." It was time to fight back. "And don't tell me there weren't any to find. I'm not so stupid, I don't know when something is wrong."

"And you didn't think to ask?"

"I did, remember? You just brushed it aside."

"And why do you suppose that was?"

"You tell me. You're the one who keeps secrets."

We were both shouting now.

"Did you really need another reason to feed your insecurities? Another excuse to question my commitment?"

His words hit me like a blow. I stepped back too shocked to respond. Insecurities?

He shook his head, his mouth a tight grim line. "This isn't working is it, Mikey? I feel like I'm walking on eggshells the whole time. Constantly having to reassure you. Any wonder I can't talk to you?"

Shaking with anger, I retorted, "And you thought you'd deal with that how? By lying to me?

"I never lied to you."

"It amounts to the same thing. You think I can't tell when you're keeping something back? You think commitment only works one way?" I was on a roll, getting into my stride. "Just what was I supposed to think? Of course I thought it was Brandon. Who else was it-"

He cut across me, voice raised. "He tried to kill himself."

I froze where I stood and the words died in my throat. We faced each other in silence and, for the first time, I realised how drawn he looked; the dark patches under his eyes, the worry lines etched into his skin.

A clock on the wall behind the desk counted down the seconds, breaking the silence with each intrusive tick. Footsteps clattered across the floor above and, somewhere outside, a car door slammed.

It took a few moments for the full impact of his words to sink in as I stared into his troubled face.

"What happened?" The words came out barely above a whisper.

"An overdose."

He stared at me a moment longer, face grim. And then his shoulders dropped, and he fell onto the couch, all the fight gone out of him.

Of all the emotions, anger is the one that men are most familiar and the most comfortable with. It's the one behind which we hide what we perceive to be our weaknesses. All those frailties and vulnerabilities that make us less than men. Anger appeals to us because it helps us keep control.

But there are times our anger fails us, and we can no longer rely on it to protect us from the fear and pain and loss we try to hide.

And then we must learn to let it go and deal with those feelings now exposed.

I sank onto the couch at his side and wrapped an arm around him, holding his head in the crook of my neck with the other hand, and we sat like this in quiet surrender until the last vestiges of anger had drained away.

He was shaking. "It all got out of hand while you were back in London. Texts and phone calls. And he came down a couple of times."

"He didn't want to let you go?"

I couldn't quite connect what I'd heard with the image of the man I remembered; that carefree manner, the open trusting face and wide boyish grin. I remembered his excited chatter and the way he bounced around when he moved; energetic, and with a zest for life.

"I only met him that once," I said. "He seemed such a cheerful soul."

Nathan pulled away and sat upright. "You only saw that side of him. You never saw how needy he was, how demanding, how…" He faltered.

"How insecure?"

His mouth twisted into a wry smile.

I returned his smile with one of my own. "You sure do know how to pick your men."

"None of this was about us, Mikey. I hope you know that. I was in a bad place." He cupped the back of my head and pressed his forehead to mine. "And I'm sorry for that." He leaned back. "It was so wrong."

"Hey, come on. Let's get real here, shall we? It's not like I've made it easy for you."

"I should have told you."

"And I should have trusted you. What I did was shameful. I knew that as soon as I did it. I would have given anything to undo it."

"You must have been worried sick to do such a thing."

"I thought… I never… I never really understood your…" I struggled to find the right word. "…your friendship with Brandon. I guess I never wanted to. I hadn't realised just how much you meant to him."

"I never promised him anything. After you and I... you know... after we went our separate ways, I didn't want to get into anything heavy. I didn't want another relationship."

There was a sinking feeling in my stomach.

Hindsight is a wonderful thing. It was so easy now to see how the consequences of that ill-considered decision to leave him behind all those years ago had damaged him as much as it had me. It had left him less than capable of committing to a stable relationship. And even after all this time, the fallout from that decision was still blighting our lives.

I squeezed his arm. "I'm so sorry this had to happen."

He pulled a face. "We make our choices. And I guess we have to live with the consequences."

"How did you find out?"

"The day of the London conference, his sister called me." He pushed himself up from the couch, moved over to the window, and stared out into the bright clear day. "She was angry and held me responsible for what happened."

His usual proud erect posture was no longer evident. He seemed diminished, his shoulders slumped.

This wasn't the Nathan I knew. He was usually so confident, so sure of himself, it was easy to forget that he was susceptible to the same weaknesses and frailties that beset us all.

"I hope you don't blame yourself. It's like you said, we all make our own choices. And that was his choice, not yours."

He turned to face me. "I have to take some responsibility. I should have seen the signs. Understood what was happening."

I didn't know how to answer him.

"I agreed to visit him after his discharge from hospital," he continued. He screwed up his eyes and fell silent. When he spoke again, there was a tremor in his voice. "That wasn't an easy meeting."

I held up a restraining hand to stop him going any further. I didn't need the details. I could imagine how traumatic it must have been. For both of them.

"His family are taking good care of him," he said. "So I thought it best not to see him again. It would just complicate things."

"I'm sure you're right."

He sank down onto the windowsill as if suddenly weary. "I talked with his sister again a few days ago. Just so she could keep me up to date."

"She doesn't still blame you, does she?"

Shaking his head, he said, "I don't think so. She understands now how it was between us. She doesn't bear me any ill will. We met up for a meal. It helped clear the air between us. That's why I went back to London."

That was one mystery solved at least. And a timely reminder of what an idiot I can be when I get it wrong.

I said, "You've been so down recently. I knew something was troubling you. I wish you'd been able to talk to me about it." I searched his face, puzzled. "Why didn't you tell me? I hate to think you had to go through all that alone."

The smile faded. "I was ashamed. I should have thought more about his needs and not just my own. It was selfish."

How ironic. He could as easily have been talking about me, about the way I had treated him. "This is me you're talking to. Who knows better than me what that's like. I would have understood."

He stared at me long and hard as if seeing me for the first time. "I wasted years blaming you for what happened between us. I should have tried to understand. This has made me realise how easily we can hurt someone without meaning to."

"Then I'm sure you must also realise how bitterly I regret it."

He nodded.

I said, "A few months ago, we made a commitment to each other. Remember what you said? If we're going to make this work, we have to be honest with each other, discuss our problems."

"I remember," he said. "I should learn to heed my own words."

"Yes, you should. We'll do that in future then, shall we?" I tempered the admonishment with a smile.

He returned the smile and said, "Deal."

Relief washed over me.

These last few days, he had seemed distant, distracted, even hostile. And I had presumed that the fault was mine that somehow I had let him down. But maybe that was my guilty conscience. I guessed it would be a while before I had enough confidence in our relationship to feel secure. Even so, perhaps it was a good time to take stock.

"All this time, I thought it was about Rusty. I know you said you accepted there was nothing—"

He cut me short. "Mikey, stop." He pushed back against the arm of the couch and stared at me from under furrowed brows. "I don't like the guy is all. Never did. But I never doubted you. I was angry with you for not telling him about us."

"I wouldn't have blamed you if you had thought the worst."

"Listen to me," he said, "and listen good." His tone was firm. "I know you're having a hard time adjusting to a new lifestyle. You've made that obvious. But I also know you wouldn't be putting yourself through that if you were going to screw up by having a relationship with Rusty. Okay?"

"Okay."

"We're not going to get very far if we build our relationship on blame and regret, are we?"

"No argument there," I said.

"Good. Then don't let me hear any more of this crap, okay?"

I responded with a mock salute. "Yes, Sir."

We grinned at each other and then his smile faded. "I'm glad we talked," he said.

"Let's keep on talking, shall we? And you'll let me know if there are any developments with Brandon?"

"Sure I will."

"Why don't you take a break? I'm sure we could both use one."

He glanced over at the pile of files on his desk and pulled a face. "If only." He squeezed my thigh. "Why don't I call you later? Dinner maybe?"

"Sounds like a plan." I rose to my feet. "Will you be okay?"

He nodded up at me and tried a smile.

"I'll leave you to it then." I nodded towards his desk. "You look like you have enough to keep you going for a while." I headed for the door.

"Mikey?"

With one hand on the door handle, I turned to face him.

"I know we've had our problems," he said. "And there have been some rough patches along the way. But I'll never regret us."

I held his gaze and said, "I'll remind you of that next time we're in the middle of a blazing row."

"Don't make it too soon."

He was still smiling as I closed the door on him.

CHAPTER THIRTY-FIVE

I left the Elan in the station car park and made my way home on foot. My head was still buzzing, full of disparate conflicted feelings, and I needed time to sort them out.

Lost in thought, I was only dimly aware of the hustle and bustle of others around me, as I passed through the town. The sun was high in a clear azure blue sky, and a cooling breeze blew in from the coast, bringing with it the rhythmic sound of waves swashing against the sea wall. But I was in no mood to enjoy it. My mind was elsewhere.

Part of me was relieved, glad not to have been the basic cause of Nathan's recent sour despondent moods. But I was bemused too. Why couldn't he have told me about it? Had he not felt he could rely on my support?

And then there was Brandon. Poor broken Brandon. And loathe though I was to admit it, I had to accept that I had sought my own future happiness at his expense. When Nathan ended their relationship in favour of ours, I hadn't given a second's thought to how much it may have hurt him.

Instead of carrying on to the end of the High Street towards home, I turned off to my left and headed towards the Fairview. I needed company, and if Karen wasn't too busy, perhaps I could persuade her to join me for lunch. If anyone could help raise my spirits, she could.

The place was heaving. I wound my way around the busy tables on the terrace and narrowly avoided being tripped by a couple of boys chasing each other around the edge of the terrace with a yapping terrier at their heels.

An enquiry at the reception desk led me to a harassed-looking Karen helping to serve meals in the restaurant.

I caught her on her way to the kitchen balancing a tray of dirty dishes. She made it clear that lunch was out of the question.

"It's just something I dream about in my more lucid moments," she said.

"It was just a thought. I'll leave you to it. Catch you later." Seems I was going to be stuck with my own company after all.

As I turned to go, I caught sight of Marcus and Carol Farrow at one of the tables by the window. Judging by the sneering expression on his face and her tight-lipped response, they appeared to be in the middle of a heated discussion.

I tilted my head in their direction. "I see the Farrows are squaring up to another fight. Does that man never stop arguing?"

Karen wrinkled her nose. "They've been hard at it since they arrived."

The reasons for this current sparring match weren't hard to guess at. No doubt she'd now learned of his affair.

Seeing them here had given me an idea. "Have they been here long?"

"About fifteen minutes. They've not been served yet."

"Good."

With the two of them out of the way, I would have an opportunity to talk to John Farrow. Presuming, of course, he was at home alone. Part of the missing puzzle in the investigation into Candy's murder were details of her more immediate history. Where she has lived before arriving in Elders Edge and who she had associated with could all provide pointers to other lines of enquiry. And in the course of her relationship with John Farrow, despite adopting a false identity, she may well have let slip information which could prove useful.

He had steadfastly refused to believe Candy's motives in forming a relationship with him had been anything less than honourable. As a consequence, he had been defensive when questioned about it by the police and may have been less than forthcoming about her past. Perhaps if I spoke with him, he may open up. It was worth a try, anyway.

"Where do the Farrows live?"

"Up at The Heights on the Charwell Road."

The Heights was an area considered to be at the top end of the residential market so I wasn't surprised that someone like John Farrow would live there.

"What number?" I asked.

Karen narrowed her eyes. "Why do you want to know that?"

"Just thought I'd take a look at the house," I said, trying to sound casual.

She folded her arms. "You're not interfering are you, Mikey? You know how Nathan goes off on one if you get too involved."

"Of course I'm not."

She didn't sound too convinced, but she gave me the details, anyway. I pressed my lips to her forehead, thanked her, and said my goodbyes. She was still glaring at me as I left.

It was too much of a hassle to walk back to the Elan so I walked up to the Heights. It was only fifteen minutes away, and it gave me time to work out what I wanted to say.

The house was a grand affair. Set far back from the road, it was a large Gothic-type-mansion of a place built of weathered black stone and reached along a winding gravel drive via an imposing arched wrought-iron metal gate.

John Farrow answered the door.

The man I remembered from the interview at the station was tall, sprightly for his age, and with an erect military bearing. This was no longer the same man. He seemed withered, grey featured, and with a slow slouching gait. The drastic change was a shock.

I introduced myself, explained my role in the investigation, and asked if would answer some more questions.

He agreed. But with a lack of enthusiasm that suggested he couldn't care less one way or the other.

He showed the way through a large oak-panelled lobby to a well-stocked library off the main hall. A large window overlooked a tree-lined side garden and the other three walls were fitted head to foot with bookcases, each one stacked full with books of all sizes and colours. The man was obviously well-read.

He showed me to a brown leather armchair at the side of an empty fire grate and sank into its twin on the other side of the hearth.

I explained that I was tasked with building up a profile of his fiancée as a means of assessing any possible actions and motives that could have led to her murder.

"I'm sure you'll want us to do all we can to find her murderer," I explained.

"It's not going to bring her back is it?" his voice was flat, monotonous, with no trace of emotion.

This was a man in the depths of despair.

"No, of course not. But we need to catch whoever did this."

I prompted him, as gently as possible, for any relevant information about Candy's past. With some coaxing, he told me how they had first met, a few months after his wife's death from a stroke. She had knocked at his door after her car had broken down nearby and asked to use the phone to call a friend to come and pick her up. Later, she had returned with a bottle of wine As a thank-you present.

"Such a charming thoughtful woman," he said. "We soon became good friends."

Something about that particular scenario rang alarm bells. But I mentally filed the information away for future consideration.

I steered him around to details of her background. "What can you tell me about her past? Did she speak about it much?"

"She told me everything. Why wouldn't she?" The look of defiance on his face slowly morphed into one of pain. "Though of course, after what we've all learned over these past few days, I can't be certain how much of it is true. I can only suppose the poor woman must have been running from something terrible. If only she could have confided in me. I might have been able to help."

Piecing together the fragments of information John Farrow had gradually gleaned from his late fiancée during their relationship, I was able to build up a picture of a woman who bore no resemblance to the one portrayed by Rusty.

The image conjured up for the benefit of Farrow had been of an upper-middle-class woman, the daughter of a barrister father and doctor mother, from Mayfair, one of London's more fashionably select areas.

The more he told me, the more I realised that none of what he had learned from Laura Carrington, aka Candy Bayliss, was even remotely near the truth. Eventually, realising I would learn nothing about her true background, I brought the discussion to a close, thanked him profusely for his help, and took my leave.

On the way home, I thought over what he had told me. Two things struck me as significant. The first was the manner of their meeting. About three years earlier, I had been involved in a case where a woman had conned a wealthy widower out of his life savings. I had learned there was a pattern to this kind of crime, known as the sweetheart scam, where lonely wealthy men were targeted by confidence tricksters, usually through obituaries in the local press which identified them as being recently bereaved. Such men were often vulnerable and open to such scams. The circumstances of John Farrow's meeting with Candy, turning up on his doorstep as she did, seemed to follow that pattern.

The other significant aspect of John Farrow's story had been the details of Candy's fictitious past. It was the sort of background that would have appealed to someone like him. Almost as if it had been invented for that very purpose.

Much as I disliked the man, I was beginning to think that there was something to Marcus Farrow's claim after all. That Candy had set out from the start to fleece his father. And if that were the case, if she were nothing more than a con artist who knows how many enemies she may have made along the way.

I was still musing over this when my mobile rang. It was Nathan. He'd made some headway with his workload and was taking a break. He was still feeling bad about our row and apologised again. We agreed to meet later that evening for a meal and I arranged for him to pick me up at the cottage.

By the time we'd finished our call, I was back on the High Street. Instead of turning left towards the police station to pick up the Elan, I decided to pick it up later, and turned right towards home instead.

Almost within sight of the cottage, I became aware of a vehicle behind me, the sound of its engine getting louder as it approached. It was moving fast.

Too fast.

I turned to face it.

A battered old red transit van rattled towards me, hugging the wall.

It bore down at high speed, throwing up a cloud of dust from beneath its wheels.

With no pavement on this side of the road, I stepped back and pressed myself up against the embankment wall to let it pass.

It gathered speed.

Only at the last moment did I realise it was heading straight for me.

A clattering rampaging heap of solid bone-shattering metal.

Moments from impact.

Only one way to go.

A burst of adrenaline tore through me, my body reacting on automatic.

Turning, as a dizzying blur of red filled my vision, I grasped the top of the wall and, in one fluid movement, hoisted myself up and over, hitting the ground on the other side, arms flailing, grasping at thin air.

The steep slope gave way beneath me.

I tumbled down the embankment, bringing along a shower of scree in my wake.

I grabbed out at anything within reach in a desperate attempt to slow my progress; handfuls of weeds, loose stones, clumps of grassy earth, and all the time vaguely aware that the van had stopped somewhere above me.

Brambles tore my hands and sharp embedded rocks, dug into my flesh as I rolled over them. But nothing was enough to stop my rapid fall. I hit the ground at the bottom of the slope, bruised and bleeding, with a force that knocked the wind out of me.

Gasping for air, I tried to clamber to my feet but slipped again on the loose gravel and scrambled on all fours to the safety of an old sandbox by the disused railway line. From behind it, I peered up at the wall above.

A dark-clothed figure in black balaclava and sunglasses stared back at me.

And then he was gone.

The door of the van slammed shut, and it screeched off into the distance.

I tried to stand but the pain in my leg was too much to bear and I sank back to the ground.

Fishing in my jeans pocket with a trembling hand, I dug out my mobile and called Nathan. "I'm not sure I'll make it for dinner tonight," I said. "Someone just tried to kill me."

CHAPTER THIRTY-SIX

"Nothing too serious," said Dr Marks. "Just some bruising and soft tissue damage. But try to keep off that leg for a while."

Nathan said, "Don't worry, doc. He won't be going anywhere." His tone of voice didn't invite argument.

I was laid up at home, lying full length on the couch, exposed leg up on the arm, with Nathan and Dr Marks from the local surgery hovering over me.

Examination over, Dr Marks snapped shut his bag, gazed down at me over the top of his spectacles and, in the sort of tone usually reserved for people of limited intelligence, said, "And the next time you think about taking a shortcut across the town, may I suggest you use the road instead? It would save us all a lot of time and trouble."

To avoid possible public alarm, Nathan had decided some discretion was called for about the reason for my fall. Apparently, presenting me as some sort of idiot who launched himself over the embankment wall as a means of shortening his journey across town was considered more appropriate. Any objections I had to this approach were shouted down amid claims that I was an idiot anyway, so it didn't really matter how it looked.

Nathan saw Dr Marks to the door and as he closed it behind him and turned to face me, I braced myself for the inevitable verbal battering.

He had already made his thoughts clear on what he called my indiscriminate and reckless disregard for my own safety. I suspected I was about to feel the full force of his displeasure.

"Are you completely stupid?" His tone suggested he'd already decided the answer to that one.

He'd been quick to respond to my phone call, arriving with Lowe in tow at the scene of my fall within a few minutes. But once he'd helped me back into the cottage, sent Lowe off to check on the red van, arranged a flying visit from the doctor, and satisfied his concerns about my health and well-being, he must have decided it was now time to challenge my ability to make intelligent decisions.

"What the hell were you thinking of, leaving your car at the station? Did you not stop to think about how exposed you were?" He paced up and down as he fired his shots at me.

"I can't stay in the car all the time?"

"You can at least make sure you use it as much as possible. Where did you go anyway?"

"What does that matter?" The last thing I wanted was to let him know of my visit to John Farrow and provoke him into a diatribe about my interfering in police matters. That would just be adding fuel to the fire.

"It matters because someone may have been looking out for you. And knowing where you were and when could help us check around and learn who else was in those areas."

"I went over to The Fairview to see Karen."

"Was that after you left the station?"

"Yes.

"How long did you stay?"

"Not long. She was busy."

"And then where did you go?"

I considered telling him I went straight home. But I knew he would question the timing and know it wasn't true. I'd have to try something else instead.

"Nowhere in particular," I said. "I just went for a wander around."

He stopped his pacing, turned and stared at me, frozen in place, his eyes hard and cold. There was a long silence while the world held its breath.

And then he exploded. "A 'wander'? You went for a 'wander'?" He made it sound as if it was an act so outrageous as to be almost unbelievable.

"What can I tell you? It was a nice day. Aren't I allowed to stroll around and enjoy the weather?"

The look of incredulity on his face was all the answer I needed. He said, "Are you sure you didn't bang your head as well?"

"Besides," I said, ignoring the question, "this whole episode has its positive side."

He spluttered. "Now I know you must have some brain damage. Perhaps I should call the doctor back and have you checked out again."

"Listen to me. It proves I was right all along. Rusty's friends are being targeted rather than Rusty himself."

"And you thought you'd test this theory by wandering around the neighbourhood, trying to provoke an attack. Very clever."

"Oh please, Nathan. You know that's not how it was."

"You are absolutely certain it was a deliberate act? Not just a reckless driver?"

"A balaclava in this heat? The guy was obviously disguised. Yes, I'm certain."

"Well from now on, I don't want you wandering off on your own." He used the term 'wandering' as if it was a dirty word. "You stay close to home and use your car when you need to go out."

I responded with a sarcastic, "Yes, sir."

Before he could shoot me down again, he was interrupted by a knock at the door, and Lowe entered.

Lowe nodded towards me, and said, "All good, Mikey? The doc give you the all clear?"

"The doc did, yes. The Chief's not so sure." I shot Nathan a scornful look and got a withering glare in return.

Lowe looked confused but said nothing.

Fortunately, Nathan now had other concerns to focus on so he let me be for the moment. To Lowe, he said, "Any sightings of the van?"

Lowe's expression suggested he wasn't bearing good news. "We found it. In a back road on the other side of town. But it had already been reported stolen. The timing suggests it was taken not long before the attack."

A sigh of exasperation from Nathan. "Forensics on it?"

"Yes, but I'm not expecting to find anything useful."

"Well, try anyway." Nathan glanced at his watch. "And I have to get back to Charwell." He turned his attention back to me. "And I want you and Naylor staying put. In the meantime, I'll have the patrols stepped up." As an afterthought, he added. "Where is Naylor anyway?"

I shrugged. "No idea. I've not been here all day." Just for devilment, I added, "Maybe he went for a stroll."

That earned me another withering look, and I felt a pang of guilt for winding him up. He had a hard enough job to do without my recalcitrant behaviour. He was looking after my interests after all. And the added burden of coping with Brendon's suicide attempt didn't help. I should try to be more supportive.

"Sorry," I said. "I promise to be good. Whatever you say."

He answered with a grunt. And then, "Just stay put and rest up for a couple of days."

"I haven't finished looking through the files. I could be working on those while I'm laid up."

"You can see them down at the station." He turned to Lowe. "Can you pick Mikey up in the morning? I'm going to be tied up in Charwell all day."

I had hoped to go over to the station that day but I didn't argue. It wasn't an argument I would win.

Lowe agreed and said his farewells before heading out to his car.

Nathan was about to follow when I called him back. "Hey." He turned in the doorway, a quizzical look on his face.

"Just wanted you to know how much I appreciate you. I'm not such an idiot, I don't know when I'm well off."

"Is that why you never listen to anything I say?" He shook his head but his tone had softened. "You're the bane of my life at times."

I grinned up at him as he turned to leave. "Love you too," I said.

CHAPTER THIRTY-SEVEN

I'd already gone to bed before Rusty returned home that night. So I wasn't able to bring him up to speed on developments until the following morning. Much as I expected, he didn't take the news too well.

He sat at the kitchen table, head in hands, a steaming mug of black coffee, untouched, in front of him. I sat in silence across from him and waited until he'd had time to take it in.

The air was rich with the aroma of freshly ground coffee and, in the background, the radio regaled us with a jolly jingle whilst extolling the virtues of a new brand of washing up liquid.

Eventually, Rusty looked up with tired eyes and said, "It's all getting too much."

I said, "There's no reason for you to stay in Elders Edge, you know. You'd probably be much safer back in London. It's easier to get lost there."

"That's what the Chief said. But I figure that's more about getting shut of me." He treated me to a feeble grin.

"Then why don't you?"

"I could ask the same of you."

"This is my home."

He bit his lip while he regarded me. And then, "It's easier here. Easier to draw him out. A small place like this. I want them to get this bastard. I owe it to Candy and Jenna. So I'm going nowhere. This is where I make a stand." Another weak smile. "Besides, who's going to look out for you, eh?" The smile faded. "This is all on me. My doing."

I tried to reassure him he wasn't to blame. "The killer is responsible. Not you."

"Even so."

I nodded my understanding. In his place, I'm not sure I would have wanted to act as a magnet for a killer, but I guessed it was his way of assuaging whatever imagined guilt he felt. And so, perhaps it was best to let it be.

Lowe came by just after lunch and drove me to the station.

I settled down to work in his office and, while he made some calls, I flipped through the forensics report again to make sure I'd taken it all in. A phrase caught my attention as I scanned through it.

Red and yellow.

A thought struck me. A faint glimmer of something I'd missed.

Lowe was still on the phone. I looked up from the file and waited for him to finish his call.

"Do you have the file for the Woodside Cottage theft?" I asked.

"Sure. It's in the cabinet. What's the deal with that? You have some thoughts?"

"I just need to know what was taken."

Lowe looked puzzled, but he fetched the file, anyway. He stood before the open cabinet drawer and searched through the file.

"Here it is," he said. He seated himself at his desk with the file in front of him. "All the towels were taken, some cleaning materials, a small rug, and a poker."

"A poker?" A chill ran down my spine.

"Does seem a strange collection of items. But they'll take anything these days."

"What colour was the rug?"

Lowe checked the file again. "No mention of it. Just the manufacturer's name and the style." He looked up again. "Why do you need to know?"

I dug into my jean's pocket and pulled out my mobile. "Give me a sec and I'll tell you. There's something I need to check first." I tapped in Martha Stubbs' number.

She answered, surprised to receive my call.

"Everything is all right at the cottage?" She sounded concerned.

I assured her that all was well and explained that I was calling in a professional capacity about the theft. "I need to know the colour of the rug that was taken."

"It was the same as the rug I replaced it with. I got the original from a store in Charwell and they had another one in stock. Why? Has it been found? Have you caught him?"

I had to disappoint her but assured her the police were still working on the case. I finished the call by promising her the police would be in touch as soon as there were any developments.

Lowe was drumming his fingers on his desktop and frowning. "What was that all about?"

"The stolen rug was red and yellow. Same as the one at the cottage. The carpet fibres on Candy Bayliss's body were red and yellow."

He stopped his drumming and stared at me long and hard. "You're not suggesting there's a connection?"

"You need to ask?"

"Come on, Mikey. Bit of a coincidence isn't it? You just happen to be living at the murder scene?"

"It makes perfect sense. There's a logical progression. Think about it."

The puzzled look suggested his thinking wasn't getting him very far, so I enlightened him. "The only reason I got the tenancy in the first place was because you learned about the vacancy after receiving the robbery report, right?"

He accepted this.

I continued, "And you said yourself that I was lucky to find somewhere at such short notice during the holiday season."

"Okay so far. But I still don't see—"

I interrupted him. "We're presuming that whoever killed Candy came from outside the area. And whoever that was would have had the same problem. Remember what Martha Stubbs told us? Her last tenant got the place only because she'd had a last-minute cancellation. He and I had been in the same situation. Faced with a limited choice. And that limited choice was the same. Woodside Cottage."

Lowe stared into space with a glazed look and I waited until he had thought over this information.

"There is one thing you're forgetting," he said, "Whoever killed

Candy, killed Jenna too - in fact, we know there were two of them - and he or they tried to kill you. So if the killer, or one of the killers, was staying at Woodside Cottage, why didn't he stay? And where is he now?"

"Why would he want to hang around at the scene of his murder? Far too much of a risk. There's always the chance of leaving evidence behind. And he hadn't yet met Martha Stubbs, remember? So she wouldn't be able to identify him. Far better for him to scarper while the going was good."

He stared out into space again, a pensive expression on his face, as if he couldn't quite make up his mind what to think.

"Look," I said, "what's the harm in checking it out? You could get the forensics guys to give the cottage the once over. Fingerprints maybe."

"Wouldn't have thought there's much chance of that after all this time. Besides, it's time-consuming and expensive. Which is why we didn't bother dusting for prints before. Just not worth it."

"For the theft of a few items, maybe. But we're talking murder here. And it's not been that long. Besides which, there aren't many prints to eliminate. Me and Rusty. You and the Chief. Karen. Martha Stubbs. And the two electricians who wired up the alarm system. It has to be worth a shot."

Sometimes, getting Lowe on board was like dragging a dead weight up a steep hill.

Another long pause while he thought this over and then a slow nod. "Okay, let's do it."

Finally. So, maybe it wouldn't move the investigation forward, but anything was better than sitting by and doing nothing.

CHAPTER THIRTY-EIGHT

Three days later, a couple of operatives from the forensics team arrived accompanied by Lowe.

Rusty was bemused by the whole idea. "You seriously think this is where Candy was killed?" he said. "It seems a bit far-fetched."

He leaned back on the couch and looked up at me, his expression a mixture of mirth and scepticism.

Lowe and I were standing in the middle of the room while the forensics guys, smocked and gloved, carried on with their work, one of them dusting the window frame, the other, at my specific request, the brass companion set in the hearth.

I wearied of having to go through my reasoning, yet again, explaining what I considered to be the logical progression of events that brought me to that conclusion. But I was still being met with doubts.

To be fair to Lowe, despite his misgivings, he had agreed to put my theory to the test. He had come down with his team and was directing them to objects that I had suggested may be more likely to yield results.

Even so, he was still baulking at having to carry out the task. "I hope you realise how much fingerprint analysis costs these days. Especially on a limited budget. And then, of course, we still have to obtain the permission of anyone who's likely to have been here. And this is a holiday cottage after all."

"And Mrs Stubbs is the finicky type when it comes to cleanliness. So she usually has a thorough clean through before she re-lets."

"Which means we're not likely to find any useful prints from before your tenancy."

I was becoming increasingly exasperated. "I said 'usually'. She told me herself that she'd not had time for a thorough clean job before I moved in. Which means there's a high probability of finding prints from the previous tenant but nothing before that."

Lowe begrudgingly accepted my argument.

I pressed on, still agitated by his negative attitude, and letting it show. "And there's only been a handful of people here since, most of whom will be more than willing to have their prints taken. The only two I'm not sure about are the electricians who fitted the alarm. But as the alarm is fitted high on the wall and no one else would have touched it, it's reasonable to presume that any prints on it belong to them and can be used to eliminate any other prints of theirs in other parts of the cottage."

"Okay, okay, for God's sake. I hear you." He was losing his cool.

Rusty sprang up from the couch and joined us. "Hey, come on you guys. We're all on the same side here." He took me by the arm.

I acquiesced and drew in a deep breath in an attempt to calm my fraying nerves. "Sure we are. Guess the strain's beginning to show." I slow-punched Lowe on the chest. "Sorry, Richard. My bad."

"You and me both," he said. "Sorry, man."

"Tell you what, Mikey," said Rusty, "Why don't you and me go for a drive. Leave these guys to get on with it. We could both do with a break. We can stop off somewhere for a drink."

Lowe said, "I wish I could join you."

I said, "Sounds like a plan. And we're only in the way here."

Rusty grabbed his car keys from the coffee table. "We'll take mine," he said.

We left the forensics team to their task, overseen by Lowe and, minutes later, we were motoring along the high street towards the edge of town.

"Do me a favour," said Rusty. "No talk about this whole fucking sorry mess. I just want to get away from it."

"Fine by me." I was as eager as he was to leave our current woes behind.

"Good. Then let's head out to The Partridge at Colten Drey and make a day of it. I hear they do a good pint there."

They did indeed. It was also where his sister had seemingly met her murderer. But it was probably best not to enlighten him about that for the moment.

We passed the rest of the journey with little talk as we sped on our way. Rusty and I had known each other long enough to enjoy each other's company in comfortable silence and by the time we pulled into the car park at The Partridge we were both feeling more relaxed.

We ordered pints at the bar, headed out through the back door, drinks in hand, and found ourselves a bench at the far side of the beer garden. We sat in the shade of a large oak that spread its branches over the fence from the roadside beyond.

Rusty gulped down a large mouthful of beer, wiped his hand across his mouth, and made a self-satisfied sound in the back of his throat. "We should be enjoying ourselves in this sort of weather," he said, "not having to go through this nightmare."

"Hey. I thought we weren't going to talk about it."

"Kinda hard not to," he said. "And after what happened to Jenna, you know, that's down to me. She didn't deserve that."

"You can't blame yourself for someone else's actions," I said. "Though it might be best if you curtailed your social life for a while." I grinned and added, "Looks like the celibate life for you."

He leaned towards me, elbows on the table, a knowing grin spreading across his face. "Unless I found something nearer to home."

"Yeah, right. That would do wonders for my relationship."

He leaned back again, a quizzical look on his face. "Your guy doesn't like me does he?"

I stiffened. That came out of nowhere. "Nothing to do with you, I assure you."

"He's not the jealous type is he?" I opened my mouth to deny it but hesitated. That was all the confirmation he needed. He grinned. "So I'm right. He thinks I'm a threat."

I tried to put his fears to rest. "No, he doesn't. I once thought he did, but that's more to do with my own uncertainties."

He looked puzzled.

"It's complicated," I said. "I've let him down in the past."

That sparked his interest. "So, Mikey's been playing away from home? Bad boy. Does that mean I'm in with a chance after all?"

I leaned away and shot him an old-fashioned look.

"Just kidding," he said. "Well half-kidding. Though it looks like we're going to have to make do with each other's company, anyway."

I pulled a face. "I think I can just about bear it."

"Let's hope this theory of yours is right. Or we're going to be stuck with each other for a long time yet."

Only then did I realise how much was riding on my being correct. My own relationship as much as anything else.

"I hope so too," I said.

CHAPTER THIRTY-NINE

It was another five days before we got our answer. Lowe was the one who broke the news. It was late morning, and he'd called as soon as the results were in. Rusty was sprawled out on the bench at the end of the garden, enjoying the sun. I rapped on the window to attract his attention and pointed to my mobile as I took the call.

By the time he reached the house and stepped inside, I'd already learned the bad news. He learned it too from the expression on my face.

I sank onto the couch, grimacing, and shook my head for Rusty's benefit as I continued my conversation with Lowe. "So what prints did you get?" I asked.

Lowe was apologetic. He knew how much I'd hoped for a positive result. "Just the ones we expected. Everyone who'd been at the cottage since you moved in."

Rusty seated himself beside me on the couch and listened to my side of the conversation with a clenched jaw.

"Nothing on the companion set in the hearth?" I said. Part of my theory had been that the missing poker had been used as a murder weapon. And if so, the murderer would have probably left his prints on the T bar which held the tools.

"Sorry, Mikey. No other prints anywhere."

"And the rug?"

"I have a separate report on that." The sound of papers being shuffled. "The analysis confirms the fibres could well have come from the rug in question." He made a disparaging sound. "Unfortunately."

"Unfortunately?"

"If they hadn't, at least it would have shown conclusively that your theory was a bit wide of the mark. As things stand, it's neither one thing nor the other."

"I'm not sure it matters, anyway. We still didn't get any prints."

"Quite. And the rug is a common enough make. The fibres could have come from any number of different sources."

Rusty was watching me intently, and I pulled a face at him as Lowe and I said our goodbyes. "Thanks for letting me know, Richard. I guess it was worth a try." I ended the call and pocketed my mobile.

Rusty said, "So nothing new?" He sounded disheartened.

"Sorry," I said. "I feel like I've let you down."

"Screw that," he said. "Sure, it's a bummer, but none of this is on you." He tried a smile. "Just means you'll have to put up with me a bit longer."

"I guess everything has its downside," I said, and grinned.

He growled at me and gave me a playful punch to the chest. "Say what," he said, trying to sound more enthusiastic, "let's go out and drown our sorrows somewhere. It would do us both some good."

I made my excuses, pleading the need to get on with some work. My publisher's deadline had long since passed and I was nowhere near a final draft of the book.

He accepted the excuse but opted to go for a drink, anyway. "I need to get away. Get some air."

Once he'd left, I settled at my desk and tried to focus on my research delving into the twisted psyche of yet another notorious psychopathic killer. It was hard going. Sometimes, I had to wonder how this sort of subject affected my own psyche.

Fortunately, I was interrupted by a call from my agent, Jerry, with details of time and place for the upcoming award ceremony. I finished the call and was keying the details into my iPad diary app when my mobile rang again. It was Karen.

"Richard said you might need some company," she said. "What's all that about?"

Laughing, I said, "Just work pressures. But he's right, I could use some company right now."

"And I need a break so why don't you come on over?"

"Much as I'd love to, I need to slog through some more work first. Why don't we meet up for dinner later?"

"Deal. There's something I need to discuss with you, anyway."

"I'm intrigued."

"It'll wait. See you later."

She rang off, and I turned back to the papers and notes scattered around my desk. But it was no good, and, after three wasted hours, I gave up. I couldn't concentrate. And so I shuffled the papers away into my messenger bag, and threw it, in disgust, onto the couch.

Vowing to knuckle down to some serious work later, I went to my bedroom, laid out some clothes for that evening, eschewing jeans and sweatshirt for once and settling for a pair of lightweight stone-grey cargo pants and a light-blue short-sleeved pilot-style shirt. Satisfied with my choice, I ran a bath and took a long leisurely soak, trying to free my mind of anything other than the prospect of a much-needed relaxing evening in the company of a good friend.

By the time I was dressed and ready to go, I was in a better frame of mind.

It was still early, and so I busied myself with a few domestic chores to while away the time. I washed the dishes that had been left in the kitchen sink for most of the day and then made my way around the cottage emptying the wastepaper baskets and trash cans into a black plastic rubbish sack ready to leave at the front of the house for the refuse collectors.

It wasn't until I reached the bedroom that a sudden shock of realisation hit me. I stood dumbfounded, staring down at the wastebasket. Why hadn't I thought of it before?

I knelt down and grabbed the handful of screwed up receipts and scraps of paper I'd dropped in the basket a few days back, the contents of the small wooden box I'd found in the loft. It had been among the assorted objects Martha Stubbs had stored away just before I moved in. That meant, in all likelihood, these scraps of paper had been left behind by the previous tenant. And who knew what they may reveal?

I sat on the edge of the bed, smoothed out the crumpled papers, and went through them one by one. Most of them, receipts from supermarkets and takeaways, were weeks old. Disappointingly, they were all for cash purchases, so no chance of tracing the buyer through a credit card number.

Two of the more recent ones were local. One I recognised as a convenience store in town and the other was the National Garage on the Charwell Road. I scanned the listed items on each of them, the convenience store first. Just some tinned food and confectionery. I didn't expect much more from the garage receipt. It itemised some purchases from the shop.

I ran a finger down the list and froze.

There, among the more mundane purchases, were two that stood out. A balaclava and a pair of gloves

A tightness gripped my chest, and I struggled to keep my breathing even.

What kind person would buy a balaclava and gloves in this kind of weather? In the middle of a heatwave? The obvious answer was one who wanted to disguise himself. The same one who had tried to run me down for instance.

My hand trembled as I scanned the receipt for more details. I noted the date and ran over the past few days in my mind, trying to place it in the context of recent events. It would have been a few days before Candy Bayliss was murdered. It seems I may have been right after all. Our murderer, whoever he was, had stayed in Woodside Cottage.

I can't have been the only one to have thought such a purchase unusual. Whoever had served our man at the garage must have considered it strange too given the weather conditions. And that shop assistant may well have remembered who he served that day.

My watch told me it was almost time to head on out for my date with Karen. But first thing in the morning, I would go over to the garage and make some enquiries. For the moment, it was probably best to keep my renewed suspicions to myself. If it came to nothing, it would be just one more disappointment for all involved. I shoved the receipts in my pocket and went out to the Elan.

I tried to put it from my mind as I drove over to the Fairview - there was no point dwelling on it until I'd had a chance to check my findings - but without success; Karen sensed my mind was elsewhere.

"You want to tell me about it?" she said.

"About what?"

"About whatever planet you're on at the moment. Because you're sure as hell not down here on planet Earth."

"I'm sorry," I said. "My head's buzzing. There's a lot going on right now."

We were seated around the dining table in Karen's private suite at the back of the building. The Fairview staff were busy catering to the evening diners and Karen preferred to stay out of the restaurant to avoid those who saw her presence as an opportunity to interrupt her with business matters. She had arranged for the kitchen to serve us here and we looked through the menu while we talked.

"So Richard was right," she said. "You did need some company." She fixed me with a shrewd look. "You and Nathan okay?"

I made a sound that was supposed to pass for a laugh. "Ask me again when this Goddamn investigation is out of the way. Personal relationships aren't a priority at the moment. I hardly see him. But you should know what that's like."

"Of course I do. But it's not always going to be like this. Things will ease off eventually."

Before I could respond, one of the serving staff, a young woman with a winsome smile, tapped on the door and stuck her head around the door. "Ready to order yet?"

Karen nodded her assent and chose calf liver pâté for starters followed by a char-grilled sirloin steak. I opted for goat's cheese and red onion tart, and a pan-roasted fillet of sea-trout for the main course.

Once we were alone again, I reminded her she'd wanted to discuss something with me, and asked what it was.

"I've sorted out a date for Nathan's birthday dinner. It's tomorrow."

"Tomorrow?" I blanched. "Bit short notice isn't it?"

She folded her arms. "Right. And you have such an inflexible work schedule, you couldn't possibly change it, could you, Mikey?"

"I'm not sure where you get the idea I can do as I please. I do have deadlines, you know?"

"So work's more important than your partner?"

"I didn't say that." I was indignant. "You're putting words into my mouth."

"Good. So you'll be there?" It was a statement rather than a question, and she didn't wait for a response. "It's a surprise, so don't let on. Richard's working over at Charwell with Nathan and he's going to drive him back to Elders Edge on the pretext that his input is needed for a case meeting at the local station. But he's taking him to The Dog and Duck instead. We're having a meal there."

"So I'll meet you there?"

"No. I'll pick you up at the cottage tomorrow evening. Then you and Nathan can let your hair down and not have to worry about drinking and driving. Okay?"

I definitely wasn't going to argue with that. And so we arranged a time.

We were interrupted again by the arrival of our starters. I was about to tuck into mine and said, "Did you order wine?"

"Oh hell, I forgot."

She threw down her napkin and was about to rise from her chair when I stopped her. "Stay put. I'll go get us something from the bar. My treat. Pinot Grigio?"

She accepted my choice. I hurried out to the bar and was able to grab the attention of one of the barman.

"What can I get for you, Mr MacGregor."

This time I recognised him immediately. Andy Burns. The young man from the garage.

I gave him my order but before he could fetch it, I interrupted him. "I know it's a long shot but there's something you might be able to help me with."

I dug the garage receipt out of my pocket and handed it to him. "I need to trace whoever bought these items from the garage." Pointing to the list, I said, "See there? The balaclava and gloves? Not what you'd expect someone to buy at this time of year. Not in this sort of weather. It wasn't that long ago, and I thought you might remember something about the person who bought them. A description maybe."

His cheerful demeanour changed to one of puzzlement.

"Sure I remember him. I see him around often enough. But so do you. He's a friend of yours, isn't he?"

"What?"

"I've seen you talking with him in here. And you came to the garage with him that day. It's Mr Naylor. The guy whose sister was killed."

CHAPTER FORTY

I sat at my desk and stared down at it. A blank computer screen stared back at me. Around it, scattered documents lay untouched and unread.

The clatter of dishes and smell of roasted coffee drifted out from the kitchen where Rusty was busying himself with breakfast. I had declined to join him this morning, pleading the need to get down to some urgent research. Truth be told, the only research I was interested in was re-evaluating past events in light of what I had learned from Andy Burns the previous evening. In the meantime, Rusty was the last person I wanted to be around.

I was so confused. I had returned to my dinner with Karen, my mind awhirl with conflicting thoughts. I was too stunned to make sense of Andy's revelation right then and tried to pass off the rest of the evening as if nothing was wrong. Of course, Karen picked up on my mood straight away but put my doleful disposition down to the pressure of work.

Now that I was able to give more attention to my concerns free from distractions, I went over the past events and considered each of the points raised in turn.

If Rusty really was implicated in his sister's murder, why would he even ask for my help in having the case reevaluated? It wouldn't make sense. Especially as it would also focus attention on an investigation that he would, in such circumstances, prefer to be kept low-key.

So too, Mia had seen Candy face up to her tattooed aggressor and would have recognised him as Rusty if they had been one and the same. Unless, as Jenna had said, there were two of them

And then there were the circumstances of the first murder, the one we had all assumed was a case of mistaken identity. Hardly likely. Rusty wouldn't mistake someone else for his sister, no matter how alike they were.

The more I thought about it, the more convinced I was that Andy Burns had been wrong. He must deal with dozens of people over the course of a working day. It would be easy to get them confused. Maybe I should find time to talk to him again, challenge his recollection.

"Here. You look as if you need this."

I was startled out of my deliberations by an interruption from Rusty as he placed a mug of coffee in front of me. "You were miles away." He grinned down at me.

As the world came back into focus, I forced a grin in return and thanked him. "It's easy to lose yourself sometimes," I said.

He was still beaming down at me, coffee mug in hand. I searched his face for signs of... of what?... of a murderer? So what did a murderer look like? I already knew the answer to that. It's not as if I hadn't learned a few things from my years of research. A murderer looked just like everyone else. But even so. That open smiling face. The boyish charm. So easy going. Someone who had been a good friend when I needed one. Could this be a murderer?

"You okay?" he said. The smile faded to a frown. "You look like you have the weight of the world on your shoulders."

"Sure, I'm fine." I turned away. "I just need to tackle some of this and all will be well."

He hovered by the desk a moment longer. "I'm taking my coffee out into the garden," he said. "We shouldn't be wasting days like this. Join me?"

"Much as I'd like to, I really must get on with this. I've been putting it off too long."

He shrugged. "Your loss," he said, and headed off to the garden, leaving the back door open.

I turned away from the desk and watched him saunter down the path, not a care in the world.

This is the man who had just lost his sister to a brutal death, been close to another woman who'd been stabbed to death. Shouldn't he be mourning their loss? Shouldn't he be feeling less buoyant, more melancholy? Or was I reading too much into his behaviour? Maybe he was just trying to stay upbeat.

I turned back to the desk and stared at the wall against which it stood. I needed to figure this out. What to do. Should I tell Nathan or Lowe? Let them deal with it? And what if I was wrong? What would that do to my relationship with Rusty?

Another thought struck me. The credit card Nathan had found on the bedroom floor. What was it Rusty had said later? He thought he'd lost it some time ago? I recalled knocking over the wastepaper basket in the bedroom and scattering its contents. What if that card had been among those other scraps of paper? Had maybe fallen unnoticed under the edge of the bed? Which meant it would have been among the papers I'd emptied out of the trinket box, the box I had recovered from the attic.

So many possibilities. And so easy to make assumptions, draw the wrong conclusions.

That's when it occurred to me there was a means of putting my mind at rest. If Rusty was our man, he would surely still be in possession of the balaclava and gloves. And as soon as he was out of the way, a search of his room would settle the matter. So now I just needed to find a convenient time.

I picked up my coffee and joined Rusty in the garden. He was spread out on the garden bench, leaning back with his head against the trunk of the beech, eyes closed.

"You were right," I said. "We shouldn't be wasting days like this." I dropped onto the bench at his side.

He opened one eye and smirked. "You saw sense at last."

"Any plans for today?" I asked, trying to sound casual.

"Nothing specific." And then as if on impulse, "We could drive over to The Partridge if you're up for it. Make the most of it."

I groaned. "I wish. But I really must knuckle down to work."

"In that case..." He slapped me on the back. "...I'll get out of your way. I'll go soak me up some rays down on the beach."

Despite the attraction of a lazy day in the open air, he didn't seem in much of a hurry to get out there. For most of the morning, he loafed around the cottage, made endless mugs of coffee, and eventually locked himself in the bathroom for an inordinate length of time before finally appearing in time to make himself some lunch. I was getting more agitated as time dragged on.

At one point, on his way back from dumping an empty baked bean can in the recycling box outside, he stopped by my desk and faced me with a frown on his face. "Are you sure you're okay?" he said. "You've been on edge all day."

I faked a grin. "I promise you, once I have this draft under my belt, I'll be back to my usual vivacious and scintillating self."

He chortled and returned to the kitchen from where I was regaled by the sound of his cheerful whistling and the ping of the microwave.

Minutes later, my nostrils were assailed by the smell of toast and he returned to the living room, carrying a tray which bore a plate of baked beans on toast. He sat on the couch, tray on knee, and tucked into his lunch while I mused over some research papers, pretending to read them.

Lunch over, he went back to the kitchen, and I heard him fussing around as he washed his plate and cutlery.

"Hey, don't waste this weather," I called out. "The day will be over before you've had a chance to enjoy it."

"Okay, okay." He appeared in the kitchen doorway hands raised in surrender. "I know when I'm in the way."

Eventually, after deliberating about what to wear, he headed out to the car. I crossed over to the window and watched him climb into the Cabriolet and drive away.

At last.

I waited for the sound of the engine to recede into the distance. For a while longer, I stood by the window, my hands pressed down against the sill, and took some slow deep breaths. This wasn't something I was looking forward to. It was as if the act itself, what I was about to do, was an act of betrayal, and yet made my suspicions even more real, more certain.

With a rapidly beating heart and a tightness in my throat, I mounted the stairs and made my way to his room.

The second bedroom, Rusty's temporary domain, was smaller than mine. Just large enough for the single bed, small dark wooden bedside cabinet, and matching single wardrobe.

I started with the cabinet. The drawer at the top contained just some loose change, assorted underwear, and several pairs of socks. The cupboard underneath was where he kept his footwear, two pairs of sneakers. Nothing else.

Next, the wardrobe. Apart from the hanging space which held an assortment of casual clothes; jeans, sweatshirts, three jumpers and a jacket, there was just one shelf running the full length of the wardrobe just above head height. It appeared to be empty, but I ran a hand over it, searching at the back for anything that was out of sight. Nothing. I checked the pockets of the jeans but found only a few used tissues.

So far, so good. My increased sense of relief was balanced by an ever-increasing sense of guilt.

Now for the suitcase. I closed the wardrobe doors, stood back, and checked the top. It was bare. I found the case in the other usual storage space. Under the bed. I pulled it out and tested its weight. It wasn't light enough to be empty, and something hard and solid slipped to the bottom as I raised it from the floor.

Unusually, it was secured by two padlocks. Not that it would be a problem to get it open. I went back to my own room and returned with a couple of paperclips. The old two-paperclip trick, easily learned by anyone with access to the internet, would make easy work of it.

I heaved the suitcase onto the bed, bent the paperclips into shape, and inserted the hooked one into the first padlock. Applying some downward pressure, I pulled the clip in the direction the lock turned, and pushed the other straightened clip into the back of the lock. As I lifted the straightened clip and raked it towards me, the pins clicked. I turned the hooked clip and opened the lock. First attempt. Not bad. The other padlock took a few more tries but soon gave way.

I opened the case.

And tensed.

Nestling among spare underwear and towels was the hard solid object that had slipped to the bottom of the case.

A gun.

Not at all what I'd expected. Why would a reformed ex-con need a gun? Not so reformed after all? A souvenir of old times? That in itself suggested not all was as it seemed in the private life of Rusty Naylor.

Gingerly, I felt around the inside edges of the case and under the towels, trying not to disturb them too much.

My hand came up against something soft nestled within the folds of the towels. I pulled it free.

A black balaclava.

My stomach churned.

Even as I looked down at the object in my hand, I tried to tell myself it was of no significance. It was just a balaclava. Why wouldn't he have one? It didn't prove anything.

And yet every new revelation led me closer to the inevitable conclusion that I so desperately wanted to avoid.

Rusty was a murderer.

There were still many unanswered questions, but if Andy Burns was right about that receipt - and it now seemed almost certain that he was - then its significance was obvious. That screwed up scrap of paper that had lain hidden away in the attic these last weeks showed beyond all doubt that whoever had purchased that balaclava was staying in this cottage before I moved in. And, if my original theory was correct, which I'm sure it was, had killed here.

And yet I still didn't want to believe it. Didn't want to believe it could have been the man I called a friend. Didn't want to believe that the murderer's fingerprints had been here all along because I was sharing a home with him.

I had to be wrong. Despite so many coincidences, whatever evidence I had found was no more than circumstantial. It was all a mistake.

A noise from behind me.

"I knew you were up to something."

I spun around to the source of the sound, and the blood drained from my face.

Rusty was standing in the doorway.

Too late to act, I saw the table lamp stem he carried in his hand only as he raised it.

The last thing I remember, the one thing that finally put paid to all my doubts, was the outpouring of hate that filled his eyes, and twisted his features into a grotesque expression of undiluted rage.

And then the makeshift weapon came down hard against the side of my head and darkness closed in.

CHAPTER FORTY-ONE

I fought back a wave of nausea and pushed myself up to a kneeling position as my surroundings swam back into focus. Despite the hot weather, I was cold and cramped, and a shiver ran down my spine. The throbbing in my temples increased as I raised my head.

Rusty was seated on the edge of the bed, gun in hand, looking down at me, a sardonic smile playing across his lips. That violent rage had subsided but his eyes were hard and cold.

How could I have got it so wrong and not seen him for what he really was?

"So it was you all along?" I said. "You killed your own sister?"

They were more statements than questions. The answers were obvious. Why else would I be sitting here with a gun in my face? And that genial easy-going style and friendly nature had all been a pretence, the mask behind which lived the psychopath. Because that's what he was. There could be no doubt about that. I had only to think back to that disfigured body in the woods, to remember the obvious pleasure with which her killer, this man, had displayed his handiwork, to know what I confronted here.

I had been far too close to Rusty for far too long not to see him for what he was. My want of friendship at a time of need, of someone to confide in, share with, had blinded me to the nature of the person beneath the facade, had made me all too willing to accept the surface appeal, the facile charm and flattery.

But now I could mentally step back and see him objectively, I could read all the signs that singled him out as the pitiless specimen of humanity that he was, devoid of emotion, unable to empathise with others. And I cursed myself for not seeing those signs earlier. I recalled the pity play, the constant appeal for sympathetic reactions to the dysfunctional childhood and negative external factors that forced him into a life of crime. None of it had been his fault. He was always at the mercy of circumstance. And so he would evoke in others a sense of pity, to weaken their resolve, enabling him to manipulate and use them for his own ends. And I, who should have known better, had fallen for it.

And now I was about to pay a heavy price for my lack of insight.

He shifted his attention away from me and I followed his gaze to where the balaclava lay on the floor a few feet away.

He looked back at me, shook his head and tutted, a display of mock concern. "Such a shame, Mikey. You had to go and spoil it all, didn't you?" He stared at me, a sour expression on his face. "I knew something was wrong. You've been twitchy and moody all day. Not like you at all. And you couldn't wait to get me out of the way, could you?"

In the circumstances, I wasn't in a position to argue. So I said nothing.

"Just as well I thought to come back when I did or who knows what harm you could have done." He leaned forward, forearms rested on his thighs and pointed the gun at me. "Such a simple thing to get wrong." He nodded towards the balaclava. "I should have got rid of it once I'd done with it. And after all the trouble I went to trying to put you off the scent. Such a nice little distraction, but you still got there in the end."

It took a moment for it to sink in. "The bullet?" I nodded. "Yes, of course. You sent it to yourself."

He grinned. "Stroke of genius really, wasn't it? Had you all running around in circles."

"And jumping over walls."

He laughed long and loud at that. "Yes, that was so funny. The look on your face as you went over that wall. It was priceless."

"Nice to know someone was amused."

"You've only yourself to blame. You're the one who said my friends were targets."

"And so you thought you'd help me prove it."

"What are friends for if they can't help each other out."

"Well you sure had me fooled."

The grin faded. "But not for long, unfortunately."

I leaned over to one side, relieving the pressure on my legs, and shifted them from under me. I spread them out before me and leaned back against the wardrobe door.

He tensed as I moved and trained the gun on me.

I help up a restraining hand. "Just making myself comfortable. Might as well make the most of it before you shoot me."

He chuckled. "Glad to see you haven't lost your sense of humour."

"That is what you intend to do, isn't it? Shoot me?"

"It's not as if you leave me much choice, is it?"

Of course, I knew he wouldn't think of doing it here. He'd learned enough to know the risk of leaving evidence behind. It would be the woods again. His location of choice when disposing of his victims. And that's where my chance lay to get away from him, out in the open, away from the confining space of the cottage where I wouldn't stand a chance. All I could do for the moment was play along with him.

"And Jenna? Did she leave you no choice either?"

A long slow sigh. "I'm afraid not. My fault. I got careless." With his free hand, he pushed up the sleeve of his right arm to reveal a tattoo, a red and green serpent coiled around his arm. "So easy to forget the obvious sometimes."

"I remember now. The day the Chief came round and told us about the confrontation in the High Street. She overheard him. She heard him describe the tattoo of the man they were looking for. It was you, wasn't it?"

"Such a stupid mistake."

He looked down in admiration at his tattooed arm. "Brotherhood. Solidarity." He looked up again. "It's important to show your loyalty."

"A gang tattoo?"

"We all had them."

"That's what she meant, wasn't it? There were two of them. She meant the tattoos. She put two and two together."

"Not straight away. But she began to wonder why I'd tried to keep it hidden. That woman wasn't as dumb as I'd thought."

"Did you have to kill her? Couldn't you have talked your way out of it?"

He shrugged and the corners of his mouth dropped. An expression of nonchalant indifference. "Too much at stake. I just couldn't risk it. It was best to settle the problem once and for all. I invited her over to talk it through. Told her to take the quick route through the woods. All I had to do was turn off the alarm, slip out of the back gate, and meet her on the way. It was soon settled."

My blood ran cold.

His eyes held no trace of emotion as he dismissed the taking of someone's life with such casual disregard, as just a problem to be solved.

"So the man who confronted Candy all those months ago was one of your gang?"

He didn't answer, just grinned in acknowledgement.

Sitting on the hard wooden floor like this wasn't particularly comfortable, and I was cramped. "Look, can I get up from here? It's not one of the cosiest places I've ever squatted in."

He waved his gun towards a wooden chair within reach by the wardrobe. "Just there."

I grabbed its arm, pulled myself to my feet, and sank into it.

"You're surprising calm for someone in your situation," he said.

That was a joke. I was anything but calm. My heart was racing ten to the dozen. But I couldn't let it show. The calmer I seemed, the more relaxed he would be, and the more likely to let down his guard.

"Maybe I can talk you out of it," I said. I knew I couldn't, of course. But as long as he thought I saw it as a way out, it would help allay any suspicions he might have about my attempting an escape. "You don't have to do this. You could leave now. Be on your way before anyone knew you'd gone."

"And stay on the run all my life? I don't think so."

He glanced down at his watch and scowled. "Parents are just finishing the school run. I guess we'll have to give it a few more minutes. Less likely to bump into anyone taking a shortcut through the woods."

He sounded annoyed as though what he planned to do was just some minor inconvenience he needed to deal with and resented being delayed. The best way to keep him calm was to keep him talking.

"I still don't understand," I said. "Your sister. Why did she have to die? And Tammy Page?"

He guffawed. As if I had just cracked some huge joke. "I promise you," he said, "if you knew my sister as well as I do, you'd understand all too well."

He stood up and waved the gun towards the bedroom door. "Time to get moving," he said. "Time to get it over with."

A tightness spread across my chest and, as I rose to my feet, my legs weakened beneath me. He followed behind as I made my way downstairs to the living room.

At the roadside window, I pressed a hand against the sill to steady myself and a movement from outside attracted my attention.

It was Karen.

Catching sight of me in the window, she smiled and greeted me with a cheery wave from the other side of the road as she climbed out of her Mondeo.

CHAPTER FORTY-TWO

I whirled towards Rusty, a wrenching tightness in my gut, my mind racing. "Karen's here." I'd completely forgotten she was picking me up.

From his position at the bottom of the stairs, Rusty was out of Karen's line of sight. He snarled. "For fuck's sake. How many more of you do I have to deal with."

I pointed a threatening finger at him. "Don't you fucking dare harm her. Even if you shoot me, I promise I'll find a way to stop you. I mean it."

"You're in no position to make threats."

I braced myself, ready to throw myself at him if he dared touch her.

A knock at the door.

He faltered momentarily and then grabbed a jacket he's left thrown over the back of the nearby chair, and draped it over his arm, hiding the gun.

He crossed over to the door, keeping his eyes on me, and said, "I want you standing there where I can see your face. Try anything stupid and you'll both pay for it. Now get rid of her."

Rusty's scowl evaporated as the door opened and Karen stepped inside. The smile with which she greeted him fell from her face when she saw me.

"What are you playing at Mikey? You're not even ready." She glanced down at her watch. "We have to be there in thirty minutes. We'll only just make it as it is."

Before she could launch one of her verbal attacks, she stopped herself short, aware of the despairing look on my face. I needed to think fast.

"What's wrong?" she said.

I drew in a breath and readied myself for the barrage of questions. "I can't go," I said.

"What?" She shouted out the word. "What is this?" She turned towards Rusty. "What's going on here?"

Rusty shrugged. "Search me. I only just got in."

She turned back to me, a look of astonishment on her face. "What's happened?"

I held out my clasped hands, an act of contrition, and said, "Karen, you know I wouldn't back out if it wasn't important. I just can't make it."

"Why?" It was a demand, and I needed to find an answer.

There are times, those times of greatest need, when our minds, unbidden, come to our aid with a sudden flash of inspiration. This was one of those times.

"It's old man Gray, Sylus Gray, I have to go see him. I have no choice. It's the old trouble again."

"Sylus Gray?" she repeated the name, not understanding. And then the light of recognition dawned in her eyes. "But Sylas-"

I had to stop her. "Yes, he's been taken ill again. It's much more serious this time."

Over her shoulder, I could see Rusty was becoming increasingly agitated. He was scowling again. "What's with this guy?" He sounded suspicious.

"He was in the force with Nathan's father way back. Retired now, but we always stayed in touch. He's not had a good time of it these last few months. He's been in a private nursing home for a while now."

I turned back to Karen. "Nathan will understand," I said. "Just let him know." I tried a weak smile. "I'm sure he'll forgive me once he knows why."

"But what...?"

She was about to demand an explanation but I cut her short. "Sorry, but I have to go. It won't wait." I said to Rusty. "Could you let Karen out, while I get ready."

She frowned. "Do you need a lift? I can always phone Nathan."

"No, really. It's quicker if I go through Tinkers Wood. It's just the other side."

"Is that wise? I thought Nathan had warned you off going out alone without the car?"

"I'll be fine. Honestly."

Rusty was already holding the door open, forestalling any further debate. She shot me a wary look, nodded to Rusty, and left.

Rusty closed the door behind her and said, "Nice move. Everyone will think you were off on your errand of mercy when you were attacked." He ditched the jacket, throwing it over the arm of the chair, and waved the gun towards the back door. "Turn off the alarm and let's be on our way."

I tried to play for time, pretending to search for the alarm fob, and, once I'd found it, deliberately fumbling my attempts to turn off the alarm.

It would be at least twenty minutes before Karen made it to the Dog and Duck and, even then, it may take Nathan a while to understand my message. If he did at all. Looking for an opportunity to turn on Rusty was still my best bet but, if all else failed, Nathan was my last hope.

I eventually turned off the alarm, mindful of Rusty's growing agitation, and opened the back door.

"Keep moving."

I made it to the end of the garden, unlocked the gate, and turned to face him. Maybe there was still time to talk him out of this.

It would be pointless appealing to his better nature; he didn't have one. The only possibility of persuading him to abandon his intended course of action was to persuade him of the risk to his own well-being.

"What if someone sees us?" I said. "How will you explain that away?"

"Not a problem. It's easy enough to keep the gun out of sight and I'll just say I walked some of the way with you." He laughed. "Later, I can tell everyone I was concerned for your safety." That seemed to amuse him and he was still chuckling as we headed towards the forest path.

From behind me, he said, "Stay off the path, we're less likely to be spotted.

I veered off to my right through the untrodden undergrowth, and, half turning as I walked ahead of him, said, "I take it we're heading to the old cottage."

"Got it in one," he said. "Where else?"

Where else indeed. It was all part of the game. The psychopath's power play against his opponents, against society. Disposing of me at the scene of his other murders would give him a macabre sense of satisfaction, a gleeful pleasure, the sort of low-level emotional boost at the limbic level, the only sort of fleeting emotional high that would appeal to his psychotic nature.

I thanked the fates that I had, at least, got that right, had anticipated the twisted logic that would make him choose this place.

I made my way slowly, stumbling now and again to hinder our progress even more but he became ever more agitated at each delay and I had to be careful not to annoy him too much.

As we neared the broken walls of the old cottage, my heart pounded and a trickle of sweat ran down my spine. Once inside the walls, he brought me to a halt, and ordered me to turn around. "This will do nicely," he said. "Almost the same spot."

But for the occasional squawk of a gull overhead or the rustle of some small creature in the undergrowth, there were no other sounds. The trees stood quiet around us, as if holding their communal breath, watching and waiting for the inevitable conclusion to our journey.

I turned towards Rusty, and stared into his calm impassive face across the rough uneven ground that separated us.

He raised the gun.

I was out of options.

CHAPTER FORTY-THREE

I had to play for time and my only hope was to rely on my familiarity with the psychopathic personality, the need for self-gratification.

"It was very clever," I said, "the way you staged the scene. Of course, not everyone would get it. But I did. You wanted us to admire your work."

A wide grin spread across his face. "I knew you'd understand. Those other idiots wouldn't have a clue, but I knew you would."

I said, "I still don't see how Tammy Page could have been mistaken for your sister. Your gang buddy must have known what Candy looked like."

He was still grinning. "That's the part you don't get. You see, Tammy's death wasn't a mistake. Candy killed her."

Now he was laughing. The expression of shock on my face must have amused him.

"Let me tell you a few things about my sister and me," he said. "While you were still playing with your toys, me and Candy was running errands on the streets for the big man while my mother 'entertained' friends in our room. My father dropped by now and again to give her a good hiding and take what little money she'd earned. Candy and I learned to look after ourselves on the streets."

"Not enough to keep you out of prison."

That seemed to amuse him too. "It was part of the life. And I met some good mates inside. Learned a few tricks too. All those lonely women on the outside. Just longing for a bit of long-distance loving. A few love letters and body-building photos and they were soon hooked." He was grinning as he thought back to it. "Next would come the tales of financial woes waiting on the outside. You'd be surprised," he said, "how easy it was. They would be almost begging you to take their money. And once you're engaged, it just comes rolling in."

"Engaged?"

"Sure. I was once engaged to three at the same time. Bigamy might be a crime but serial engagements aren't. And once I was out of prison, it was easy enough to give them the blow off."

I still couldn't see where this was going. "What did Candy have to do with this?"

"She came in with me once I got out. It was just the two of us. She was a natural."

"How did it work?"

"We started out with the angry husband routine. Candy would pick up some mark in a bar and take him home. Then I would turn up as the outraged husband and relieve him of his wallet as compensation."

He was getting into his stride now. He was enjoying this, boasting about it. I just needed to keep him going.

"Eventually, we moved on to bigger things," he continued. "The sweetheart scam. Marks were easy to find through the obits. Lonely rich widowers looking for solace. They soon fell for Candy's ample charms."

"And where did you fit in?"

"I acted as the roper. Got to know them first and assessed their potential. Then I would introduce them to Candy. And I was always around to act as muscle in case things went adrift."

Some of the pieces fell into place. Marcus Farrow had been right all along. His father had been Candy's latest victim. Though it obviously hadn't worked out as planned.

"So what went wrong?" I said.

The grin faded. "We landed a big one. A real big fish. Candy had him hooked real good. Got a Porsche out of him not long after I introduced them. She was soon stinging the old fool for all he had." He was scowling now. "But then the boys in blue caught up with me. For the driving job. I'd been doing it on the side. Ended up with a two-year stretch. While I was inside, Candy bled the mark dry then did a runner. Took the proceeds with her."

"She betrayed you?"

"Seems so." He was clearly agitated, his mind elsewhere, no longer fully concentrating on me. For the briefest of moments, I considered making a run for it and glanced around me, looking for somewhere I could find cover.

He must have caught my action and realised what I was doing. Bad move. Now he was on his guard.

"Don't even think about it," he said.

"I'm not that dumb," I retorted. "I'm not likely to get far, am I?"

"You got that right." He raised the gun again.

"So your friend spotted her here?" I said, getting him back on topic.

"That's when she 'phoned me. Spun me some tale about a relative of the mark taking exception to her. A real hard case. Said she skipped cos she was frightened of him but always meant to get in touch. Next, I hear she'd been killed. That sort of put an end to it all.

"I'm beginning to understand now. That's when you asked for my help. It wasn't her you were bothered about. You wanted a lead to her ill-gotten gains."

"It had to be somewhere. I needed to know where. Asking for your help was a long shot. But it was worth a try."

"Didn't quite work out as expected, did it? It must have been a shock to learn she was still alive."

"She always was a clever bitch. Didn't take me long to work it out though. See, I know my sister better than anyone. I knew what she was capable of."

"Are you saying she staged her own death?"

"You've still not figured it out have you? Why do you supposed she hooked up with someone who looked like her? You think it was coincidence? I figured it out straight off."

A chill ran down my spine. "She befriended Tammy just to use her? To kill her?"

Rusty smiled. "Like I said, I knew what she was capable of. We were two of a kind."

And so they were. I should have seen that coming. It is well recognised that there is a strong genetic disposition to psychopathy.

Nurture plays a part of course, but with the kind of parents these two had, the kind of parents who, given their own behaviour, could themselves have had psychopathic tendencies, it was almost inevitable they would both share the same psychoses.

He carried on with his story. "I came down here as soon as I knew and booked a place. Ironic really that I should be living back at Woodside Cottage."

"And a convenient reason for your fingerprints to be all over the place."

"Yes, nice bonus that."

"And you had no trouble finding her?"

"A small place like this? It doesn't take long. I kept a low profile. Stayed in the car while I cruised around. Spotted her shopping in town."

"Odd that she should have stayed around."

"Not really. She'd got herself a new mark by then. John Farrow. She wasn't going to let him go so easily."

"You confronted her?"

"You bet I did."

"I take it the meeting didn't go too well?"

"It went off okay to start with. She came over to stay the night. Made some excuse about visiting a friend in London. I got the big sob story about how she'd been threatened and needed to cover her tracks. I wasn't buying any of that crap though."

"And so it turned violent?"

"She turned on the charm. Said we'd sort out the cash in the morning. But after dinner that night, I caught her trying to slip a mickey in my drink. That's when the bitch showed her true colours. Went for me with a knife."

There was a movement behind him. I shifted my gaze slightly, as if looking into the distance, not wanting to alert him. Nathan and Lowe were making their way towards us across the clearing, moving slowly to avoid making a noise.

I turned back to him, focused on his face and raised my voice in an attempt to detract attention from any extraneous sound around us.

"And so you killed her."

He shrugged. "What else could I do. She went mental. I felled her with one blow. Slammed her head against the fire grate. Had to finish her off."

Nathan and Lowe were closer now, almost within reach.

"And now I understand why you moved her here," I said. "I wondered why you would take the risk. But now it's obvious."

He seemed pleased at that.

"It just seemed fitting somehow. My final revenge. The last laugh. She was the one who'd already made it her final resting place. It seemed only right to make sure that, in the end, that's exactly what it was."

"There is one thing you didn't take account of though."

His brow furrowed. "What?"

From right behind him, Nathan said, "Me."

He was poised ready to spring.

And as Rusty wheeled around to face him, he grabbed his wrist, twisted his arm, and wrenched the gun from his grasp as Lowe kicked his legs from under him and brought him crashing to the ground, howling with rage.

With his arms twisted behind his back and Nathan straddling him, he struggled in vain as Lowe snapped a pair of handcuffs on him.

Still howling with rage, he glared up at me, murderous fury written large across his face.

My legs were giving way beneath me, and my heart raced, but I was determined not to let him see how frightened I had been. I moved towards him, dropped to a crouch, and said, "What you didn't take account of was your overweening arrogance. You thought you were invincible. Well, you weren't."

I stood up and stepped back as Lowe hauled a struggling Rusty to his feet.

"How did you do it?" he said.

"It was easy. I told Karen I was visiting Sylus Gray." I spread my hands around me. "Well, here we are. This is where he lived before he shot himself. All of us long-term locals knew the stories about Sylus. They were part of local folklore. Only outsiders like you wouldn't know."

He snarled at me as Lowe dragged him away.

In the painful silence that followed, Nathan and I stood facing each other. He looked down at the gun and then back to me, a look of abject misery on his face.

I knew how harrowing this must have been for him and how distressed he must be feeling right now. And I couldn't begin to imagine the anguish he must have felt as he raced over here, the gruesome scenarios that must have played out in his mind as he wondered if he would make it in time.

A raging mix of emotions, regret and sorrow and despair and overwhelming love and need, welled up inside me and swept out towards him.

Even as the tears filled my eyes, I tried to ease his pain, tried to make light of our situation with a quip. "Before I forget," I said, "Happy birthday."

The next moment, I was on the ground on all fours, sobbing uncontrollably, my body shaking, fingers clawing at the soft earth.

And then his arms were around me and he pulled me close, hushing me with soothing words as he rocked me in his comforting embrace.

CHAPTER FORTY-FOUR

Karen had insisted on driving. "I know you three will want a drink or two on the way back," she explained.

Lowe sat next to her in the passenger seat of her Mondeo and Nathan sat beside me in the back, his hand on my thigh.

Once he'd vented his anger at me for not reporting my suspicions about Rusty as soon as they'd been aroused and after reminding me what a complete fucking idiot I was, he'd calmed down and was now more solicitous.

"Are you sure you're up to this?" he said.

"Are you kidding?" I said, "I'm looking forward to it. And besides, we owe you a birthday meal."

"This is your night," he said.

I patted his leg. "Then we'll make it a joint celebration."

We were on our way to London's Grosvenor House. It was the day of the Broadcast Awards and we'd decided to make the most of it and treat ourselves to an overnighter.

I cast him a sideways glance. "You never did like him, did you?" I didn't need to say who.

"There was just something about him. The way he looked at me sometimes when you were there. As if he were challenging me. If I had to give it a name, I'd say it was contempt."

"I'm just glad you got the message."

"It was all thanks to Karen. She was the one who worked it out."

Karen butted in. "I'm not stupid, Mikey. I knew something was wrong. And when you mentioned Sylus Gray, I got it straight away." To Lowe, she said. "When we were kids, we played in the old gamekeeper's cottage. Mikey used to try to scare me with tales of Sylus Gray haunting the place. Not that it got him anywhere."

"Yes, she always was hard-bitten, Richard. You'll need to remember that when you're married."

Lowe laughed. "I remember you telling me about those tales when we first visited the crime scene. Looks like Sylus did you a favour this time."

Nathan said, "And maybe in future, Mikey, you'll try not to get involved with psychopaths."

"It's not something I intend to make a habit of, I promise you."

"I'm just glad we got there in time," said Lowe. "That must have been one scary moment."

And not one I wanted to dwell on. I changed the subject. "Nowhere near as scary as the one Nathan has to face when we get to London."

"Oh?" Nathan sounded concerned.

"My agent wants to meet you to make sure you're suitable partner material. By the time he's finished the third degree, you'll be jelly."

Lowe and Karen laughed.

Nathan snorted. "Guess I'll have to take my chances."

As it happened, Jerry heartily approved of my choice. We met him in the foyer of Grosvenor House and once introductions were out of the way, Nathan and Jerry were chatting away like old friends. Quite a surprise given how taciturn they both were most of the time.

Later, while we settled into our rooms and changed for the ceremony, Nathan seemed much more at ease than he had been in a long time. I hoped he was finally coming to terms with Brandon's attempted suicide and not letting it burden his conscience.

He faced the mirror and struggled to fasten his bow tie. Without success. I took over the task and fixed it in place. "I have to say Mr Quarryman, you sure do look hot in a dinner jacket."

"Enjoy it while you can, Mr MacGregor. It's not my favourite mode of dress."

"Not to worry," I said, running a hand down his chest. "I can help you take it off later."

He wrapped his arms around me, a big grin on his face, and pulled me close. "If I didn't know you better, Mr MacGregor, I'd suspect an ulterior motive."

"That's the policeman in you. Always suspicious."

Enjoying the moment of shared intimacy, I cupped the back of his neck, leaned my head against his shoulder, breathed in his heady scent. And hardened against him.

He chuckled and said, "And now I have the supporting evidence."

Groaning, I pulled away from him. "Guilty as charged. Though my timing could be better."

He pressed his lips to mine briefly and murmured, "It will wait." His grin slowly faded to a look of concern. "You are okay now?"

I pulled a face and nodded. "Getting there."

"You need to talk about it?"

"Eventually."

The experiences of the last few days were still too recent, my emotions still too raw. And it wasn't lost on me that Nathan had gone through hell too. He's told me later that the rush to Tinkers Wood had been one of the worst moments of his life.

The days following Rusty's arrest had been a salutary learning experience too. Or maybe more of a wake-up call about my own lack of insight into areas of concern I should have been familiar with. The experience had been demeaning. Not that the confrontation with Rusty hadn't been traumatic enough. But to learn that I had been used and manipulated for all those months when he'd pretended friendship, made it a thousand times worse. I'd been such a fool not to see the signs, and I was ashamed. It had been a lesson well learned.

The trip to London was a Godsend. For Nathan too. Not so much the award ceremony itself, but the complete break from the horrors at home, and in the company of good friends.

"And Woodside Cottage?" he said. "Are you still happy there?"

"Why wouldn't I be? I love that place." I sank onto the end of the bed and leaned down to tie my shoelaces.

Over the past few days, Nathan had helped me remove every last trace of my nightmare house-guest. And Woodside Cottage was beginning to feel like home again.

"I just thought…. After everything that happened."

I finished tying my laces and looked up again. "I'm not going to let

Rusty's time there spoil it for me." I shot him a reassuring smile.

"Good." He visibly relaxed, turned back to the mirror, and fiddled with his bow tie. "Because I spoke with Martha Stubbs the other day. She's looking to sell the place. She'd be happy to give us first refusal. If we want it."

I stiffened. "Us?"

"It makes sense really. We live so far apart at the moment. And the cottage would be so much better than my flat."

"You mean move in together?"

"And it's such a good location. Beautiful woodland right on the doorstep. And near to the beach."

"You mean move in together?"

"And I've always wanted a dog. It's not fair to keep one cooped up in a flat. But Woodside Cottage would be ideal."

"Nathan." I had to raise my voice to shut him up.

He turned toward me, fell silent and stared down at me for a second or so. And then, "Yes, I mean move in together. What do you say?"

I rose from the bed, blinking back the tears that welled up in my eyes and said, "Are you sure you can put up with me full time?"

"Well, I've managed so far."

"You know how argumentative I can be."

"How could I fail to notice?"

"And stubborn."

"Now I've got you there. I'm the stubborn one here. I can outdo you on that front any day."

"And we'll probably fight a lot."

"So what's new?"

Feigning a look of despair, I said, "Okay, let's do it. If you're mad enough to go for it, then so am I." I leaned towards him and sealed the deal with a kiss.

I was still on a high, grinning like an idiot, when we met Lowe and Karen in the foyer.

Karen looked amazing in an emerald-green full-length sequined evening dress that set off the fire in her flame-red hair. Lowe looked uncomfortable in his unaccustomed attire.

We went into the ballroom together to join Jerry at our table.

I smiled at familiar faces and exchanged greetings with others as we threaded our way through the tables. I had to brush aside the occasional enquiry after my wife from those who weren't too well acquainted with the details of my personal life. But I was in too much of a good mood to let it bother me. And on the whole, it was a pleasure to catch up with old friends.

In anticipation of the awards themselves, the tension in the room underlying the animated chatter was almost tangible.

Jerry had already ordered wine, and a couple of bottles of Veuve Clicquot Brut Champagne were waiting for us. Microphones and a podium were being set up on stage as we enjoyed our meals and once dinner was over and the serving staff had cleared the tables, the room fell into a hush as the ceremony began.

It was a joy to share in the pleasure of friends and colleagues alike as the awards were announced and winners collected their trophies with such obvious delight. Not for a moment had I thought I might be among them. Not that it mattered. Nathan had already made my day. Receiving an award could not have made it any happier.

And so, when 'Killer Instincts' was announced as the winner of the Best Documentary Series, I was stunned.

Jerry prodded me in the chest. "Don't just sit there with your chin on the floor," he said. "Go get it before they change their minds."

In a complete daze, I made my way to the stage, applause ringing in my ears, and when I turned towards the sea of expectant faces, I was lost for words.

When I finally found my voice and stumbled through my acceptance speech, spouting out the usual clichéd acknowledgements, thanking producers and production staff, agent, friends and family, I looked over to our table and saw the pride written large on Nathan's face.

My heart rose in my throat and I faltered.

That's when it occurred to me that only one cliché mattered, which is, of course, why it's a cliché in the first place.

And so no more denials. No more fudging and skirting around the issue. It was time to stand my ground and declare myself for who and what I was.

Keeping my eyes on Nathan, I said, "I'm sure you've heard it all before at ceremonies like this, but I'm going to say it, anyway. Because it's important.

"It's a rare person who achieves individual success without the help and support of that one special person who stands by their side through thick and thin and gives help and succour every step of the way, the one who makes it all worthwhile and without whom that success is meaningless. And so I want to say a big thank you to my own special person, the one whose love and support mean more to me than anything. My partner, Nathan Quarryman." I raised a hand and held it out towards him. "Thank you, Nathan."

The wide and generous beaming smile that spread across his face, flushed with embarrassment though he was at the well-deserved applause, was the only response I needed.

Some experiences stay in our memories forever. As this one would for me. Not just for the joy of the occasion itself. But for what it promised. And in Nathan's rapt expression, I saw the promise of the life that lay ahead of us.

And I knew that I had, at last, found my way home.

IF YOU ENJOYED THIS BOOK

I'm now working on the third book in this series. If you enjoyed this one, you may wish to add your name to my mailing list to receive notification of future titles.

Please see details on my Website
GrantAtherton.co.uk

And I'd love it if you could post a review about the book on Amazon or another website. Getting reviews would give me a lot of pleasure and I look forward to reading what you think. Perhaps you could mention which parts you liked best.

I look forward to hearing from you

Grant Atherton

Made in the USA
Middletown, DE
22 August 2024

59568248R00139